MW00792067

A Piece of Peace

A Piece of Peace

PENNSYLVANIA | CALIFORNIA | VIRGINIA

Publisher, OSAAT Entertainment
Arlington, Virginia 22203

All rights reserved. This work is a work of fiction.

No part of this book may be reproduced or transmitted in any form
or by any means, graphic, electronic, or mechanical, including pho-
tocopying, recording, taping, or by any information storage retrieval
system, without the written permission of the publisher.

Reprinted Edition. Fiction

Contact the Author/Publisher:
Email: rycj@osaatentertainment.com
Visit: oebooks.blogspot.com

Copyright © 2011/2021 (RYCJ), A piece of peace.
Reprints in circulation 2011, 2012 (ebook), 2021
Cover Design by RYCJ
Cover Photo Credit: KDMorris Photography

ISBN: 978-0-982715-25-3
ISBN: 978-1-940994-20-8

Library of Congress Control Number: 2010919053
Printed in the United States of America

We're never too old to fall in love,
And it's never too late to forgive.

God Bless this Work.

CHAPTER...1

𝒞𝓁𝒾𝒻𝒻𝑜𝓇𝒹 𝓌𝑜𝓊𝓁𝒹𝓃'𝓉 𝓈𝒶𝓎 𝒽𝑒 𝓌𝒶𝓈 𝒶 𝓇𝑒𝓁𝒾𝑔𝒾𝑜𝓊𝓈 𝓂𝒶𝓃. He didn't run up to people, stopping them mid-sentence to remind them he was five-foot/nine, or decent looking, or black, any more than he sat around reminding everyone he believed in God. In God he trusted people would look at him and assume these things.

He would say he was a spiritual man however, even if he didn't put this information on full blast either. But then he was a rare breed. He still believed in help-ing strangers, whether they were indigent or well-off. A person didn't have to be barefoot, missing teeth, and have holes in their pockets before he would reach down and give them a hand. Falling was enough.

But if this sounds like a yawn too good to be true, look out, it is. Clifford had a few socio-paraplegic issues. For one, and two, he never got married and didn't have any children. These were two major issues that didn't sit right with a lot of people, namely his sister Meredith, who he grew up calling Merda.

Take a good guess why he called her that, and why their relationship was what it was. A long time ago, fifty-some odd years in their turbulent past, he couldn't pronounce her name. And when he could, he insisted on calling her Merda, since she called him Satan. She hated him on sight, calling him *'the work of Judas'* the day their mother walked in the house cradling him in her arms. She said he cried too much, and when left in her care she said he stunk, and looked like road kill, getting on her last nerve, ruining her fun, stomping on her sunshine. Going by her, the brat should've never been born. Only the devil could cook that hell up. She hated his guts.

But guess what? Merda believed in God. And told everyone about her beliefs. She said she didn't care who didn't care. She wasn't shamed of the Lord she served. God had been good to her, and indeed He had. Quite a few men serving time in the pen could attest to that. As a matter of fact, it's all they attested to; and what they would do to her once they got out, if they ever got out.

But Fine. Let bygones be bygones. It was water over a bridge. Dirt swept under a rug. Half a county of street hoods dimed out and deservingly locked up. Now Merda was a saved woman. She ratted on the friends she ran out with, and ran down to Florida a praying woman, hoping one of them didn't in fact get out.

This stuff happened years ago, her running down to Florida, and literally running on both feet, to disappear for a few years she later described as a time when she was finding herself, getting saved she said.

Found! The family found her shacking up with a guy running foul like her during *her* lost and found sin-filled years. The new guy spelled ethical work lumped together in one word. Try fraud. Or try driving up a tree and blaming it on a rich guy who'd rather pay off a poor man purporting to be hurt, rather than having his name dragged through a community rallying against loaded and toasted rich drivers who drove drunk. Merda met this man,

Parker, as he was collecting, settling to the tune of a half a million dollars. Two of a kind those two were. Ask anyone who cared about telling the truth, they were a perfect match.

Parker, and all his working parts, moved on to bank-roll the city, adding zeros behind zeros collecting on disability, SSI, workman's comp and the likes, though the man hadn't worked a real job a day in his life.

Clifford hadn't met Parker, but Merda talked up the bum, swearing to family her savior and saving grace was a prince. Yah, right. Princes didn't resort to stealing money when they could print it...with their pictures on the front of the bill, and palaces on the back. Clifford knew exactly what Merda was up to. Both him and his father, Pops, knew. She was up to her old tricks. She was a thief, just like her so called match made in heaven. A gold-digger was what she was. And not a very gifted one, though true to her last coin she cleaned out Parker's trust fund, his pockets, and nearly ruined his good relationship with Uncle Sam. Everyone back home knew all about Merda's so-called helping hand, a small matter of perception only saints could see.

But Clifford wasn't altogether a saint either, at least not that kind of saint, a loving saint, one that forgave and forgot a whole lot. He remembered it all, and swore never to forget...as long as he lived. Who could ever ignore, and forget forgive, a sister who treated him the way Merda treated him? He put her high on his unforgivable list, even as he packed up with everyone but his father, and drove down to Florida to witness a whole bunch of family firsts.

Call him cynical, or scornful, or what Merda always called him, *Satan*, but not one prostitute in the family had ever gotten married. In fact, there had never been a *known* prostitute in the family. Also, they'd never been to a wedding held at the type of courthouse where Merda's wedding had taken place. She sent out the most lovely wedding invitations made of crepe paper and tissue paper, sand and beaches, and the most bizarre thing happened. She got locked up for what no one was saying. Just as they were loading up the vans, Merda was pleading her case to police, trying to get them to believe she was really in Motel Six selling Avon cosmetics. But police didn't buy it. If only the video hadn't picked up her taking money for goods not made by Avon.

It was a big embarrassment for their mother, and Clifford felt plenty sad for Mama, but he was a happy prophet otherwise. The swanky invitations and all the lies had him fooled none. He remembered Merda, and knew her style well. The only reason he packed up and ran down to Florida with everyone else, was to hit the beaches Merda described in her many omnificent calls—the only truth he ever believed coming out of her mouth. Florida, indeed, proved to be a good place to catch plenty of sunshine…and sunbathing beauties.

All accept for an uncle, Uncle Jamison, who went along for the ride too, no one laughed about Merda's predicament. "All right Jameson," that's how Aunt Idell, Mama and Jamison's middle sister, and Cliff's favorite aunt, pronounced Jamison's name. "You know it ain't right laughing at people's pain."

But Jamison tapped him on the leg, ignoring Aunt Idell. "Hey look man, just block me if it look like I'm about to catch the garter." And Jamison doubled over to his knees. "Cause man…ain't nothing I can do with a yard girl," he howled.

Mama wasn't in the room while all this cutting up was going on. Clifford would have stopped him if she were. He didn't want to hurt Mama's feelings, even if it hurt his feelings seeing how Mama often favored Merda. He respected Mama more than anything, choosing to believe she cared for them in different ways. It wasn't her fault he thought Merda didn't deserve to be cared for at all. Not by the hateful and crooked way she lived her life in those early days.

• • •

Merda returned home the day their mother died. Despite Clifford having called weeks in advance, when Mama was first put in hospice, she slid in town with her slimy Parker fifteen hours after Mama was taken off the respirator, and three hours and fifty-nine minutes after she took her last breath.

After all Mama had done for Merda, the many jams she pulled her out of, the love and support she always showed her, and the fact that Mama would screw up the Will, putting in a clause where Merda could end up with the house, and this was the most Mama meant to her. How nice of a sister was that?

Mama had one of them funerals he didn't want to live through twice. Her home-going was nothing like Pops, who left out like an angel. One day, a few years before Mama went home, and a decade after Merda's wily wedding, Pops quietly became ill, sleeping more than his usual, after 30-years working as a traveling salesman. One morning Pops didn't wake up. Quietly, like the way anyone with an ounce of dignity would want to go, he sneaked on home. Mama just as quietly made funeral arrangements, and Merda just as coolly slipped in town... this being in the days before the Lord recovered most of her. She didn't want everyone knowing she and her saving grace were still going through *some things*, so she slipped in and out of town without much fuss.

Not this time however. Despite doing all he could to help Mama transition as peacefully as Pops, good grief Tampa Bay...Merda marched in the house her old bossy, hostile, unrepentant self. Barging in smelling like fried chicken and a nonstandard fragrance, she hugged and kissed him like always—phony, like he'd forgotten her hateful ways. The huggaroo was one of her oldest tricks. This was the hug where he would be thinking nice things about her, wanting to believe she changed…when wham! She'd bring out the sword and chop up his heart.

Sure enough, right after hugs and kisses, she pulled out that bloody sword. 'Mama wouldn't want this, and Mama wouldn't want that,' she yapped, wailing like a deluded whale that accidentally washed up on shore. "…And what are your plans Satan, now that Mama is gone!?!" she sneered, the one tirade that turned his grief into a tumulus spade.

How about first getting Mama in the ground where her soul could rest, and then *let's hope to whoever you pray to*, I don't have to bury you right alongside Mama!

Great nerve. *What were his plans?* The real question was, what were her plans? Forget Mama for the time being. He put a lot of work into the home; Brazilian cherry hardwood floors, honeycombed ceilings, spare rooms and bathrooms. He wasn't going nowhere. This was his home, the only home he had known. The home Pop paid off ten years after buying it, something a gypsy would have no respect for.

He didn't care if she *looked* cleaned up. Much older, and much wiser his foot. Though she wore 24-karat gold love nuggets around her neck and on every other finger, those shifty bedeviled evil eyes were still engraved deep in her face. And it really got beneath his skin looking at all that extra gel she worked into her scalp. Obviously, she not long ago had been in to see a beautician, likely while he was busy working on the obituary she wanted corrected; at his expense since it was his mistake he left Parker's name off the program.

That's how Mama's funeral started. Hostile. Merda yapping on about Parker and the obituary, and him hoping to keep the peace until after the funeral. After the funeral he would be more than happy to put both her and Parker's name in an obituary. Right there on the cover. He would even go out of his way scrounging up photos, ones where she was dressed like the only known prostitute in the family. Or maybe, he'd do it the easy way and use her mug-shots. And don't think his name was going in the family and friends section. No, he would leave it at: See Tampa County's Correctional List.

Real rawhide nerve Merda had telling him Mama would want that man's name in her obit. Mama barely knew Parker, and the little she did know, she didn't like.

Things went from bad, straight to Devil's Canyon. Merda escalated from 'why wasn't Parker's name in the obit,' to... 'I don't see why all this time you've been here, you haven't thought about getting a place of your own anyway. For God's sake we all thought you'd be married by now!'

We all!?! And 'for God's sake!?!' She'd be wise to leave the Lord's name out of this. It wasn't the best time to be talking like the Lord didn't know her history. Had she really read them scriptures she would've known the Lord saw and knew everything, and righted all wrongs. On this point alone, prayer was not her friend. She had not a hope in heaven, OR HELL. Had her good Lord decided to collect her debts due and owing, she'd have to borrow air to take her last breath.

Clifford left out of the house to clear his head... and get some fresh air himself. Bless Mama's heart, trying to be fair and all, but he hoped she had gotten around to changing her Last Living Will & Testament. When he dropped out of college...upon realizing he couldn't hack hearing any more of the drivel and drone from latch-key raised scholars, Mama wrote up her Will, emphasizing how **'Contingent upon Clifford staying employed'** he could have the house.

God he hoped Mama had done something about that clause in her Will, because if Merda thought for one red-herring he was going to let her have the only piece of peace he had left, she was in for a tooth and nail fight. She claimed she had changed and was saved by His blood, but hand on the Bible, Darth Vadar's mistress hadn't seen a complete metamorphosis! Nothing would save her if he turned inside out. Plain and simple, he wasn't moving out and that was that. The Will read: *'Contingent upon Clifford staying employed'*, in which case he still was.

. . .

What Merda didn't know, during all the time she was away piece-milling her soul over to the Lord an arrest warrant at a time, he was home building and polishing his life.

After dropping out of college he hadn't caused his parents one iota of trouble. He returned home and by the disappointed look in Mama's eye, but lenient hand of his father, he went to work for Linthicum. Being a courier in the mailroom wasn't the most prestigious position in the world, but it was there where he buckled down and became a man. Dutifully he went to work, helped out a great deal around the house, stayed away from trouble, didn't knock up women, and certainly never called back home to borrow money from relatives he knew good and well he never was going to repay.

He was a good son who, in their parents ailing years, made the family proud. He didn't ruin the family name, and by all accounts was the only child his parents relied on. Occasionally Mama would ask if he ever was going to settle down and marry one of *'those pretty gals'* he introduced the day before he decided she wasn't the one. But Mama didn't make a big fuss of his dating habits. Seeing how he renovated the house, creating a bigger space for himself, but also making things more comfortable for her, she left him alone.

"Cliff, honey," Mama used to call him, "on your way home today would you mind picking up my medicine?" Or, "Cliff, baby, on your way in to work tomorrow, would you mind dropping me off at the hospital? I can catch a cab back."

She knew he wouldn't allow her to catch a fifty-dollar cab ride home. He had moved up the ranks in Linthicum by this time. As an associate he could call in and arrange to take the day off so that he could take Mama to the hospital for her dialysis treatments... nothing Merda and her selfish self would have stuck her chicken neck out to do.

The kicker was the tone of voice Mama used when she was fed up...usually with Merda. "Cliff, I swear your sister is the work of the devil!"

—so then, why hadn't she gotten around to changing her last living testament... when for over twenty years, and adding some years for the time Merda spent two-timing and loyally diming-out her Clyde Burrow swathe of friends, he spent taking care of them, and working for one employer, Linthicum; and God-willing was soon due to retire?

. . .

The thing was, like the housing market drying up, so were corporations. It wasn't like it was when he started, employees counting down days left until retirement. He had been to dozens of retirement parties, envying those men, and one woman, for serving their time to finally live the other half of their life waking up whenever they felt like it, lounging in front of the television, and taking big fat sloppy vacations at the drop of a hat.

As recent as a few years ago he started counting down the days to his retirement too. Only he didn't count as loudly as the old timers had. This wasn't a day to be making it known he was soon due to retire. Executives had since turned into leeches, of the thirsty bloodsucking kind, shaving right off top layers the most senior employees. And they got rid of them for any reason.

Visit the doctor one time too many and it'd be, "I'm sorry sucker, we need someone who's accountable." Or decline a promotion, which he'd done numerous times, and it might be something like, "I'm sorry loser, we need progressive people who take on challenges."

It didn't take long to figure out what was going on. These leeches figured out they could pay four-year graduates four times less than what they were paying old-timers. Everyone was paying into a dried out archaic retirement system that had died years ago. No one was seeing a dime of the money they were, by law, forced to contribute to. Didn't take a second grade mathematician to see the math going on in the retirement system.

Merda wouldn't have understood any of this. Minimum wage workers and those chronically unemployed, or like the tub she dragged back home and had already found his place slumped in Mama's recliner, knew nothing about what was going on in the work force. They were already retired. All they were waiting on was death.

But then Mama had to die, and Merda return home, and Linthicum posture, grinning at him holding up the early walking papers they had a habit of handing out like Halloween candy.

Soon as Merda heard what happened to Mama, she threw a spoon, a fork, a toothbrush, and lumpy and grumpy Parker into a U-Haul and fled like a felon in the night up to Maryland. Clifford parted the curtains and looked out the window wondering which relative had come to pay their respects by way of U-Haul. First thing he thought was which hotel was closest. An affordable one, because this relative was going to need a place to stay that night, and cost was going to be a major concern.

That's when he caught the peacock head springing out of the cab from the driver's side, and the chiffon scarf, reddish-orange this time, flying behind her. His heart sunk as he watched her mannishly handling Parker, kicking open his wheelchair and hustling around the chair to help him throw a leg at a time out of the cab.

"It stinks in here," was the way she greeted him, as she caught a glimpse of the program he'd been working on. "You haven't found no one to clean this place before people start coming in here..." her voice trailed as she picked up the program, dusting her eyes over the front room, sizing up what she had in mind to claim at the same time.

Up to Mama's final days she kept the house clean. The odor Merda smelled was lingering lineament scents Mama used to help ease the swelling in her ankles.

But before he could answer, Merda had breezed into Mama's room and pried open a safe he had no idea was even in the house. He thought she was going after a typewriter to type up the obituary the way she wanted it written, but instead came rushing into the front room with the Will seized in her hand.

"Alberta and Idell and them will probably be over here in a minute, but I'm telling you right now, ain't nobody gettin' nothin'!" And then she asked what were his plans, and when was he moving out.

"Merda, I'm not moving anywhere—"

"—Oh, no Satan...just you wait one red minute! It says right here," the papers squeezed in her grip, "this house belongs to me, and I will be selling it!"

They argued for a minute, before he was able to get her to 'reread' the Will again. That's when he saw the clause, just as he realized the jeopardy he was in.

The day his mother went home, and Merda returned, he was in fact the last man of age left at Linthicum; hanging on by a prayer, sitting in a corner behind a half dozen new graduates, hoping to get through five more years when he could give Linthicum the thumb, walking out the door a fully retired happy man. *'Good riddance! Hope you all live out your time here in misery and hell!'*

He didn't have the age to draw on the money, but given his good health and savings he managed to reinvest, coupled by a trickling of income he got from freelance writing, his duckets...and life... were in order when she arrived. He was in good shape to tell her what parts of her body the sun was going to be shining brightly on.

Except she seized that Will, and already had her ostrich claws dialing legal imposters she plucked from her grimy past to go over Mama's wishes with a fine tooth comb. This was no time to be grand-standing. This matter could easily get bottled up in probate courts, given the stamina of legal imposters in cahoots with the values of Linthicum types who had children to get through college.

So Satan, on this long walk around the block, got to working on a solid plan to save his piece of peace.

CHAPTER...2

The plan came out of nowhere. Because honest to goodness, he had no plan. It was Friday and raining crocodile tears, an ominous sign, like every other grisly Friday preceding it, that a heartless layoff was on the horizon. Somebody, on that day, on that beltway, was getting the axe. It could've been the twerp who kept cutting in front of him, despite no one getting anywhere fast. Or it could have been any one of the 1.3 million motorists who'd hopped on the 495 outer-loop to be sitting behind a tin desk by 8:30AM. Most likely though, it was him. Being one of so very few old-timers left, he had every inclination it was he, and not the twerp, the dipshit, or the 1.3 million other epithets he had for pain in the ass drivers who should have been on a chopping block, instead of him!

So why hadn't he called out and stayed home? He could've been cozied up in his study, adding more keystrokes to his partially finished novel, listening to pitter-patters pelting his bedroom window instead of watching rain hailing nails at his brand new Mercury Cruiser.

Wasn't no way Linthicum was letting him retire quietly and peacefully, not by the way these nails railed against his window. Even the gods had crunched the numbers, depreciated its assets, and closed their budgets. None too sorry to report, he had to go. He rode out his luck long enough. *'Get out of here…exit life, you sorry misty-eyed loser!'*

Only five miserable years to go and the dark cloud finally caught up to him. He could almost make out his name, strung together between the pitch of pelts pinging the windshield and loud claps of thunder and lightning promising his goose was as good as cooked.

For a split second he felt sorry for himself. He hadn't done a thing wrong. He kept to himself. Minded his own business. And did what was asked of him. Well… and then again… he actually had done one thing wrong. Year after year he sat idly by, hiding out in the confines of his comfy shrine, watching his peers getting shafted, glad it wasn't him.

Shame on him. And lame of him too. If anything, one thing all barrel-chested novelists should've known, and a moonlighting published novelist no less, was how to deal with villains. A plot thick as the annals of fiction should've been lurking in his back pocket, laying in wait to turn this shamrod show around and let the corporate leeches learn a thing or two about the real loser.

But he kept postponing making a move, fearing his fleeting payback thoughts wouldn't amount to a hill of beans. Knowing his luck, the old slip and fall he mused on, figuring to ride the trip into long-term disability, and from there, right into retirement, would've gotten him only as far as a kangaroo court. He may have been a good writer, and an even better dreamer, but his acting was the pits. How people could get on stage in front of full audiences making those silly dramatic faces, playing out ridiculous skits to start with, were a cringing embarrassment. This loser just couldn't do it.

But he indeed thought about it, practicing the fall by kicking one foot with the other…kind of like tripping himself in the midst of foxtrotting, except (and of course) this was no fancy dancing. This was a very deliberate shuffle where he could even make his shoe come off. It looked silly rehearsing in front of mirrors, but if his guts were half the metal in his head, he'd get through the slapdash script and bankroll the real crooks from front to back. In other words, he'd get to retire early and wipe out Linthicum to cover all the losers they had thus far ripped off.

As the Mercury inched around the beltway parking lot, crawling an inch every twenty minutes, he pictured the party Merda throwing him upon hearing Linthicum let him go early. It was all in the news, talks of massive layoffs, and her eyes happily flickering every time an anchor ran those dismal unemployment numbers. He watched her crusty fingers, anxiously reaching for a phone as she asked how his day had gone. He might've been born late one night, but he wasn't born blind. She had her pulse on all the snakes in her address book.

Begrudgingly the car slugged on, him cursing the rain and scoffing about traffic, telling himself he needed to come up with a surefire plan. Mean-mugging a prick reading a newspaper, probably about congestion on 495, and a woman applying eyeliner, both leaving wide gaps between traffic, enough room to swallow a semi whole, wasn't going to stop Merda from sic'ing her rattlers on him if he, in fact, was getting canned that morning.

Looking at his watch, and then at the clock on the console, his first plan of no action was he didn't want to walk in the office late. Not on this day. If the signs were right, as the burning ulcer in his stomach now indicated, then he wanted to get the news before there were any witnesses. No one could see him walking out of Human Resources with his head tucked down carrying a box with his desk trinkets hanging over the top like the media figured out, bad news traveled fast. Merda also had a host of church friends who loved putting people on prayer lists.

• • •

He arrived at work finding it eerie dark and quiet, and gloomier inside. The only life flourishing in the office were the generators generously pumping heat into the building, anticipating those at the front of the nightmare on Interstate 495 rushing into the kitchen to hit the switches that would get the coffee machines brewing.

But he wasn't a coffee drinker. In fact, he hated that his desk was so close to the kitchen. He heard things he'd rather have not heard, how he honed in on picking up the layoff signs. One snicker and someone was in there flirting. Two snickers and a whisper, and someone was being set up. Three snickers and if he couldn't log on to the system…it went without mention.

Served him right, perhaps. While everyone was busy partying and screwing over people to get rich quick, and just for the hell of it, he was busy working on novels and missing signs of a love to share his life with. He should have married Angelica. Although she was a root canal too sweet and wasn't all that pretty, he was sure Mama would have remembered the Will and rewrote it so that he and Angelica would have a place to stay. But he told Angelica, who was up to calling him five/six times a day, with the sappy-happy sweet 'honey-do' sickening voice, to decrease the calls to once a day. She agreed, but didn't tell him she started calling another man five/six times a day on the days she cut back.

He lost her, but quickly picked up another young woman. She wasn't as sweet, and even less prettier, but she was good company. All he had to do was dial up her number and she would race over to the house like a racehorse, please him for all of ten minutes, and then gallop back out of there. He couldn't remember her name, it was a long time ago, but she was a good one. He pulled off one novel on account of her gallop. Made a few grand off the novel too.

After that he saw women here and there, mostly there, until he met Marcella. Now, if there ever was a woman who should have been the one, it should have been Marcella. The woman didn't speak a lick of English, but seemed to love his novel ideas, yessing anything he said, until Pops got sick and died. She was Pop's nurse. But he should have gotten that woman's number since they were sleeping together on occasions. The agency who sent her wouldn't release it, and the woman never called the house again.

That was his fault. If only he made it legal because he really liked that woman. If he had gotten down on one knee and asked her to marry him he was positive she would have said yes. At least he thought he was sure. Speaking no English he wasn't always certain she understood him. Plus, he wondered what her personal life was like. It sounded like an awful lot of them in one house. Her husband, she assured him in hand motions, was out of the picture. She hated the man. He left her for another woman when they arrived in the States. But she kept talking about these hermanas and hermanos and tias and tios and primas. Sounded like they all lived in the one house with her.

Graciously it was still dark in the office. He dropped his lunch sack on the desk and looked around. There was a chance there was one project left with just enough meat in its budget that an old wishful gaining centurion might have just enough gumption to sink his teeth into and hang onto. But just in case, he looked around for something to throw, or maybe a wall to punch. One where his fist could go clear through and leave his mark.

Sitting down at his desk he started to turn on the computer. For reasons unknown, though given the clearly punctuated signs, he couldn't bring his finger to mash that little circular button. It always took a while for his system to load up, old as it was, but in this case, on this miserable day, he was sure his system would take even longer to load. Like forever.

"Clifford, can I speak with you for a minute...ugh, in my office," came Shirley's nimble voice crawling over his shoulder, sending a familiar chill up his spine.

It didn't take a clairvoyant to know what Shirley wanted. Her intentions couldn't have been clearer had she walked up on him holding an axe.

"Don't bother," he retorted as a surprise to even himself. He hadn't planned to snap about the layoff, telling Shirley, "I'll show myself to the door." His plan was to first evade all rainy Fridays, and if perhaps, Shirley caught up to him on the following Monday or the next Tuesday, he planned to do like one of the other old heads had done. He was going to get down on his hands and knees and beg for his job. If that didn't work then he would try the skit he'd been halfheartedly rehearsing. Things worked better ad-libbed anyway, like now. He had no idea he was going to get all snippy with Shirley.

Too bad no other employees were in the office. Another skit he played out (in his head albeit), was going out like a maniac. May as well if his next stop was skidrow. Security was always looking for trouble anyways... like his Armageddon colleagues. During the drag, hopefully by his feet, he planned to recite every bit of gossip he overheard coming out of the kitchen.

Shirley is a slut! She's sleeping with Paul and all the men on the third floor. Cathy is cute, but everyone says she has bad breath. Robin has herpes and Frank is a fake, a fraud and a freak. He's sleeping with his dog.

He wanted to say all that, and MORE, except he lacked opportunity...and guts. He was kind of like Fred, one of the few old-timers he admired for not going out too much like a chump.

Fred went in HR and begged to keep his job. He told Shirley he would do anything...and was granted his wish. His salary was trimmed down and he was flown to a place located in the Pakistan mountains, a position no one had a thing good to say about it because the job was always open. Clifford had seen the 'vacant' posting many times. It was the only job open on the board. And now Fred had it, and they hadn't heard from him since.

This was his cue but he didn't take it. He didn't want to be hauled off. And he didn't want the job Fred had taken either. The craftily worded announcement chilled him; *'Exciting travel opportunity to train a diverse group of people on skills you'll oversee from implementation to completion.'* The location was listed in excruciatingly small font. Looked similar to the location Fred selected, at least it was located in Pakistan, though by the spelling of the city, given there were more z's and k's in its name, it likely was an entirely different mountain altogether.

Blinded by frustration he hit the elevator call button so forcefully that the covering cracked. He wasn't angry with no one but himself. Individually, to include Merda for the moment, no one had done a thing to him. No one except one. Linthicum. But then Linthicum was nothing but an eleven-story brick building. He was willing to bet if he walked over to any company official, they wouldn't recognize his name from one of Fred Douglas's third cousins.

It was too late for planning now. He had to go with the instincts he was born with, which was to quickly exit the building before his photo ended up captioned above a CNN headline.

He had backed out of the parking garage before it concretely registered, he just lost his job! And as he jumped a curb and blew a stop sign he noticed there was one still left! He wasn't the last. There was still a sole survivor. Charlie Willbanks stood almost directly in his path, meekly waving, trying to get him to stop. But his foot was stuck to the accelerator. Charlie jumped back as he breezed on by, perfunctorily aware that if he knocked off a dozen or so baby-boomers in one go, it might open up a dozen or so more spots. *Right? Wouldn't it?*

Obviously he wasn't seeing clear. The wild dazed look in Charlie's eye told him this. He really wanted to stop and say something; something like, "blow up the building, Charlie! It's okay!" Except that wouldn't have been right either. *Would it?*

He kept going, foot pressed to the metal, zipping out of the garage and over-shooting an island, turning out of the lot on two wheels. He was amazed at how well his new Mercury performed. Car salesmen were the worst lot of scum-sucking crooks, but not Feldman & Sons, the men who sold him the truck. They hadn't shafted him. They swore the baby he drove off the lot would give him one heck of a road performance, and they hadn't lied. Slippery wet roads and that baby hugged tight to the asphalt, spitting at everything it passed.

By the time he got to the first traffic light his foot let go of the pedal some, though the engine continued grinning plenty. Seemed like it was saying, "more, more," egging to show that red light a thing or two, more.

The light turned green and he sat there, debating whether to turn around. He shouldn't have left out like that. Mama told him time and time again about not pooping where he ate, or burning bridges! *'What was he going to tell Merda!?!'*

Maybe he should've gotten some documentation that he could take to a civilized attorney to prove he had been scammed. *'Oh, yeah right, Mr. Wronged. Good luck with that sucker!'*

In this fusion of self-doubt and bulimic distress he missed his exit and ended up on Georgia Avenue. It was an exit he missed many times, but those were times when his mind was less foggier. He could see the road ahead and knew which turns would get him back on the beltway.

This day he couldn't remember a thing. So he continued on, forgetting how long Georgia Avenue stretched on. A lost motorist could be hours riding out Georgia Avenue.

The rain continued coming down, the wipers going tit-for-tat matching his anxiety. Even the defogger got to huffing, or maybe it was him breathing that hard. He heard the piece of plastic blathering behind him, louder than normal, the result of a crook trying to take from him what didn't belong to them either. He couldn't win for losing, and his losing streak was running like a bow-legged knock-kneed man down a dusty racetrack at an amazing clip. Couldn't this much bad luck be slated for just one person.

Going down Georgia Avenue, the long stretch that it was, he caught a bundle of people in his quarter-after view, not more than a fingernail tip away from his rear passenger door. A large woman cloaked in a burqa was busily hustling children out of a double-parked car, one by one, pulling them out by the left arm. *'What in the devil was wrong with her... leaving those kids wonky on their feet in the street like that!?! Couldn't she see she was putting them in danger!?! A deranged man who just lost his job had rubber on the road!'* He could've swiped them all left! They'd be gone forever... like what the backspace key did to erroneous thoughts.

He started to blow the horn, for the hell of it, but a man more deranged than him darted out of nowhere and rushed up to his driver side door, pressing an unhinged smutty face against his window. "Got a dollar?" the man begged, smearing an ugly gummy grin against the glass.

It was still happening. He could see it clearly, a bow-legged knock-kneed creature inherited from a grim dream had butted into his lucid state. In the dream he was winning the race, against the bow-legged coughing and gagging creep lagging behind. Nowhere near the finish line, and that was for either of them, the creature however was catching up, in fact closing in on a win.

Clifford tried to ignore both...that being the leviathan in his head and the maniac pressed to the window. The second the light turned green he was putting the heat back on the metal. At least that was the intent because without warning the deranged maniac went behind his back and whipped out an instrument of what looked like could cause mass destruction.

Before blinking, seeing in a flash two feet go up in the air, the lunatic flipped on the hood of the car. In that same split second, still unsure what the deranged stranger held in his hand, he would have sworn to any dieter it was possible to shed fifty-pounds in less than a second.

Clifford only realized he wasn't in imminent danger of watching his life, liberty and or limb fade to black when the maniac began fiercely wiping his front window, smearing grease across the windshield with what turned out to be a squeezy.

Tapping the horn Clifford hissed, "get off the car, man! Come on, get off the car!" He wanted to call the maniac an unpleasant name, and threaten him for good measure, but was afraid he might have to live up to those words. So he kept tapping the horn and gas pedal, doing what he could to get out of this nightmare.

But the maniac stayed there, no bucket, so no clean water, but wielding a squeezy busily smearing filmy dirt across the windshield. Horns blared behind them, yet no one but him seemed to see the madman on the hood. As cars sped around them, some motorists flipping him the bird, not a soul had an ounce of empathy. People could care less about his predicament, or the maniac's obvious brush with death. This couldn't be real.

In the many years he worked at Linthicum he heard a small collection of happenings witnessed by colleagues on this stretch of road, but nothing like this. The worst he recalled was a colleague being assaulted by a hungry homeless woman reaching inside her car and grabbing a bagel out of her hand. The pastry-jacker ate the dough on the spot, right in front of a mile of monolithic bumper-to-bumper witnesses.

Clifford continued to tap the gas, brake and horn. "Get off the car! Move! Get off!" he begged, but the man hung on.

Desperately looking around, hoping one of the angry witnesses piling up behind might have mercy on him, or at least the maniac, he pleaded for at least one warm-blooded soul to come to his rescue. But no such luck. Like the woman in the burqa, this man too could have been permanently hurt. All he had to do was show everyone what his baby could do. Who could live with something like that on their conscience? Apparently many. Because every one of them blew around him laying on them horns and flipping him the bird as if they wanted to see blood first.

Was humankind reverting back into itself? Returning to the barbaric behaviors technologies were built to escape? A lady resembling Godzilla, face contorted and unhuman-like, nothing even Ifukube could imitate...a probable distant relative of the first dinosaur by the look of her stretched bloodshot eyeballs and uneven row of broken razor sharp teeth, angrily swerved around him and passed him the finger. She was more unnerving than the derelict still strapped to the hood of the car. Her pit-less hate, like the other creeps blowing their horns, zeroed squarely on him. Those people on the road that morning were plus positive proof they either were void of a human conscience, or 100% nuts. And, perhaps, that included him too.

Coming to his wits end he reached into the ashtray and scooped up a fist full of iron. Quarters, nickels, dimes and pennies seized in his grasp, he flung the coins out the window with one foot mashed on the brake and an elbow rolling down the window. It was a maneuver that belonged in Baileys and Barnum Circus. Coins went everywhere; landing in the street and on the hood of the car. One coin hit the man, apparently in one eye, because the maniac rolled over the hood, playing both parts of cops and robbers as he held his face. It was a hellva class-act, a class-act he wanted to give Linthicum…and Shirley, but didn't have the nerve to do.

Laid flat on his back the maniac started kicking and screaming, "You got me! You got me! I'm out! I'm out!" Clifford sat there and watched. With his throat swollen and chutzpah in his socks he wondered what was going to happen next. With the way his luck was going, when the maniac ran out of act he could wend up in the nut house for real, dropped off by the nut taking off in his car. Why hadn't he gone on and given the maniac the buck he asked for in the first place? This entire act could have been over and done with.

The maniac stopped screaming and opened the one eye to assess his damage, suddenly seeming to realize what hit him. *'Money! It was raining money,'* the Fruit Loop appeared to think, after peeling a silver coin off his cheek and carefully examining it.

In a wild sweep the dizzy fool went from crazy to crazier…if that was possible. Rolling over the hood he dove into another Broadway act, scooping up as many coins as he could. The light must've changed a thousand times by the time he was satisfied he hadn't missed a coin. And had a skycam been reporting from above, as the insanity backing up traffic the length of Georgia Avenue surely communicated, every bit of blame would have been placed 100% on the one motorist too civilized to take his foot off the brake.

Crazed and dazed, but elated, the maniac rushed over to his window panting, "thank you sir. God bless you. I really appreciate this." And just like he appeared, he danced away, disappearing into the fog that created him. The only evidence of his presence he left lying on the hood of the car.

Unsettled Clifford got out of the car and grabbed

the mangled squeezy, laying it on the seat beside him. What in the devil, he sighed before a horn blew. Guess the bow-legged man won that one!

. . .

Right off he blamed Merda. If she hadn't been wound up in the picture, the entire morning wouldn't have gone the way it had. He'd probably still be at work hearing about some other poor sap escorted off property. But all praise due and owing to Merda, the bow-legged bastard ran him down and trustworthy as the sun would rise again and again, was coming back around for as long as the sky was visible in his eyes.

He couldn't get out of his head how often his sister went to church, like religiously, every damn Sunday. He overheard her telephone conversations, bragging about all the philanthropic missionary work she was involved with. Mondays and Tuesdays working at the children's home, allegedly cradling homeless children with her love. Huh? Wednesdays volunteering at the battered women's shelter, purportedly showering homeless women with her support. Stop the presses…and your lying! Thursdays she claimed she was down at the soup kitchen ten hours a day, feeding homeless families meals. Pure blasphemy! Did homelessness mean anything? Or was it her mission to add to the homeless population…to give her lying self something else to brag about?

At sixty-five and pushing it, Merda still was a good-looking woman. *Cough, cough.* He heard her bragging about that too. Behind Parker's back however. So her legs were a little long and not in the best of shape, but it did make her look taller. And so her complexion was a little blotchy and wrinkly around her eyes and lips, but at least the light patches allowed people to refer to her as a redbone. All she had to do, which she did, was jazz up the tinseling of copper hair on her head by moussing it into cute little curls and garnishing her leftovers with fake lashes, nails, and enough jewelry to open another Zales. And oh, add on the cooing mooing voice and everyone saw her as a mesmeric rejuvenated savior.

Truth was, the way he saw her, Merda's heart was little more than a balled up knot. And how he knew this was by simple things such as how she had handled her infertility issue. Instead of trying to adopt a child, which thanking every angel she worshipped she hadn't tried, she settled the matter by adopting dogs she boasted she had been collecting and saving her whole life—the liar she was...unless she was referring to the flea bags she collected mating and dating.

Indeed in the holy half of her life she returned home dragging in mutts, the first a Beagle...found deserted on a highway, emaciated and fearful. A day later the mutt, still emaciated, and even more alarmed, took off again.

So he suggested getting a small dog, one she could maintain easier, given the hours she and fatso did nothing around the house. But no, she was set on larger breeds. She claimed their temperament was better.

Well, along came Mr. Chef, a big gruffy looking Saint Bernard, and fat ass Harriet, a boxer. Forget the fact that the dogs didn't get along and tore up the house after left alone for under an hour, those two animals almost tore Merda to shreds. Too bad they failed. Mr. Chef and wide ass Harriet growled at Merda only a short few 17-hours before they were on a road trip back to the pound.

Mr. Bean was the best, a Terrier mix so lonely that his connection with Cliff was instantaneous. Of course she picked up on their friendship and right back to the pound he went too. A day after Mr. Bean she came back with another double wham gram slam.

She brought home Dutchie, a Dogo, and Echo,

an Eskimo. That's when he knew for sure she was trying to kill him. Both dogs hated him, from the first day their eyes locked. Echo, nine months, and Dutchie, two, tore after him one paw out of the car. He almost ended up in pieces; head in three states and torso spread across the globe. *'Hello, it's Cliff down here. I know it's a partial toe, but this partial toe belongs in Maryland.'* Couldn't convince him Merda hadn't planned the attacks, so anxious about him leaving...by any means necessary.

On the beltway, the rain continued coming down in a steady maddening pace, forcing the wipers to work twice as hard. According to Mama, in every one of those clouds contained a silver-lining. Only he liked a better folklore. Going by his circumstances, the silver linings he made out, ripping long jagged seams in the sky, were best described as cold-hearted streaks of lightning...alas... God up there cussing somebody out. That was the lore he was going with. God had to be listening. Fired, laid-off, or even if he QUIT, he wasn't moving anywhere!

CHAPTER...3

Barnes and Noble, book haven of America, that's where he ended up on that cheerless day. Tacoma Park was a few exits before the ramp that led him home, and just where he found himself loafing half a day away. He couldn't face Merda broken and spineless. He needed an escarpment of other aromas, like wafts of coffee, books, and a filmy sunshine pressing its breath against a huge floor to ceiling window to rasterize his thoughts and get Merda off his back, and maybe even fatso out of Mama's chair.

His mother wouldn't have wanted this and his father for damn sure would have burned the home down to the ground before letting Merda get her grubby hands on his real property. He never trusted Merda, ever since that day she stole his legally registered and licensed gun and gave it to one of her Clyde Burrow friends who used it to commit an armed heist. This incident happened in the early days of Merda's growing transgressions. Five long years it took Pops to restore his upright reputation. It's why when he heard Merda had supposedly cleaned up her act and met a really *nice young boy*, he grunted and looked the other way, refusing to talk about what he thought of her so-called improvement. And when he heard she was marrying the really nice boy, and everyone got to making plans for that big trip to Florida, he claimed he lost his nerve for flying, despite his flying all the time, and never mind the fact that they all drove to Florida.

Clifford made his way up a galley of stairs and sat in a far back corner of Barnes and Noble. Dressed in hum-drum fall colors; plaid shirt, gray slacks and honeycomb colored loafers, with his cocoa complexion and a million and one everyday look, plus a pound of books in his lap he meshed seamlessly among drifters, loners and people basically interested in minding their business. It was un-likely he'd find relief in the many tomes he selected, but one after another thumbed through them anyway.

The home-keeping book he flipped through first. He always liked Martha Stewart, but thought she'd gotten the shaft too. So, it was a little tough seeing her with a roll of paper towels in hand, and smiling on the cover of a book. How could anyone have that big of a smile on their face after being shafted like that? Disturbed by the hallow look in her eyes he dropped the book on the floor and moved to the next.

The parachute book bothered him too. He hadn't gotten past the first page before the question, 'what color was his parachute' burned his eyes and turned his mouth to chalk. The question he wanted answered was why he felt like hurting the book. The son-of-a-gun on the cover didn't look a day over ten.

But *Shit My Dad Says*, that book hit him in the gut... hard. Reading and laughing, he had almost reached the center of the book when he realized hours had gone by. Before he knew it, he was standing in front of a small girl staring across a counter at him. She must've asked if she could help him because it dawned on him that she wasn't the only one waiting on a reply. A guy breathing down his neck, and a line of nasally afflicted customers weren't happy about his silence either. "Aye buddy, you might have to point to what you want because ain't no Miss Cleo's in here," snarled the neck breather.

If he was a thug he would've capped on the guy, but instead looked straight at the barista and asked in his head, *'Miss, can you please call a manager to come kill a book?'*

Funny as silly string, the Espresso artist actually read his thought! Indeed he met his first real psychic hearing her say, "Sir, I'm sorry but we don't ring up books here! You'll have to purchase your book downstairs!"

"Oh, no, no, no," Clifford stammered, giddily hobnobbing from one foot to the other as he removed the Shit book from the counter. "I'll have a toffee nut ice-blended Frappe," he grinned like a cheese ball.

He still got back a stank face, and a stankier face when a large woman wearing a bracelet of keys around her wrist had to stop playing with a calculator to ask him to step aside and describe a drink no one within the sound of his voice had heard of. Several eye rolls later, and a lot of extra boiling pots he finally got the Frappe but be damned if he had a dime to pay for it. Digging in his pockets, feeling for loose coins, he ended up extracting little more than lint. *'Ain't this about nothing,'* he scoffed. All he needed was seven lousy cents, or an unanimated barista that would forgive that part of his tab. He even suggested that if a few lousy coins was no big deal she would let him use her tip jar. But the big barista was adamant. No dime. No Frappe. And No! He couldn't pay by credit card. According to a sign scotched-taped to the credit card reader, this Frappy Joe's didn't accept credit cards for purchases under $10... *the bunch of white collar snobs they were.* But the satire of it all. He bet that squeezy guy was probably enjoying a cup of Joe...and a burger...with his spare change, while he faced a big bad barista, and a bunch of benighted customers eyeing him as the broke bad joke.

"Never mind," he huffed, leaving the half read Shit book on the counter and schlepping out of the store.

And that's when, looking to his left and seeing Dress Barn, that he smiled. It hit him at once; the panhandling derelict, the sarcastic drifters, the Shit book, Linthicum, Merda, and a tax-free vengeful skit to pay a whole lot of nobodies back.

He smiled recklessly to nobody and everybody. Merda talked a lot about divine intervention, and man-o-man was he not now lapping up in the thrill of it. This would be a throwback at life, slapping in the face anything that ever pinned him to the underclass. All of his life he tried doing the right thing, keeping his head low and emotions dialed down. Now it was time to get even shafting all the villains who shafted him. For once, he was breaking the rules. Satan was pulling on boxing gloves and throwing a few punches at life too.

Full of bitter hope, he walked into Dress Barn and stopped the friendly face that greeted him at the door.

"Hello, welcome to Dress Barn," replied a young girl armed with a clipboard and bargain basement smile. "Let me know if I can be of assistance," she hummed, turning to greet a customer on his heels.

But he stopped the girl, catching her by the arm. "You look like you do a lot of shopping here. I'm going to need your help," he said.

Sssh...he wasn't flirting like usual. He really did need help. He hadn't bought a stitch of clothing for himself, other than socks, and maybe briefs on occasion. Full fledge shopping for clothes was something he never did. Just so happened, his father was one of the best dressers in the DMV—District of Columbia/Maryland/Virginia area. Lucky him; between the sharp suits he inherited from Pops, and his galloping lady friends who treated him to gifts he could wear, he never bothered to know his neck size, leg length or waist measurements. Even Merda, and this was a classified omission he'd kill to keep, but even

Merda bought him a few things to wear.

"Cliff," she asked one day, weeks after moving in, "is that Dad's sweater?"

He had to look at what he was wearing. He got lots of compliments styling and profiling in Pop's threads, but it was unlikely Merda was flattering him. "Yes, it is," he warily told her, suspecting in addition to wanting the house, she wanted the clothes on his back too.

"Cliff, how are you going to meet someone dressed in Dad's old clothes? That sweater has to be old as me. I remember Dad wearing it when he used to walk me to school!"

WoW! Now that was a long time ago! He couldn't fathom it, let alone picture it. Dinosaurs kept creeping up in his view, blocking out sight of his beloved Pops holding the hand of something so extinct. To Merda's credit, something else that bust the bunions beneath his feet to admit, she didn't look as old as he preferred to describe her. Still, she didn't have it, like her old Welcome Back Kotter decrepit behind had her believing. But then the next night she came home carrying environmental-friendly large paper shopping bags. Inside were hoodies, denims, and one rigid leather jacket—the kind Fonzarelli wore. None of it was his style. He was a more khaki-sweater dresser, when he wasn't suited up in one of his father's light-weight worsted wool suits, no more than three buttons. But then Merda had always kept up with the hoodlum type styles, gangly fashions he avoided.

And yet, and even so, Merda shopped for him, too. Embarrassing to admit, but the God's honest truth. He was outside his league shopping in Dress Barn.

"I'm looking for work clothes," he told the greeter. "Do you know where I can find them?"

"Umm sir, I'm not sure where you work but you might want to try next door..."

...Oh no, the Jim Crow buck ended here. This wasn't 1964 when blacks were treated like how Broom

Hilda the barista had just treated him! Insulted he asked "...but isn't it your job to help customers!?"

The greeter released the shift on her face, some-what miffed too, and hit a mental space bar cogitating the possibility that suggesting he try next door where men's clothing was actually sold, might be biased. After all, he could be shopping for that special friend. "Umm...over there in that corner we might have some more masculine brands," she timorously replied.

Clifford squinted, looking in the direction of where she pointed. "Ugh, but..." he stuttered. "...Ugh, I think I'm going to need a little help picking out what I need."

The young lady drew back. He didn't realize he'd latched onto her arm, and found out he was clutching on to her pretty desperately too. "Oh, sorry," he said before letting go. "I'm not trying to pick you up," he sheepishly grinned. "I'm just not sure what size I wear."

The greeter looked him over. It was hard to tell if she was sizing him up for girth, or truth. In the end she asked if he preferred "Dockers or denims."

He took a wild guess. "...Think I'll go with den-ims," he decided.

"But, they can't look new," he thoughtfully threw in. "Do you guys sell any beat up looking stuff?"

The young woman paused again, once more giv-ing him the up-down. "Sir, you *really* might—"

—Whatever the woman was about to say he cut her right off. "I swear," he pleaded. "This is my first time shopping for myself. I've never done this before. Usually my—"—and like garbage disposals churned up leftovers his muttering ate up that one word—*wife*. "Usually my —*muffle muffle*—buys my clothes," he supplied.

Ah ha! The revelation brought the greeter back to her hospitable senses. "Well, we do sell pre-washed jeans," she replied, eye-balling his measurements. "Looks like you might be a 16 or 18-plus," she guessed, translat-ing his 34-36 male measurements to women's sizes.

He didn't know what those numbers she flicked at him meant, given he was so far out of his lane. "I'll need a shirt too," he replied, looking as if he needed a hand getting dressed too. "...Nothing too flashy," he reminded her. "I'm more a plain dresser," he added like a goofball.

"Flannel maybe?" She sarcastically asked, though he didn't catch that drift either.

"Yeah, sure," he shrugged. Flannel sounded warm enough for the season. He had a pair of flannel pajamas he loved slipping into when it got cold.

The greeter looked around, hesitant to leave her post. "Look, I'll hold your clipboard and stand here and watch the door," Clifford offered helpfully.

The greeter was not humored. She flagged down an associate and in hyperbolic sarcastic syntax repeated his bizarre request to an even less humored hourly wage worker. The floor associate, armed with a price gun and huff galore, rolled her eyes and sort of paddled off. Clifford would have followed her, if for no other reason than to pretend he cared about what she selected, except in less time it took normal customers to grab a loaf of bread the associate returned cradling smocks, denim, plaids and flannel in a mix of styles and sizes.

"Take this over to the cashier," ordered the put-out associate, dumping a rack of severely discounted clothes in his arms. Clearly shopping for customers wasn't in her job description, but ridding Dress Barn of an obvious nut was.

"Oh, but I'm going to need beat-up running shoes too," he said looming above the pile of cheap clothes.

Both women looked at each other before returning two duplicate ick faces. No. *They did not discriminate*, but something about this customer made them sick to their stomach.

"Sir, shoes are over there," barked the associate, pointing to a shoe rack within sight. "If you need further assistance, the sales associate over there can help you!"

Clutching the colorful motley of fabrics, he made his way over to the shoe area, dropping garments as he grazed along the shoe aisle. He couldn't tell what was in the boxes, not knowing the difference between ladies or men's running shoes. He did, however, know what beat-up looked like. And all of these shoes looked 'toe' up. Skipping over the heels he came upon a pair of black Aerosoles. With a few alterations these rubbery black boats would give him just the societal reject look he had hoped on.

As a loud register tallied his total, he calculated his haul. All he needed to do was hustle a dollar out of 500 people a day, only five days a week! He'd be his own boss. Could call out when he wanted. Have Saturdays and Sundays off. And make ten grand a month! At this tally, he could fully retire in five months! No, he wasn't hurting for money. But this would be just enough tax-free money to get back at everyone on his get-back list. Even five grand a month would satisfy his aim.

A short trip down Imagining's Lane he opened his eyes to find a cashier giving him a similar look that had tailed him his entire life. First Merda, then Linthicum, followed by selected clergy members and a laundry of disgruntled people like the barista, the greeter, the snapping turtle, and now this pushy cashier demanding "$69.72" with a corner of her lip upturned.

"Wow, rags sure are expensive," he gaily chuckled, pulling a worn wallet expanded to capacity with credit cards out of a back pocket.

"Just slide the card in the reader," the clerk tersely instructed, her upper lip stiff and still upturned.

Clifford ignored her Ragamuffin keep moving look and snatched the receipt out of the printer before it finished printing. Gleaming wildly he strutted out of Dress Barn smiling at Satan Blanchard stepping up to the batter's plate to take a swing at life.

The melancholy came back the moment he walked into the house. There sat Parker, spilling over his mother's lounge chair with the TV on... the sole source of light in the front room...and fatso pointed in that direction.

Clifford walked by without greeting him. This was the norm. They rarely spoke. Unless Merda had guests over, usually around holidays when she lured in a house full of family like his favorite Uncle Jamison who made it impossible to stay locked up in his room, would he expend extra energy to share what little comradery an arsonist and a piece of work might have in common. It was just hard to appreciate a man that didn't leave the house to make an earning.

Any moment Merda would be home, nosing around in his business, always with the usual fabricated motive, when was he leaving? It was Friday, so this was the day she spent in the church, tallying donations so she claimed. It was hard to believe Pastor Edmonds had that much trust in her. For God's sake, why he refused to believe the woman was a career thief, knowing her pilfering history, was a vague secret. Thieves like her counting his money, he'd tell to guess what was in the safe. If she guessed correctly, or almost correctly ten times in a row, he'd let her volunteer as a fortune-teller...in somebody else's church.

Like every day since they had been there, he went to his room and locked the door behind him. Before they came home he used to leave the door open, but now he kept the room secured by a fairly decent Magnum 357 deadbolt. Yeah, she was sweet as pie, and saved, but the deadbolt summed up how much faith he had in her comeback. The seclusion was a nice way to put distance between them and keep the arguing and suspicions at safe levels. He only had to deal with Parker, since there wasn't much choice, given the man went nowhere, except from the frig to the chair, and maybe to the toilet. Sometimes he smelled so bad, he doubted if he did that.

Staying in the room kept him away from all of that and allowed him to write more. His latest novel, *Satan's Best Friend*, a screwball tale about the devil and an evil goddess, had picked up quite a bit of steam since their arrival. Fine-combing through the completed draft he found the main characters finally coming to life. Parker was Exodus in the story, and Merda the evil goddess of course. He got the starring role—his favorite character of all the characters he drummed up—Satan.

Merda's return home made it an easy rewrite. Before he couldn't stay motivated to keep the story going. He couldn't visualize the characters, trying to create them from a collage of mythology novels he read—namely *Gates of Fire*. Latching on to the Greek names grew to be a pain in the neck, and getting the characters beyond evil became a monotonous drain. But the idea of avenging aristocrats stayed wide-awake. When Merda and the waffle traipsed into town, he opened the document and almost in one night rewrote a whole second draft.

Grejeckula he was calling her. He liked the sinister twist to the name, and the fact that under this guise he could exploit Merda's most used deviation, pretending that he loved her while craftily exposing her secrets in complete obscurity. Ripping her to shreds was the full intent.

The tale of why he hated her Bible thumping ways was clear, beginning on a day if he lived to be a million and one he'd never forget. The Sunday he out sung the choirmaster and left the church forever. A woman with one of them wide-open mouths who sang like Mahalia, just louder, was singing. He didn't see it as no big deal, out-singing the showoff, since nobody liked her anyway.

Even when Pearl…Ms. Pearl Anker…or Sister Anker to the fallaciously pious, mouth was shut, which it rarely was, the line that split her lips apart stretched clear from one side of her face to the other. And to exaggerate the matter, she traced her kissers using a color from a multi-family box of crayons. One Sunday she used black, and painted her smackers silver, trying to standout for the anniversary service. She did. And liked to have cost the church its top tithing parishioners who threatened to cut ties with Cedar over the minstrel show. It didn't happen, but was a part of his tabulations not seeing it a big deal out-singing the showoff, even if no one in the history of Cedar Baptist Church had ever dared to do so.

His last foray with Jesus happened on communion Sunday, at the 11am service. Mass Choir was singing and Pearl, as usual was leading. Only this Sunday, which was unusual, the Youth Choir was invited to join Mass Choir singing *Precious Lord*. He loved that song, along with *Jesus is My Rock*, the song he swayed to, coming down the aisle in a two-step bump behind Mass Choir. He was in his world, dressed in his best suit…a tailored gray and blue pinstripe suit he wore two Easter Sundays in a row. By the time he sat in the front pews, he was pumped. Eyes closed, church walls oscillating and floorboards vibrating, he couldn't wait until it was time to sing *Precious Lord*. He had practiced all week in front of a mirror. And Jesus told him, *'do it.'* He was under His spell, with every intention to deliver God's chosen people to the promised land.

When the instrumentals to *Precious Lord* began and he hopped up, along with 11 other children in the youth choir, he noticed worshippers sobbing. Why? He had no clue, but concluded not enough were crying. He wanted people up out of their seats and carrying on like when Miss Brown caught the holy ghost. So he stepped up, with his small but mighty voice, pulling notes from his diaphragm like taught at choir practice, stretching open his mouth rubber-band wide like Pearl's. When he heard

Brother DeGraff's low trombone sound, he got deeper, the way his father sounded in the shower, even bending over his little ten-year old body to give the congregation a real show, something like how MJ used to do when singing '*I want cha' back*' with the Jackson Five.

For a good minute the church seemed stealthy quiet, as if the piano had stopped playing and the choirs had stopped singing. Peeking out of his semi closed eyes he spotted mouths dropped and heads turned his way, but Strap on the piano still playing, and the choir indeed still singing, gave him his cue.

That's when he took over, moving to the aisle to be sure everyone knew who that mighty voice belonged to. Generously his voice jutted ahead of everyones', Pearl's included, bringing people to their feet and tears pouring from their eyes. The congregation moved, some singing with him, others rejoicing in the aisles...waving their hands, shouting, dancing, and basically passing out as they caught the holy ghost. Cedar Baptist, that Sunday, rocked.

Clifford never saw it coming, thinking he had done the Lord's work, what Jesus...and God... instructed him to do. No one told him there were consequences for out-singing Pearl.

Merda beat him like a stepchild, all the way home. "Boy, don't your fool ba'hind know any better than to be showing out like that?! Don't nobody su'posed to out sing Sista Ankle!"

Never mind Merda's paltry diction and inaccurate pronunciation of people's names, the only reason she got to *met out* his punishment was because Mama and Pops weren't home. They were visiting a sick relative, leaving the *cannister of evil* wide open. And he may have blamed them too for the beating, his parents that being, had not they been as much in the dark as he. This all happened before Merda got lost in the bowels of doo-doo, when she was prepping for the trip, doing little nasty things like plucking him in the head and twisting his skin when their parents weren't looking. Mama and Pops were good wholesome people, but back then...so very naïve. They always told Merda 'to stop messing with her brother,' an admonishment that didn't amount to a hill of beans, though wasn't too much of a big deal since she hadn't delivered the whipping she delivered when he crossed her line out-singing Pearl.

Truthfully, and being totally forthright, while he was scared to death of her, he found ways to get beneath her skin. He liked to get sick, throwing up on her shoes right before she was headed out to one of her parties, or he'd run up a fever, crying uncontrollably so Mama wouldn't go wherever she was about to go, and stay home to look after him herself. These little fits would put Merda on a sort of like punishment too. She couldn't sneak out of the house, or sneak in one of her boyfriends after locking him in his room.

From the day he was born... until the day she ran barefoot down to Florida... she made her hate for him patently clear, and that one Sunday she finally got to do what had been in her crooked soul all along.

Feeling justified in what she considered the ultimate sin, she gave him a beating he never forgot. She beat him so bad he developed a fever. When Mama and Pops saw his swollen face and bruises over 90% of his body, sparing only the soles of his feet and palms of his hands, they asked what happened. She told them, and they scolded her. "Don't you ever whip your brother like that again," they said. Although they didn't add this part, it might've been wrong what he'd done, but that was no whipping. That was attempted MURDER!

Mama didn't come down on her like she should have. But then, kids getting the daylights beat out of them wasn't called child abuse. That's just how it was. But right or wrong, it was the last time he ever outsung anyone, especially at church. He stayed home with Pops!

What was done, was done, this being the bridge that separated his love from not only his sister, but from religion, motivating much of his writings. In his latest work, a meticulously veiled Greek story, no one would know he was writing about a 16th century unholy whore. If Merda was wrong and could be forgiven, then surely killing off the spirit that killed his spirit in literature only he knew the subtext, he'd be forgiven too.

• • •

He emptied his briefcase, dumping papers that belonged to Linthicum in the wastebasket. Many were marked confidential; some (by law) he was required to return. Too bad. They should have secured their assets when they first thought about giving him the shaft. He didn't even bother to shred them. Pay stubs, confidentiality statements, non-compete agreements, bills, notes... it all went in the wastebasket.

He went to the closet next, a room about the size of a small bedroom, and stared. A wall of suits, arranged by color like his father used to do, stared back. Ivory slid to black. Welp! Might as well get rid of them too. He had no use for them. This was it. He finally hit rock bottom. Church well into his past, Merda back on his back, the suits a vintage collection no one wanted, about as retired as he was good and fired, he filled trash bags with the old half of his life. It wouldn't be long before Merda would come clunking in the house with her knock-kneed self, so he put a pep in his step. Last thing he wanted to see... and hear... while carrying the last of Pops out of the house was bumping gums and clinking knees. Not yet. Not until he could cash in on his new life and smother her face *in his success*.

Passing Parker, looking more statue than human,

with that filthy remote sitting in his lap, a remote he vowed never to touch, he carried the large black plastic bags out back. Any normal person funking up property that didn't belong to them, might've asked if he needed help. Or at least asked what he was up to. But not fatso. He sat there staring straight ahead at a black and white screen, disturbed none about a likely crime bisecting his 'Gunsmoke' daily life. But that was cool. Of all people, fatso needed to be 'in collusion', even if it was for sitting in his mother's lounge chair perpetrating a fraud.

Clifford hurled the trash bags, one after the other in the outside dumpster and poured 100% pure ammonia on top. Merda didn't like him doing this. She said it was cruelty to animals that liked dumpster diving, tearing open his trashcans and eating his garbage. So, for extra good measure he emptied the bottle, shaking it to make sure it was completely empty. The smell kept him from peeking too long, but from partial eyesight his deed appeared well covered. He made it back to his room just as Merda hustled in the house.

"Cliff! Cliff!" she shouted, turning to Parker staring transfixed into the tube to ask, "have you seen Cliff?"

"Ugh…he just went in that room," muttered fatso.

"Cliff! Cliff!" she yelled, banging with both fists on his door. "Cliff, are you in there?"

What the heck, at least he hadn't yet turned on the PC. He unlocked the door and partially opened it. "I just got in. You need something?"

"No, I was just wondering how you got home so fast. The beltway was a parking lot when I got on."

It would have been for him too; except he wasn't on the beltway at his usual time. He was sitting comfortably in Barnes and Noble loafing through books and devising a get back plan. "Oh, I had a headache," he answered wearily. "I left early today," the best excuse in the world. It gave him two reasons to close his door without letting her further the investigation.

"You should take one of those roots in the frig with some of that chai tea. Do you want me to make you a cup," she asked headed back to the kitchen, where she spent the other half of her day.

Hell No! Though he didn't say this. Well, he didn't say it like this. "No, that's okay," was how he put it. After he closed the door he added, "I'll poison my own self, thank you very much!"

"I'll put on some water," she answered anyway, not hearing him. "Think I'll get a little myself," she sighed.

On to the kitchen she rolled that stiff high behind of hers. Not that he imagined it, caring none about what she was about to cook up in the kitchen, he pictured her squinting when she happened to catch a glimpse of what was going on outside.

"Cliff!" and she yelled out as if Parker was attacking her. It was one of those long drawn out echoing Cliffs. Sounded like her last words before falling off a cliff.

Hurriedly he unlocked the door and rushed into the kitchen, joining her at the window. Parker hadn't moved a muscle. He hadn't even bothered to lean forward. An axe wielding maniac could have been charging full on bull run ahead to do some sawing work, yet fatso sat in his mother's beautiful vintage buttoned-up leather chair like he had hoped to be embalmed there.

But in plain view Clifford saw the problem. Merda had set Dutchie and Echo free, from where she normally kept them locked in the cellar, to crap up the back yard. So there they were, having gotten hold of the trashcan, strewing trash across the yard. And like who else but him ever took out the trash?

"Don't worry, I'll take care of it," he huffed, though she wasn't half as worried as he should've been. Dutchie was lying on one of his father's jackets. Laying on it like he owned it, perhaps contemplating to wear it one day.

The moment he stepped foot out the back door, the pups were up on their feet, ears at full attention ready to pounce. Echo stood first. He was Merda's favorite. And his least favorite. Like the hateful pup-mate he was, he came at him baring his teeth and snarling. Not sure if Merda was watching from the window, and fearing taking his eyes off Echo, he felt his pockets for keys. He kept a tazer on the ring.

"Take another step you dumb mutt and I'll taze your butt to hell," he hissed.

Dogs understood language better than most people gave them credit for. Echo didn't move. But not moving wasn't all of a good thing. He needed to get the clothes back in the trashcan, and he needed to do this before Merda came outside nosing around.

He tried to be cool, acting like he and Merda's pups were on good terms...like those mutts hadn't made it clear what they would do if he stepped foot on their turf. Sure enough, as he reached for a pair of pants, out the corner of one eye he saw the fifty-pound mutt lunging at him. He flew backwards, both feet up in the air, landing on his back as in that same flash he saw himself starring in the movie Cujo. Echo pounced, literally coming out of the sky looking like the red-eyed devil people uniformly saw in nightmares.

"Get back! Get off of me you dumb mutt!" And he rolled over, James Bond style, squeezing on the tazer as he rolled. Miraculously, somehow, he managed to get Echo in the eye. The mutt squealed once and backed away, taking off in a spastic run to the other side of the yard. It looked like he was running in circles, going mad it seemed, but Clifford couldn't be sure because as he was rising from his knees he caught Dutchie sprinting his way...100-yard dash fast.

There wasn't any barking, at least not coming from Dutchie, perhaps she didn't have enough time to bark being in a brisk haste to tear a hole in his backside. In the scuffle with Echo he lost the tazer, but gained a fistful of grass and one trashcan lid, what he used to sock Dutchie in the head with.

Merda rushed out in the yard, bursting through the backdoor as if she was coming to his defense, though of course it was otherwise.

"What's going on out here? What happened? Did you forget to tie down the lid?" she beleaguered. Now, was that anything to ask with a 70-pound mutt standing his ground snarling at him?

Of course he didn't tie the lid down. But he hadn't forgotten. Damn dogs!

"Go put some peroxide on that," Merda ordered, speaking of the small puncture Echo managed to put in his leg. And off she lumbered with her high behind, to comfort Echo of course. Dutchie followed, being the smart heifer she was. Surely she wasn't coming back for more, not with Echo going off like a siren, throwing himself into the fence.

• • •

Just like Merda she thought it was his responsibility to foot the expensive emergency room dog doctor visit.

"Well Cliff, you're gonna have to help me take care of this," she whined. "I don't have that kind of money lying around."

And he did? Shucks, he just lost his job, and was contemplating a vicious legal war that could spiral them both in the pits of a deep dark novelish poverty, costing them the house and their life if things didn't go his way.

Fifteen hundred bucks the mutt doctor charged. That was a lot of loot fixing whatever got in Echo's eye. Merda asked what that whatever was, like it was his concern. But he went on and claimed he didn't know. Heck, those were her fuzzy knock-off besties. Hadn't she hocked Mama's jewelry, the pieces she never liked, and used the money as collateral to retrieve her beasty stink faces from the professional hit list trainer? Whenever he caught her with the pound-hounds, she talked like an expert mutt mind reader when all he knew for sure, was he was in a life and death fight.

As usual, he said none of that. He acted like he hadn't been just let go and wrote out a check for half the cost of the dog's doctor visit.

"And I'm going to need help paying for his meds too. Whatever you hit him with, burned his left eye and got inside his mouth!"

Now, he'd only zapped the mutt in the eye, though it was no long drawn out thriller what caused the burning inside the beast's mouth. Still, none of it was his fault, yet he paid for the meds too. Just don't ask him to take care of the damn eye. Not if she wanted her hairy pal to have any eyes.

All things being what they were, he was happy his masquerading sister hadn't gotten ahead of his plan; a pretty convincing plan he thought. He had written it all out, separated by chapters, guaranteed to be a best seller beyond Satan's Best Friend. When those puppies hit the market, readers would either love it, or hate it, but nobody would forget it.

The plan was to leave the same time, dressed in one of the two suits he had left, and drive the same route he'd driven to Linthicum for the past twenty-two years. Instead of pulling onto Linthicum's parking lot however, he would find public parking on the Northwest streets of Washington, D.C. and roam the Mall begging tourists, residents and pedestrians for spare change until he had $500, or the sun set...whichever came first.

And that's just what he set out to do, beginning day one of his industrious panhandling enterprise. Monday morning he got up, brushed his teeth, shaved, showered and before Merda's size eleven-and-a-halves hit the floor he was out the door with a cup of coffee in hand.

In a hurry, most ambitious to start his day, he hopped in his mini SUV, turned the ignition and hit the brakes when he caught a smooth-faced quite handsome KAW staring at him in the rearview mirror. Clearly there was a snag in his loosely plotted plan. This was not exactly the street bum he expected to see.

Hesitating a minute, long enough to check the glove compartment for a quick fix before the scarecrow he'd last seen detonated in sponge hair-rollers interrupted the morning, he gave up. After all, there was a man swelling up in his mother's chair who probably couldn't explain what a mirror looked like, much less had used one for shaving, yet that professional bum had a face smooth as butter.

Yeah, if the hairless fatso got away with looking like a drifter, so could he, least risking having to explain to Merda why he suddenly looked like Moses, or a black Santa. That's how the spy plot landed in his back pocket. Smiling blissfully, tap dancing 10-miles mph in parking lot beltway traffic, he mused at the *Road Runner*, resembling in every aspect Merda...huge mud flappers, rooster hairdo, and that thing tied around its neck... making tracks crisscrossing the entire state of Maryland. Gossips *like her* notoriously ate up espionage thrillers, and Satans *like him* loved laughing his low hanging arse off at all the suckers he had in mind to trick; Merda and her church sisters top on his list.

The Sheraton's parking lot was full when he arrived, so he parked on the street beside a 3-hour meter. This concerned him at first. It wasn't quite 8:30am. That meant he'd have to slug it back over to the meter at least three times during the course of his nomadic travels. He shrugged it off though, since he'd be wandering around anyway. He only had to keep track of the time; checking in at 11:30, 2:30, and quittin' time.

The Sheraton brimmed with activity. This was where he planned to change. Didn't think he was going to start out in a bus depot public restroom? This gig required he glide into it, not jump in head first. He wanted a clean, comfortable spot to change into his derelict costume. And the Sheraton, with its superb lighting, and shined to a heavenly perfection marble fixtures... bellhops bowing and attending to guests every need, provided that. Of course too, under such majesty *'wasn't all this brilliance the best way to be recognized?'*

Lo and behold if he didn't arrive at the Sheraton to discover a job fair in motion. The first banner he spotted belonged to Linthicum. *Wasn't this about a blip!? Like what were the odds!?* He couldn't count high enough the times he participated in one of these conferences, elbow to elbow with people he shared cubicles with, who the minute they were let out of their cages, and their egos roaming higher ground, that they would get to snapping their fingers, rubbing their chins and scratching their heads trying to recall how they met. It happened all the time, and yet wouldn't this be the one time when one of these same corner office tarts who ignored him every day getting to their desk, would suddenly know his first, last and middle name. Yeah, just when he didn't need visibility, he'd get it...prime time! Wouldn't recall a thing about the conference, except seeing the wart corporate finally got rid of, down on his luck.

"Did anyone see Clifford Blanchard? I saw the old geaser at the Sheraton looking like a vagabond!"

Without making eye contact, he slinked his way into a restroom and into a stall. Man, he muttered, struggling to pull on the pants. He should've tried them on. Those darn Dress Barn sales gals couldn't shop worth a lick. He couldn't tell if it was the stall or the pants that was too small. Only after he managed to get the pants on did he realize it probably were the pants. Gathered around his crotch and snatched up his butt, he decided not to tuck in the shirt, which was even more outlandish. Looked like he was wrapped in a tablecloth intended for a circus tent, or maybe a holiday celebration… like the 4th of July.

He emerged from the stall a little sweaty, and looked in the mirror. Awful. That's how he looked. Plain awful. And not in a good nomadic way. He looked like a crisp brand new one dollar coupon clipped from a Dress Barn newspaper advertisement.

Making his way back to the lobby, steering through throngs of people, he wasn't the only one espying his questionable look. A security guard; big, tall and very angry and black, stopped him right away.

"Excuse me," barked the large dark shadow stepping in front of him, blocking his view. "Where are you going with that?"

Stumped, and crazed with fear, not only hoping no one was catching the exchange but that he wasn't in real trouble, he searched himself for an answer. Perplexed he asked, "with what?!"

"With that," the dark slug barked, nodding towards the briefcase.

"Oh this," and he relaxed, dropping his arms and sheepishly grinning. "This is my briefcase," he tried to laugh off, expecting to soon be on his way.

The mass of authority muttered something into the top corner of its uniform before abruptly grabbing him beneath the arm, strong-holding him, to lead him into a hidden back office.

Who was this fifty-cent security guard with the lava mocha dark lips wearing a jacket that looked like it was hanging on a gorilla's coat hanger? He started to protest until he looked around. Several pairs of eyes curiously inspected him, staring him up and down as if at any moment one of them would knock on his head and ask if he was inside. *'Come on Clifford, we know it's you. You can't hide in there. We see you…'* before erupting into a laugh so hideous he'd have to laugh too, and admit it was him.

Humbly, with his briefcase tucked securely beneath an arm he faced a room full of law people, a few

with guns clipped to their hips, just beneath pouches holding a rack of ribs and a pot of fat back. Still, he was sure...
things would get sorted out once he was able to explain
his side of the story.

At first no one spoke, not even lava lips the big
gorilla pompously pacing as if he just caught a great *black*
shark. Clifford's guilt was assumed. So the jury took it's
time pouring coffee, tossing pencils to the next guy over,
and answering calls with, "yeah? Whadda' ya' got?"

For a good minute they ignored him... as if he
didn't have some place to be. A windshield full of tickets
and sixteen boots could end up on his car by the time he
got out of there.

"Hey, look guys," he volunteered. "I really need
to be getting to work." It was an ingenious spiel, one that
slipped out of desperation, visualizing the job the city
might do to his car and the story he'd have to trump up for
Merda.

The seated round mushy guy wearing a white shirt,
striped necktie and two coffee driblets over his left pocket... horizontal to the tie and perpendicular to his chin...
looked up. "Work," he asked as if the term was foreign to
him.

"Yes, I'm working undercover...and you guys are
really about to blow it." He wanted to call them nimrods
too, but left that part out.

"Do you have some ID," asked the stumpy mushy
coffee dribbler.

Clifford reached in his back pocket and pulled out
his wallet. Driver's license, credit cards, medical cards, he
pulled out a dozen cards, slapping each one on the table
like playing aces in a Spades game.

The round guy wheeled around in his chair to take
a good hard look at lava lips. He threw up his hands like
a wasted effort. "So what do you have on him," he asked
from a worn out irked voice.

"Ugh, I just saw the guy walking around with that

briefcase under his arm," mumbled lava lips. One thing was for sure. After this excursion, the mocha chump was getting chewed out. That much was for certain. He was not the hero in this case.

The round fella sighed loudly and shook his head, swatting the cards out of his line of sight. Disgusted, he waved Clifford off too. "Go on and get out of here," he grumbled, fanning him away.

Gladly, Clifford muttered. No one had to tell him that he needed to find another hotel to change into his spy wear. Gratefully only an explosion of laughter hit him in the back as he schlepped out the door.

"Damn, wonder what they're paying him?"

"Must be one hell of combat pay…"

"…HaHaHaHa!" the guards, minus one, howled loud enough to be heard over the lobby full of Linthicums. He couldn't have been less conspicuous if torture bait had been tattooed across his forehead.

CHAPTER...4

Note to himself. No more Clifford, or no more of the soft nice reasonable guy who tried to live on the straight arrow doing the right thing. That guy was gone, dearly departed, vamoosed, the tag stricken from his resume.

Norm was his new persona. And why Norm? He had no sincere idea. Momentarily he klept it from the Cheers character. He identified with a man wasting away on a barstool, staring down at life swimming in the bottom of a beer mug, an iodine reflection of pity he longed to flush down a toilet.

Clifford, Cliff, or Norm if he could make it stick, started up Independence Avenue, staggering and muttering to himself, practicing a vagrantness strut he planned to adopt. He never would have believed it, had he asked himself the other day, but it honestly felt good playing the polite sober drunk, just so long as he pulled in five hundred that day. Made him a little salty though, being a coward about taking them acting classes. He probably could've had one major acting career by now, had he not flagged film school. Surely he'd be much better off than what became the case, following Pop's footsteps when clearly Pop was the last of a retiring breed.

A woman digging in her purse about to feed a meter caught his attention. With her purse hung open, digging to the dear bottom of it, it looked like a fine opportunity to ask if she could spare some change.

"Ma'am...ma'am...can you please help a sick
vet..." he began, impulsively doing the bounce, a little jig
he saw homeless men who'd been on their feet night and
day doing. He bounced and bumbled his way in front of
her so he couldn't be ignored. "Please...please...a dollar
will do. So an old vet can get a cup of soup."

The woman didn't answer right away. She tried to
ignore him, shoving her face deeper in the purse. If she
could just find more coins quickly, this it might go away
and leave her alone.

But he didn't. The one thing he told himself when
he drafted the plan, he had to be persistent, career advice
he was given at Linthicum but ignored.

"You need to make yourself more visible," a capital K.A.W. wrote in his evaluation.

"Why," he asked when the KAW finally crawled
out from his shell for a face-off meeting to discuss why all
year long he said nothing about him doing less than satis-
factory work.

"Visibility is the key to success," the KAW told him,
mimicking exhausted buzzwords every walking-talking
suit used. Linthicum could've written in a memo tucking
his tail beneath his butt would propel him up corporate
ladders, and the spineless creatures these KAW's were,
would've mimicked that lyric too. Kiss-Ass-Wipes had become infomercials for every corporation in America.

So he ignored the ill thought-out advice. He was
just fine where he was. Even if he'd been told he was surfing a tidal wave, he would have rode that swell too. Better
to be above the sharks than swimming with them. And
now here he was, on level ground, where he controlled
how persistent he wanted to be.

He expected the woman to go on ignoring him, or maybe spit in his face, but she surprised him. She came up with two bills crumpled together and mashed them into his hand and hurried down the street.

"Thank you ma'am...God bless you. God bless your soul." Happily he staggered on up the street thinking two dollars was even better than what he calculated. If he doubled his expectations, he might also end up with a doubly good book. He strolled assuredly on to his next casualty.

"Sir...sir...can you please help a sick vet..." and he did the bounce, adding a nod and a little saliva to the skit, wiping his mouth on the end of his sleeve. "Just anything you can spare to help an honorable vet with the cost for a cup of tea and some hot soup," he drooled, going as far as to wipe the extra juice he let build up around his mouth on the end of both sleeves.

"You disgraceful prick," the man spat back. "You think I'm stupid! You worthless piece of scum! You need to be thrown beneath a cell for perpetrating a fraud!" And he spat on his shoes!

'Oh God! His shoes!' He looked down and realized he must have left the running shoes in the car, or at home. His Bremen leather loafers were as polished and shined as two shoes could ever get. He lost his nerve, genuinely staggering over to a wall to brace himself.

'Come on Cliff, you can do it. You can't let a small set back like this get you down brotha'. Think five hundred a day... five hundred tax-free dollars a day for just one year Cliff...or rather, Norm. That's all. You can do it brotha'.

That was the spiel he was giving himself when a voice hit him from his blind side. "Hey, hey my man," came a flat raspy voice heated by so much funk he could feel scales warming the right side of his face. "You got anything you can let me hold?"

He turned his head to meet a crusty mouth and a hardened scabby hand held out in front of him. Those were *my man's* beauty traits. The pair of crusted grapes juggling around his head was the revolting edge of this dude. And the hole between the grapes, oozing with a palpitating puss was the side that almost made Cliff turn around and run all the way home and hand Merda his house keys.

Any other day he would've been shooing this person away. Far away! But this person was now him, in a real personal way. He didn't fear him, nor pitied him, but in an errant moment rethinking what he was doing, he happened to look down at the man's feet. Swallowing hard he managed to ask, "say my man, how about you trading me my shoes for yours?"

My man looked down at his feet, his eyes lighting up like Christmas. "Cool, cool. I like them there shoes," the guy said, bracing himself against a wall and hurriedly kicking off a grubby pair of battered running shoes. By God did this man's feet stink. His feet stunk like a skunk swimming among dead fish.

Clifford squeezed his eyes shut trying to fend off the odor. There was no way he could stick his feet in those shoes. He wanted to rescind the offer, but it was too late. My man was already out of the smelly shoes, nodding his head spasmodically looking towards the ground. Not all the drool trickling out of his mouth was due to the inability to close his mouth. He wanted the shoes so bad he could taste them.

Cliff took one last long look at his loafers, shoes he wore countless times in to work, staring at them while KAWs talked progressive talk about building bridges, knocking down walls, and skipping up stepladders.

With his eyes squeezed tight, he slipped out of the loafers to trade his good KAW shoes for one miserable pair of funky running shoes. Any shoes were better than no shoes. October wasn't the best month to be walking around DC naked around the feet.

My man jumped right into his shoes and busily

got on his way, snapping his fingers and spinning small doughnuts dancing down the street. "Hey, thanks my man! These shoes here feel real good," he called out with one last spin, arms raised high as if he'd hit the jackpot.

Nauseous, Cliff again looked down at the running shoes my man left behind. They looked so hot that a puff of steam seemed to be rising above them. Easing into the shoes felt like stepping into eggs, cow gut, and vomit. His stomach quibbled as he stepped into the left shoe, and he almost spit up his guts when he eased into the right shoe. When he got both feet in, squishing and sinking as he tried standing on his full weight, he was thankful the contents of his stomach hadn't left his body. Carefully he took a step, then another, telling himself he could do it. A few more steps and he giggled at his image creeping by a large glass window. He thought he looked vagabond good. Like a perfect reflection of a man living on the streets. The shoes were an instant hit. The new pre-washed jeans and long flannel night-shirt hanging to his knees got along well with the squishy shoes.

Before long he was walking at a good clip, part of the way skipping and singing, not realizing it was almost noon and that he had another four hundred and ninety-eight people to nudge out of a dollar, barely enough to pay the tickets accumulating on the meter he forgot to feed.

• • •

Merda got home first. She usually did. And just like she also usually did after arriving home, she went straight to his room to check to see if he'd locked his door. That morning he hadn't. He was so excited about his new venture he ran out of the house with just the briefcase.

Toeless black shoes he bought the other day sat in

the middle of the floor in his bedroom. It was the first thing Merda noticed. She bent down and picked them up, examining how the toes were cut out of what looked like a brand new pair of...women's running shoes!

She knew it! She knew something was going on with Cliff. It wasn't normal for a fifty-two year old man to never settle down and make a family.

"Have you seen these?" And she shoved the running shoes beneath Parker's nose.

He leaned back. *No, he hadn't seen the running shoes.* "What about 'em? Who's are they?" he asked.

"What about them? Who's are they," she shouted. "These belong to Satan! That's who!"

Parker looked up at her and shook his head, trying his best to spread open his eyes and appear concerned. No one ever heard him, but he grumbled it a lot. He wished Moo-Moo would mind her business. Things were so much more peaceful when she did. Besides, why was she so bothered by Cliff? He wasn't. Cliff never bothered him. Maybe if she stopped advising those lawyers about how much law she knew...from her past experiences... she might've already had the house and wouldn't be seeing Satan at all.

Merda rolled her eyes at Parker... hard. The man was no help. Head was as useless as his legs and all the rest of his non-working body parts. She took her squawky-scratchy shrill screech to the kitchen where she got on the phone with her good friend Theresa. The two had been friends since Crockett's *fake* coonskin cap craze. Both of them used to run the streets hard back in the day, before parting ways to invest in Avon *'and whatnot'*...while *going through some things*. The friendship resumed after they found Jesus, and returned to their old stomping grounds.

"Do you think Cliff might be gay?"

"Well, you know your brother has always been a little strange," Theresa replied. She knew Cliff when he was running around with the snotty noses and poop in his pants. She used to wipe his nose...and butt too. Only she wasn't as mean with him like his sister. She was the one who got him a date for senior prom. She got her cousin Jackie, who at first didn't want to go, but returned home talking about how nice and wonderful Cliff was.

"Oh no," Merda shrieked. "Ain't no way in the hell I'm lettin' a cross-dresser breathe underneath the same roof that covers my head!"

"Well, what you gonna do Mary...kill him?"

Merda got silent. *That was a thought.* The Bible did shut the door many times over on turpitude, and getting it on with the same sex was a moral iniquity, so who hath cared if she rid the world of a blatant sinner.

"Mary?" she heard Theresa's waiflike voice call out. "Have you talked with Cliff? Did you ask him?"

"I'm holding the evidence right here in my hand," Merda snapped.

"Wait...what evidence," Theresa asked.

"These shoes!" Merda shrieked. "I just told you he has a brand new pair of women's running—"

"—Aww Mary," Theresa whined. "The shoes could belong to anybody. Maybe he's working on another one of them books...or what if he had a woman over?"

"So I should be looking for a woman with ostrich toes?!" Merda quipped. "Terry, you and I both know these shoes don't belong to no one but Satan!"

Merda recounted the other day's events, him getting home before her and acting fishy out there in the yard, fighting with her dogs. She had to take both dogs to the vet after he almost poisoned them; intentionally she was sure. She told him a million times not to pour ammonia in the trash can! "I started to turn his butt in for animal cruelty," she told Theresa. "The only reason I didn't is because I don't want him to miss our next hearing. Ain't no way he's getting this house!"

That was too much information for Theresa. She kind of liked Cliff. Merda was on her own. She needed to put that mess on an altar and let someone far more spiritual pray over it. "Ephesians 6:18...Mary! You gotta pray girl, PRAY!" she told Merda.

"Yeah, I'ma pray alright," Merda replied back. "With a helmet and thy sword!"

Just to think what this might be doing to her parents trying to be at peace in heaven. It was just too much to bear. She threw the shoes out in the yard for her dogs to chew on and returned to her room and got down on her knees. She was serious about the Word. She wasn't one of those sometime Christians. Mess with her and you was messing with her God!

She opened an old weathered Bible, one she found in Mama's vault, and read parts of Revelations, from the very old testament. "One of the elders saith unto me, Weep not...behold, the Lion of the tribe..." she mumbled before closing the book and using both hands to pull herself up off the floor. Quietly she berated herself for calling Cliff Satan. The pastor of her church, Pastor Edmonds, spoke about how she treated her brother...last Sunday. Well, not personally. He more so told the congregation to 'keep the tongue from evil...' and 'to not let the lips speak guile,' neither word she had been able to follow.

Cliff was just too darn willful... something like their father. The both of them, just as obstinate as an old mule, which...and to tell the real truth... it wasn't even Cliff that was on her mind as the pastor preached. It was his darn bad ass boys!

Right there in church, within direct line of his view, beneath the almighty pulpit and his righteous voice, he and that First Lady of his saw them boys cuttin' up, like they did each and every Sunday...kicking the pew with them expensive brick Buster Browns they dressed them spoiled brats in...making all that noise and disturbing worshipper's like Elder Butler who had every right to get up, in the middle of service, and straighten those bad ass boys out. Had them cut-ups kicked the back of her pew she wouldn't have just scolded them, she would have straightened them out the same way she did Cliff that time he cut up singing all over Pearl. *Talking about it wasn't his fault! Lying on Jesus claiming God told him to show his tail. God would've never told him to do such a thing!* She sho' did. She straightened that fat tail right out, the minute they got home! She gave him a whipping he not only deserved, but a whoopping he'd remember for as long as he lived. She could say one thing. It was the last time he pulled that stunt!

This was what sometimes infuriated her about Cliff. He just wasn't right. The boy was born damaged. Mama had no business having him. She just had him too late. Her and Papa were past their time to raise him right, though the good Lord knew she *at least* tried.

Cliff used to look like *Humpty-Dumpty*, with his big fat butt, trying to eat them out of a house and home. So she stayed on that juicy round ba'hind, wobbling around the house thinking it was okay to embarrass her in front of her friends...belching and farting and throwing up in her shoes! And ooo! She hated to see him cry. He made the ugliest face...turning them sausage lips upside down looking like Ronald McDonald the clown!

Too bad she left when she had. God as her witness she would have straightened Cliff out had not a higher calling called. Unfortunately he was left in the care and custody of an unsophisticated mother and hoary spiteful father so bitter that he didn't even attend her wedding to properly give her away. These two people could never help Cliff learn how to be a man. What a shame. Though what was done, was done.

...Well, Almost! And hang on...

She could let a lot of stuff be bygones, except but for one. No one was getting between her and Jesus. Christ never intended for two men, or two women, to share one bed. Never. It was immoral, and an outright sin. And everyone whoever touched a King James *version* of the

Bible knew the wages of sin was death. Come hell over high water, wasn't no way she was letting Cliff embarrass her again. She was not Mama, nor Pops! First of all, entertainers belonged on Broadway. Not up on the altar serving God. And secondly, Over Her Dead Body!

She greased her lips…and knuckles…waiting to hear his car pull up in the driveway. On this matter, Christ was having the final say.

• • •

Around the same time Merda was inspecting the shoes, Cliff was still be-bopping along the Mall gloating over his earnings…a ringing $2.00, plus a few coins picked up off the street. Grand salary…*thus far*; $2.17, to include the Canadian coin, every cent spent on bottled water. The *five-n-dime* clerk didn't hassle him too much, other than yelling at him for trying to slip off the foreign coin. She told him to take his water and get out of the store, "and don't let me see you back in here AGAIN!" she shouted.

Bopping on, in the spirit of his new gig, working into the shoes my man pawned off on him, he lost track of time. He forgot about driving into the city. And by the squish in the shoes, he forgot he even owned a car. All in his head was what was going on between his toes, and what his toes might look like once he stepped out of the shoes.

He made it to a Metro underpass, couldn't recall the name of the building, but it was a white ashy building, the spot where he stopped to hang around a few guys hoping to pick up a better script. One of them, the one he learned was Blue, wanted to know where he'd been.

"I just got out," he said, going into his act. Didn't know how it came to him to say this, or if the guys would buy it, but the words came out naturally.

The tall one, the one they called Hagerstown, stood there inspecting him, almost as if he wanted to laugh, reading him like the flake he was.

"Awl man, dat ain't Deep. You thought that was Deep," laughed the one with no visible legs and one arm, making the chair he was sitting in spin.

Hagerstown smirked and Blue squinted. But Cliff didn't stop his act. Can't say it didn't take a lot of nerve, because it surely did. He had a lot of nerve smiling with all of his good, clean, brushed teeth, and strolling over to a few guys who knew the streets years better than him, suited up in his crisp new dress for less clothes.

"Who you?" Blue asked with this giant chip on his shoulder, mad because he wasn't Deep, but crashing their party as if he was.

Indubitably my man's shoes held magic because they added more bounce to the skit. "Man, I remember you from the ward," he grinned with his nerves of steel. "Oh, you don't remember? We was in the ward together."

"Naw pimp. You don't know me," Blue said looking him dead in the face, his snarl upstaged by a tarnished capped tooth.

Cliff stopped smiling after that. His act needed to be tweaked a bit. "Man, you was out of it. I thought you wasn't gonna make it," he lamely added.

He didn't make it obvious, but he counted the exact number of seconds before he'd know whether he was walking away or going to be carried away. Exactly five. If Blue didn't lay into him in exactly five seconds he just might make it out of there with at least a full chapter for his next novel, and a full rack of teeth, taking testimony directly from what remained in his hippocampus.

Slowly a hideous smile tailored Blue's face, turning his complexion from dark, to darker, and lifting a corner of his mouth upstaging the capped tooth which looked more deranged. "What? Is you a NARC or somethin'?" And he looked him up and down.

'First, tell me if you got any drugs and I'll let you know,' Cliff mused. He didn't dare say this aloud though. By his count, and he started recounting after Blue's last reply, he had shy of 3 seconds remaining. "Shit...they couldn't pay me enough!" Adding the shit, added creds. Without it, he was a NARC for sure. And a geeky one at that. At least that's how he felt.

He started walking away when an arm caught him around the neck from behind. He felt something hard and blunt poking him in the side. And he smelled Blue's breath. "Where ya' boyz at? Where dey at? Let's see if they come save ya' ass," Blue chuckled, breathing funk so dank and stank into Cliff's neck that his entire body curled.

This startled the new drifter for a second. He made it all the way to one in the count, when Blue laughed loud in his ear, smacking him with a kiss in that ear too, allowing him to relax some.

"Ah ha! You ain't no damn NARC. How you know me? Was you in General?" Blue continued laughing with the watchful Hagerstown looking on, and Simp in his world still spinning them semi circles in the wheelchair.

"Yeah," he answered, sullen and thrown off script.

"Deez fools over here talkin' bout Steele is on our side. I say Steele ain't shit. What 'chew see?"

Hagerstown waited. Before he intently watched. Now he openly dared Cliff, challenging him to say more. Taxing him with that wily stare that said he'd been drinking since he was a child, hard 100% proof alcohol, eyes so red they looked pulled from a dragon and sewn into his face. But through the scarlet veneer was an astute glare that said he read him well.

Cliff looked at Blue good and hard, careful not to let Hagerstown's vilifying grin distract him, and coolly told him, "I don't know no Steele," and he turned to walk off.

He knew what happened when there was a crowd. He'd seen this bunch at Linthicum too many times. They huddled in groups and tested newcomer's spine and backbone. Too much of either and they would team up to break one or the other, or both. It was the only time he witnessed such a valiant effort of team camaraderie.

"Hey my man...where you headed off to," Blue apologized.

"Gone up to twenty-first," he tossed behind him, adding more bounce to his step, thanking every harking angel that had come to his rescue.

"Awl Pimp, what's on twenty-first," Blue called after him. "Bring us back a sammich," he teased.

But Cliff kept bouncing, pacing his dips to how good he suddenly felt. What were them fools doing talking politics anyway? What did they know about Steele and Pelosi? He caught up to a man going by Roscoe not more than 500 yards from the politicking trio...hawking jewels. These didn't appear to be jewels of the Nile... like rare blue diamonds. These glassy objects looked like home-made crafts; polished stones and pebbles drilled and fed onto thin wires. Roscoe called them his African collection. He'd been making and selling them for a few months, he claimed.

"Well, what's this one here do," Cliff asked, coming out of his pocket with a fist full of his own crumpled dollar bills he'd planned to use for just such a purpose. It was a transient crack to show Roscoe he was a veteran of doing business on the streets, careful not to repeat the offense as what happened with Blue and Hagerstown. Beneath the canopy of dreadlocks and smell of incense Roscoe looked like a fairly decent businessman that if he quickly connected with, just might protect him from the likes of dudes like Blue.

"Those are stones from Istanbul...brought them back after serving two tours in Turkey," Roscoe explained.

"Two tours in Turkey?" Cliff asked acting surprised.

Roscoe jerked his head to one side. "Oh, you've been there?"

No, he hadn't. And had Maryland, DC and Northern Virginia not been so close, counting as one state, the furthest territory he could claim on a worldwide map, was the outer loop of the beltway…and Florida.

"That's a long way from home," Cliff said bouncing, nodding as he fumbled with the ties on a cloth bangle. "I don't like flying, so I could've never gone so far away."

It was Roscoe's proudest moment. He smiled wide, showing off gaps between all 26 of his exposed teeth. He had done something many men were afraid to do, plus served his country, proof displayed across an eight-foot table. In short, he could lie through every tooth and Cliff would have to believe it.

"Did this come from Istanbul too," Cliff asked, speaking of the cloth bangle he held in his hand.

"Yes my friend. Everything here is a product from Istanbul. That there comes from head wraps men and women wore back in the early 1800's." Roscoe leaned into Cliff and sort of like whispered explaining intricate details about the bangle. "See, that's raw silk," he said pointing at a thin blue thread weaved through the fabric. "Well, it's been treated to keep it from wearing," he admitted, lowering his voice even more before abruptly remembering its selling feature. "It was worn by a spy, who ultimately was killed for treason," he said with his chest puffed up.

Immediately Cliff put the bangle back and picked up a less interesting bangle. This one was a silver wire that looked reshaped from a large paper clip. "What's this one do? I need something for luck!" he chuckled. Shoot! He'd wear a garter belt, hosiery and heels if it was the only choice between that and something a dead man, or woman, had worn.

"Now that's your lucky piece right there!" Roscoe cheered, the typical Rasta businessman he was. Clearly he didn't know any more about where his knockoffs originated than the little old Turkish man who probably pawned them off to clean out his tent.

"Great!" Cliff cheered too. "How much?"

"For you my friend, it's fifteen," Roscoe said as if doing him a favor. "Grab two and I'll take twenty," he tossed over his shoulder, hustling to the other end of the table to greet a family of tourists with a near identical sales pitch. 'These are rare pieces from Africa,' Cliff heard him tell the misty-eyed shoppers. 'Everything is a hundred percent handmade, imported from East Africa!'

While Roscoe presented his rare jewels, Cliff laid a twenty dollar bill on the table and discreetly toggled the Rasta merchant's elbow. "Here you go my man," he said leaning into Roscoe's shoulder. "You've got some good stuff. I'll be back."

"Boss! You sure you looked at everything," Roscoe exclaimed, surprising the heck out of Cliff.

He spun around, his brows arched and lips parted, asking speechless 'you talkin' to me?'

Roscoe laughed, leaving his customers to guide Cliff over to a rack of colorful dashikis. "Yeah boss, you look like a man trying to find his roots," he chuckled. "I want you to check these out," he said, separating the rack of textiles Cliff wouldn't touch to blow his nose on.

"Check 'em out," Roscoe continued. "They're only thirty—"

"—Look my friend," Cliff chuckled throwing up his hands. Enough. He'd already shaken twenty out of him, and hadn't even taken the second bangle offered. "I like your hustle but I'm all out of scratch," he said.

"Where you from," Roscoe abruptly asked.

"Maryland...Baltimore," he replied without pause.

"No. Where are you really from," Roscoe countered.

Cliff cocked his head to one side, as if Roscoe was wearing a t-shirt announcing he was from Jupiter.

"Man, you from Af-free-ca," Roscoe said pointing in Cliff's chest, enunciating every word and each syllable in Africa. "And don't you forget that, no matter what 'da settlers try to tell you," he added with the pointing.

"Ah yeah," Cliff replied, or more like muttered. "Ugh, I've got to get back out in the streets..." and he peered the 500-yards over to where Blue, Simp and Hagerstown were still cutting up. "...so I don't end up like them," he eased off his tongue nodding towards the trio.

Roscoe narrowed his eyes and looked over to where Cliff nodded. "Yeah," he sighed, his eyes watering but without blinking added, "war'll do that to a man."

"Vietnam vets, huh?" Cliff muttered, about to move on again.

"Nam!?! Aww, naw boss. Those cats came out of the Storm like me!"

Cliff turned back around to take another look. The one in the chair with the blanket draped over his legs, Simp, even if he had all of his teeth, he looked no less than seventy. Hagerstown too. Height aside, to look in his eyes, how wise but tired they looked, he would have guessed he might have been hanging in the background of General Patton's crew. The inspection warned him; he was no good guessing ages. Note to himself: Laugh long, loud, and hard. After that, get plenty sleep.

"Boss, I don't know what your hustle is but you far from them cats," Roscoe said. "Rain or shine they're out here," he murmured, keeping his eyes trained in their direction. "The big cat used to be an LT before getting chaptered out. And the cat in the chair ain't even thirty," he said shaking his head and turning away.

"Man," Cliff shook his head too. "Every day?"

"Yeah...every day they're out here. They're harmless though," he laughed, "long as they're on their meds."

Cliff walked on, less the bounce however, so regaled by the lilt of encounters that hadn't once reminded him to check a clock. Down twenty-two dollars and 17 cents, he hadn't considered his loss. A day ago, dressed in the KAW suit and shoes, he would've hoped the people he met didn't stand near him at newspaper stands, or bypassed him when asking for spare change. He shooed them off his windshield, and crossed the street when he encountered them fencing their goods. Telling the truth, the lowest common denominator the world proffered, were street people. But 24 hours later, moving into their circles, standing beside them, mimicking their dialogue, eagerly trying to measure up, learning their routine and smelling their breath, trading them for shoes and phony jewels released him from a 20-year long lurid nightmare. Basically Cliff had forgotten about the $500 a day.

He made his way to a coffee shop, hankering in this gifted mood, where he pulled out his precious $2.17 bottled water. If only he had brought a book with him, maybe he might come up with another idea as brilliant. He untwisted the cap, took a sip, burped, sighed noisily, and accidentally overturned the bottle, catching sight of the most lovely goddess in the world.

To one side of this goddess sat a triplet of trashcans and on the other side of her was a shopping cart filled with dark green lawn-size trash bags. She seemed to be looking his way though he couldn't be sure. This woman was so faint in features he had to block out the trees shading her expression to find her face. With a rapidly beating heart, fearing any moment she might disappear, he hopped up. He couldn't risk losing her now, not with so much of his life spent searching for this woman.

Quickly he searched for a reason to share her space, finding nothing but an empty Styrofoam cup and balled up used napkin some tacky creatures, probably tourists, left behind. In one swipe he scooped up the garbage and made his way towards the woman not paying him a lick of mind.

Those seven steps it took getting near her, the most worthy steps in his life as far as he was concerned, were the longest steps he'd ever taken. This mirage of perfection could have been committed, or taken, or not interested in spending a second with him, let alone for the rest of his life! And of all the days and ways he tried picking up women, smearing on designer colognes and dropping bank receipts... *intentionally face up*...and here he was, dressed like a bum!

None of that mattered. He was desperate.

"Hello darling," he smiled, tossing the contents in his hand in the trashcan. "Nice weather, huh?" He didn't feel like a fool for running the lamest pick-up line in all courting tactics on her. The woman deserved the best.

She smiled back, feebly, and went back to staring off in the distance.

"On a clear day they say you can see forever," he offered standing in front of her, watching her, waiting to see if he could catch her taking her next breath. Before the layoff he would have never had the nerve to walk up to a woman with his intentions and lay these sorrowful lines down on a beauty as stunning. But that was before, and she was different. He could tell by the way she ignored him. His presence neither bothered her, nor alarmed her. She took him in like she took in the gentle zephyr dipping her thoughts in that far out place where he longed to one day share.

But for a very good reason he had to wake her. "You wanna shack up with me?" Now this was his best pick-up line. Not only was it lame, drastic, and absurd, but it was obvious, salient, precise, and the surviving sword he had left to get her attention.

"I'm doing just fine," she shyly giggled.

See, he was in. Without wasting a beat, he pulled out a chair and sat at the table beside her. "My lady, I can see you're doing just fine, but my question is would you like to live with me?"

Honestly, he was dead serious. Looking at her fragile slim fingers, thin shoulders, delicate face, and watching her face flush and blush, he meant every word. He wasn't leaving without her consent.

"So what do you say," he persisted.

"Where do you stay," she meekly giggled.

"Oh, in a big old house a little piece from Tacoma Park," he smiled as if answering a young child.

"Tacoma Park," she giggled, brightening up, if this was even possible given how lit up she already was. She looked like a diamond. "What are you doing all the way over here!?!"

If a tangerine could talk, he imagined they would sound alike. Sweet and tangy. "I'm out scouting for a woman to share my life with, and I believe I've found her," he smiled.

The thing was, he could freely admit this. No other woman was competing for his time and attention. This delectable beauty had no competition at all. Besides, had he not said these words in this exact sequence he would surely have lost her.

The lady didn't answer. She stopped giggling and blushing however, staring at him as if she was seeing him for the first time.

"Miss Lady, I'm serious…well…" and he moved into an unrehearsed verse. Actually, not much he'd said or done that day had been rehearsed. Most of it was off cuff and off script. But this was a different off the script. A feeling had crept inside him and he was running with it. He could tell this lady was no push over. She didn't run off with anyone. She had principles. Morals. She took her time to carefully consider what he was asking.

"…Truth is," he reluctantly confessed, sure he was a sentence away from getting dumped again, "…I really came out here to see if I could make five hundred bucks a day panhandling—"

"—five hundred dollars!?!" she shrieked, her brows disappearing into her hairline. "A day!?!" She shrieked again, laughing in his face. "Man, you some kind of fool if you think you can make five hundred a day out here." And then she looked at him with the warmest smile, though tilting her head she still questioned his sanity.

"…If that much could be made, no one would be

out here looking for work," she continued. "All these stores would be empty," she chuckled, fanning her tiny hand around like Vanna used to fan hers on Price is Right.

Cliff nodded. He thought the same thing too. Just so happened, his ambitions outsourced his common sense. The KAWs always said if he worked hard and long enough, anything was possible...and yeah...their rhetoric hypnotized him.

"Well, how much do you think I can make?" he asked anyway. She sounded convincing...like she had verifiable proof.

"You might make enough to buy a cup of coffee... if you're lucky," she snickered.

"Okay then...so what's the most you've ever made?"

"Aah," and she looked up at the sky thinking back. "One time I got fifty dollars, but..." she interjected, lowering her voice "...that was just from one person," and just like that her mood spiraled down to the ground. She didn't want to talk any longer about why the person gave her fifty dollars. It took her to a bad spot, killing the light inside of her.

"Okay then...if you won't tell me how I can make 50 bucks, then at least let me prove to you what my house looks like." Merda would probably kill him, but did he care? No. He'd would kill her back. This was the woman he wanted to share the second half of his life with. This was the heroine of his next novel. My Dearest Love.

"Mister, I'm really fine just where I am."

"Miss Lady, I already told you I can see that. But what's it gonna hurt if for one day, at least, you visit a place you've never been?" He changed his voice, and he played with his eyes, trying to nosedive inside her, aiming to hear her laugh again. "I'm a real good cook," and he winked. "I'll make you a nice home-cooked meal, and run you a nice long hot bubble bath," he teased. "I'll even let you sleep in my big warm fluffy bed..."

"…With you in it, I bet," she grimly retorted.

He lifted up, disappointed. "Aww, come on… Look, I'm not trying to take advantage of you. I really want to prove to you I mean what I say." And he looked around, hoping to come up with something more convincing.

"I don't even know your name," she prudently shot back. "How am I supposed to know if you're not Jack the Ripper, or a Ted Bundy!?!"

"Miss Lady," and he stood, bowing in front of her, "you are absolutely right. Please accept my apologies. My name is Cliff-Clifford Maurice Blanchard, and I have nothing to hide. Now, tell me your name." And so okay, he was returning to his old self, a person he never truly left. But this angel deserved not to be lied to.

He thought she said Debbie, except her name turned out to be Tebby, even prettier. Offering her name had to imply consent, so he held his breath as he extended his hand, which by God, she accepted.

Felt like little more than a few branches of straw he held. "Here, let me get that," he said stepping between her and the shopping cart she reached for. "You have a man now. No more pushing and heavy lifting for you."

They walked a short distance away to where she'd been staying in a hotel for drifters. A dozen tenants lived in the building, sharing a bathroom on each of the upper floors over a restaurant. For only ten dollars a day they got a private bedroom and access to meals in a cellar served out of the restaurant's kitchen where they also did laundry.

It was a fairly decent setup, though Tebby's bedroom was shoebox small. In a 5x5 square foot of space, and a closet large enough to hold an umbrella, she managed to squeeze in a daybed and bookcase, and the miserable squawking shopping cart, really a wire laundry basket, packed neatly with folded clothes and stuff belonging in a bank vault.

"So, guess this explains that," Cliff chuckled, looking up and around and back over to the shopping cart.

"Why you say that," she asked, her voice catching him by surprise. There was no caroling in her tone as she busied herself returning folded clothes she normally kept in a box beneath the bed. "Like, exactly what does that mean…this and that?"

She wasn't smiling when he looked at her. A cynical grin had replaced a girlish guise. He cleared his throat and turned his head mumbling words even he couldn't make out.

"Cliff, you aren't the only one trying to make ends meet in this world," she replied. "What if I told you I was a professional panhandler too?"

She got him good on that one, teasing him when she smiled and winked. That's how the day shot by so fast. He had forgotten about needing to feed a meter. Unlike what he recalled being the case at Linthicum, watching clocks mercilessly, seeing every second tick by in a slow agonizing drawl, this day breezed by. He couldn't wait to get home and write. It was a good chance he could have his love story wherever books were sold, by the end of the week!

"Where are you from," Tebby asked as they headed towards K Street where he parked.

"Well…let's see…I was born in Chow, Maryland. Attended Howard for two years—"

"—you went to Howard!?!"

"Yes, I did," he answered officiously, quickly settling her curiosity explaining how many hustlers were college educated as well.

"I know that," she rowed back, giggling as a tagalong. "I went to Howard too!"

Surprised by the admission but holding his ground he fought her on it, "you went?! You mean you're still going don't you?"

"No. Them people were too snooty for me. I had to get out of there before I turned into one of them," she offered, clearly downplaying his compliment.

They fell into a silent stride for a while, her sandals lightly clapping against the ground and him clumsily wandering among the stars, car horns and the reality of his great fortune. Nothing could erase the euphoric buzz dancing around his head ...until suddenly the meter he forgot to feed dawned on him. The windshield probably was going to be plastered with tickets. Oh well, whatever it cost him, would be worth it. The city's penalty, no matter how healthy, couldn't put a dent in the prize he just won.

They walked up one side of K Street, and down the other, and around a curvature corner. Cars parked back to front lined the street, but his car wasn't there.

"I can't believe this," he muttered, "...someone stole my damn car!"

Tebby looked up at the sign screwed to a pole and frowned. "Cliff, how long did you leave your car here?"

Hands on his hips, looking around anguished, trying to figure out what next, he answered in a fog without looking up at the sign. "Since this morning," he replied annoyed, a reflex away from pulling out his key fob and pressing the panic alarm. This was his normal reaction, what he did after visiting Safeway and forgetting where he parked. Except this wasn't a suburban lot, spread out a good mile and paved in a village patronaged by, give or take, 11,000 law-abiding residents, of which less than 1% had a criminal record of any kind. He wasn't in his neck of woods. In this instance, worst case scenario, if he pressed the panic alarm not a gosh darn thing was going to happen. That's why he hated big cities, especially DC. *Too many crooks, from the top down.*

Trying to retrace his memory from that morning he angrily insisted, "I know I parked right here in front of this damn—"

"—Cliff," Tebby softly butted in. "They towed your car."

CHAPTER...5

Bitter Hench Men & Towing was the least of his concerns. He and Tebby hailed a cab. Or more like they snatched a cab. The first few cabs he tried to stop drove by. Light on, cab empty, the cabbies took one look at him and Tebby, and stepped on the gas.

"The nerve of these towel head evangelists!" They'd been in the country a few days and already was trying to reinstate slavery. But then, a black African flew by too. Same thing. Light on, cab empty and the black man gassed it. So Cliff whipped out a credit card and held it above his head, high in the air, waving it like he just didn't care, with Tebby standing behind giggling her little cute head off. It happened again. Another cab flew by.

"Okay, watch this," he told Tebby. "The next one won't stand a chance!"

He grabbed Tebby's hand and walked near a couple who'd just left a hotel. Probably internationals headed to dinner, or to make a business deal they preferred to be on time for. They were hailing a cab too. The square-shouldered white man dressed in an Italian designer suit, and his lovely companion dressed in a Vera Wang gown. Sure enough a cab raced up the street, light on, empty, and 911 stopped dead on the dime at the lovely couple's feet. The dude with the blocks for shoulders attempted to open the door when Cliff stepped to him.

"Sir, my wife and I were out here first. Do you mind letting us have this cab? I'm sure another one will stop for you a lot quicker than for us."

As the cab driver snatched around, looking back and forth from left to right, desperately trying to catch what was going on, the couple stepped back, reluctant to get in this cab at all costs. They only were trying to get to dinner…or this important business meeting…on time, and of course alive.

The cabbie didn't like it. Looked like an octopus with a dozen tentacles flailing about, intent on exiting the cab. "No! Get out! I'm taking them!" shouted the cabbie, struggling to untangle himself trapped by one seatbelt. He only managed to get a foot, and mostly his voice out of the cab.

"Cliff, let them have it," Tebby pleaded, retreating, staring in absolute dread at the torture pulling apart the cabbie's face. His brow hairs stood up and out, past his hairline, at least several inches away from his skin. His nostrils resembled a double-barreled shotgun. And his eyes looked like they'd been borrowed from Chuckie, the fictional Halloween character, and pasted beneath his forehead.

"No!" Cliff replied, grabbing Tebby by the arm and pulling her inside the cab with him. *Aaah, just the way he pictured it in his novel. The hero saves the heroine.*

"What are you doing!?! Get out! Get out!" The cabbie cried, rolling over in his seat, still saved by the seatbelt, as he reached for his radio.

Cliff leaned between the seats and snapped pictures of his credentials as the square shouldered man stopped the cabbie. He tapped Joshua Alvarez Sorrentino, badge no. 659401-22 on the arm and told him they no longer wanted to ride with him. "Please, take them and go!"

The cabbie drove wildly, a scene clipped out of you name the best action flick, as the angry hornet ran lights, turning corners on two wheels, the tires screeching and squealing as he raced to the garage. But it was a ride of sheer bliss, Tebby holding onto Cliff and him imagining they were on a theme ride of a lifetime, the navy sky lit and screams peeling around them with his arms tightly wrapped around the only woman he loved at first sight.

• • •

"Where have you been!?!"

That was Merda standing at the door, hand on hip and large pink curlers haphazardly hanging onto pieces of her hair. Women had stopped wearing these sponge rollers back in the 70's. She looked Neanderthal-ish. *His opinion.*

"You aren't my mother and you aren't my wife," Cliff spat, grabbing Tebby by the hand and brushing by the homosapien to head to his room.

"Cliff, you know this isn't right," Merda cried as he closed his door in her face. "And take off your shoes," she shouted through the clinking of him deadbolting the door. "You know we don't wear shoes in the house!"

"Cliff, are you sure it's okay for me to be here," Tebby whispered.

"Of course. This isn't her house," he replied, placing his keys on the nightstand. "Soon as I evict her ba'hind we're gonna have the whole house to ourselves!"

Tebby crunched up her face but didn't say anything. Obviously something wasn't right, but a cursory view of his bedroom stole her attention.

"Let me show you around," he said. "So you know

you are in good hands..." he smiled, guiding her by the arch in her back like the princess she had become. "This in here," and he opened the door beside his bed, "is my lovely sitting and writing room."

Hesitantly she poked her head inside the room, and popped open her mouth when she saw what was inside. She would call this rather large room, larger than the closet she expected to see, a shrine. Inside was a huge leather recliner, and on top an executive desk was an old typewriter, two opened laptops and a desktop. Filling the remaining space were standing wooden globes and reference books swaddling stanchions of many heights.

"It's amazing," she sighed, peering around the room, looking up and down over walls of books.

"When I hit this switch," and he turned a wall switch midway, "...we get music," he grinned as Bach's cello filled the room. "You like that?"

She smiled, her eyes twinkling as she looked up at the ceiling.

"You can't see the speakers huh?"

And she shook her head no.

"Come on, I have one more thing to show you," he said guiding her to the opposite side of the room. Giddy with delight, how could he have ever guessed meeting a woman like Tebby? Had he seen her in his future, Merda long ago would've been past tense. There wouldn't have been a door to shut in her face. Other than the front door.

He couldn't wait to see the twinkle in her eye when he showed her the bathroom. But slowly sliding the door open he watched her face shrink. It was hardly the reaction he expected. "What's wrong? You don't like it?"

Inside the white marbled room with gold accents was a his and her sink, a walk-in shower, claw tub, and a toilet she couldn't see, hidden in a private enclosure. The shower head, spigots, door handles and light fixtures were gold chrome, designed in the latest advent-garde motifs... swan neck taps, LED lighting, regency handles and motion sensors that turned the contraptions on and off by movement and hand claps. Looked like he hired a science freak to build a bathroom inside a glass castle.

"It's fine Cliff," and she turned towards him. "I just don't understand why you have to be beggin' when you have all of this."

"Sssh," he whispered, putting a finger to his lips. She wasn't loud but he didn't want her to worry. For sure, it was a lot to take in. Cinderella only existed in fables. Of course, any woman would be leery walking into such a fairytale.

"Don't be afraid," he explained. "My sister is not as frightening as she appears. Besides, she only hates me," he sighed.

Tebby stared at him, her lips separated, but pursed in the form of a smile. "Cliff, I'm not afraid of her," she said. "I'm just wondering what you are up to."

"Okay, how about this," he said. "What would you like to eat? Anything you want, I'll cook it, or make it appear…"

She sighed, deeply. "Cliff, I don't think I'm ready for this…" and she paused, "I mean—"

"—Just name it," he pleaded. "Do you want to try the hot tub? It's a good way to relax…it opens the pores and extracts anxiety…"

But she put up her hands and shook her head. "No Cliff…something's not—"

"—Tebby, Tebby…" he said cupping her ginger face, kissing her forehead and both cheeks. Gosh, she smelled so sweet, like she hardly needed a bath at all. "Darling, Miss Lady, My Love, I'm not going to take advantage of you. I promise."

She didn't speak, so he nudged the small of her back. "Go ahead," he nodded towards the bathroom. "I'll get some towels and get you all set up."

Before she started protesting again, he brought out plush towels, ivory and gold, and laid them on the bed.

"I'm going in my haven," he said pointing to his literary sanctuary. "Take your time. Get comfortable. When you are ready we can discuss what to eat," he coolly added.

Another thought hit him as he was about to turn and head to his library. "Hey, I saw all those books in your bookcase. You must like to read?"

She smiled wide. "Yes, I do," she replied, lighting up from the inside.

"Welp, come here. I want to show you something." He turned the light switch inside his sanctuary to its full position, rolling forward a portion of the wall. "Look."

Covering her mouth she gasped. "Oh my God... it's amazing," she sighed, moving closer to touch the books she initially thought might be wallpaper.

"Take your time...browse all you want..." he smiled, slipping into his writing chair and firing up the PC. "I'm about to get in the zone," he chuckled. "To start working on our story..."

• • •

"Cliff! Cliff!" She yelled like the house was on fire.

He rolled off the couch and stumbled to his feet, looking around for the flames or signs the house was coming apart. It took a few seconds to realize it was his sister yelling like that.

Stumbling to the door he unhinged the latch, turned the deadbolt and peaked out. "What is it?"

"It's eight o'clock. You're late!"

It took another moment for it to register what he was late for. "I already called out...but thanks," he mumbled, again closing the door in her face and relocking it with a vengeance.

Almost sleepwalking he slid in his bed and snuggled up to the pillow, forgetting all about Tebby, and that she was beneath the covers too. All he wanted to do was get back to where he left off in his dream, which first meant erasing a scornful cancer from his thoughts. *Ooo! She was such a thorn in his backside!*

It took several grunts and a major shift in position to get comfortable…before realizing there was a foreign object in bed with him. Oh My God! Tebby!

He threw back the comforter and sprung out of bed as if he had hopped in bed with a boa constrictor. It had been a long time since hopping up that quick. He was a good twenty pounds leaner, and shot hoops half the day. Luckily he landed on both feet, but not without knocking a candle off the nightstand and making a heap of noise trying to break his stumble.

Quickly putting things back in place he looked over at the tiny lump on the other side of the bed noticing it hadn't budged. She had to be a pretty hard sleeper to sleep through the noise…plus all the yelling too.

He started to wake her, to make sure she was okay, when the covers seemed to move. "Hey, are you awake in there," he whispered, careful not to startle her.

So far he had done a superlative job building her trust. Before they had fallen fast asleep she had checked out the books in his library, enjoyed the hot tub, and let him feed her mussels, which she had never eaten before. They didn't talk much, him being on his best behavior to not give her a reason to bolt. Mostly they felt each other out, under candle-lights and Bach playing as he shared what he put in the mussels. After dinner she curled all 4′ 9-inches of her up in a chair she claimed to have seen in Macy's …with Santa sitting in it, the reason she looked so small curled up in it, since she wasn't 4-foot 9-inches, but 5-feet 1-inch. In 52 years it was his most romantic date. He ended up retreating to his writing sanctuary where he eventually curled up on the daybed, and she so obviously ended up in his bed.

He looked down at her laid so contrarily still that

it dawned on him something could be wrong. He debated touching her. *What if she had stopped breathing during the night? Maybe it was the mussels? Some people were allergic to shell fish. He could have accidentally killed her with the mussels she had never eaten before. Merda was right. He should've thought better of bringing a transient home and letting her sleep in his bed. There wasn't a jury in the world who wouldn't suspect old strange Cliff of foul play and throw a book at him.* That's how writers like him thought. He could concoct a murder plot in the time it took most people to raise their eyebrows.

The thought terrified him, but not more than losing the love of his life. Holding his breath, he waited, staring intently at Tebby's contour wishing he knew magic. A snap of the finger and this little thriller would be done and over.

He started to peel back the cover, to put his hand on her chest to check for a pulse, but slipped into one of his writerly crypts where he was cautioned against touching her. His paw marks would be all over her. He'd be convicted for sure if she really was dead. And if she was alive, she could wake up and accuse him of something far more incestuous. She also could lift up and turn out to be a three-head unicorn, or worse, *a three-head transvestite unicorn.*

Pacing around the bed he tried to think of the best way to stop a tragedy. There was still a chance he could save her. He could be letting precious seconds tick away.

He opened and closed drawers...clanged glasses and walked around the bed shaving. Actually, turning on his razor served two purposes. If Merda was outside with her ear pressed against the door, which he suspected she was, it might convince her to leave, thinking he was getting ready for work.

But Tebby didn't budge. Whoever he brought home was either a really hard sleeper, or really dead. He got even more scared, pacing faster, rubbing his head harder while chanting, *'Please dear God, forgive me!'*

He made a lot of promises to God during the pacing, before deciding to hop in the shower. His mother used to say all the time, 'the best way to get on the right side of God, was to come clean.' In this maddening moment it meant, washing his behind.

In the shower he continued praying and pleading. 'It's on you God. May Your Will be done.' If God couldn't do it, well… no one could. He made a lot of promises as well. He was going to stop calling Merda, murder, and the fatso, fatso. Likewise, he was going to church more, and taking another stab at reading the Bible. Of course too, if worse came to worst, all these promises were null and void. If Tebby died, he didn't want to live. There'd be no point. Close the book. The story was over. The end.

Except he walked out of the bathroom and there she was sitting in the center of the bed with her knees drawn up to her chin and arms locked around her legs.

"Oh, so I see we're up," he sighed, too relieved to be startled. The fear had numbed him so completely that he didn't realize he was naked until Tebby pointed at his midsection and he looked down.

"What's that," she asked pointing at an old battle scar covered with a tattoo he had since removed.

"Oh, that," he blushed, adjusting the towel to cover the scar. "That's what happens when fake insurance gets you a fake doctor who uses his fake scalpels to fix a fake story," he chuckled.

"You're strange, Cliff," she giggled. "I never met no one like you."

"And I never met anyone like you my dear lady," he smiled, admiring her large indulgent eyes set in a bare face about as big as his fist. "Anyone tell you how pretty you are?"

Bashfully giggling, she buried her face between her knees. "Why would someone tell me that?" And she fell back on the bed drawing the covers over her face. "I'm not pretty. I'm too old to be pretty."

He slid beside her, careful not to slide too close. "So, how old is old?" She certainly wasn't acting old. She sounded and looked like a grade school girl.

"Say...are you ticklish?"

"No! Don't tickle me," she ordered, popping up. "I have to use the bathroom," and she slid the other way out of bed.

Just a few short minutes ago he was kicking himself, making bizarre promises to God, and preplanning what he was going to do to the house if and when the police came for him. And now he was back to lusting over a lady slinking by like a whisper, congratulating himself on the treasure he found. She couldn't have been more than twenty-five, if not still in her teens.

. . .

"Thirty-five! No way!"

"Yes way..." she smiled, dipping a strawberry into a bowl of whipped cream to suck on. She obviously didn't know how seductive she looked, twirling the strawberry around the bowl, dipping it and out of whipped cream to suck on. She was one giggle away from an erotic film.

"You're just trying to make me feel good," she said.

This was true, what he loved about her most. Her innocence. Any woman who didn't realize sucking on a strawberry dipped in whipped cream, in front of a full grown man who still got erections, was teasing, she had a lot to learn. She only needed to look beneath the table to appreciate his point.

"But, why'd I want to do that," he asked anyway. He couldn't wait to hear her answer.

"To get in my pants," she flatly replied.

And Aaah! So she wasn't so naïve. And still, there it was again. The virtue. Who would openly admit to such a thing? "If I wanted to get in your pants, we'd already be touring utopia," he capped back, his leg quivering so happily that his knee was a tremor away from clearing the table.

"Okay…I'm done," she said pushing the bowl away and brushing her hands together.

"No, please…have some more. I want to watch you eat. I like the way your lips curl around the strawberry," he gushed, licking his own lips.

"Cliff, you're a strange man…"

"…I know," he laughed. "You said that already."

If she was thirty-five, then he was five, however the math worked out. Because of her, he didn't get to write so much as one sentence…for any of his works in progress. He sat up all night playing Star Wars, and fell asleep dreaming of deserted islands and offing a million Merda's trying to end up stranded with his soul mate.

"Why are you staring at me like that?"

"Because I'm painting a picture," he smiled, using the space between them as his canvas to trace the curves of a mistletoe. "I'm seeing you and I," he openly flirted, "at the altar of love," he teased. "One day I'm going to write our story," he told her.

An original love story was what he had in mind. He wasn't exactly sure how he would begin, but its contents would writhe in passion. Like *Lawrence of Olivia*, or *Bridges of Madison*. Something romantic to conquer racial and social divides, traversing continents to stay on lips and tongues, engraving their story on hearts and minds forever and ever.

Tebby was skeptical though. "How you gonna write a story about us when you don't even know me?"

"All I need to know is sitting right before me."

"Yeah…" and she made no pretense of challenging him. "Well, then tell me how this story is going to go?"

Okay, so she got him. He had no clue how the story would either begin or end. He ran wild with the middle ...the two of them meeting and living happily thereafter.

"We don't need to know the intricacies," he explained. "All we need, is to experience it..." he gushed.

Tebby leaned back, and for the first time looked like a real person. Before she almost had this ghostly quality, as if he reached over and tried to touch her, she would disappear.

"Cliff, stop fooling around with me. You just sittin' over there making stuff up," she giggled waving off his corny made up tale. "You don't have no story cookin'," she laughed.

For the clever lady she was showing herself to be, he closed his eyes and began reciting what he thus far had. *"She came by white knight, trimmed of voguish coils, buttons, dear zibellinis, and orange blossoms in her hair. Trite to the touch, demur on the vision, he batted not an eye, nor wasted nay carrying her away..."* and he stopped there, opening his eyes to see her staring at him, and not as if she were waiting on more, but as if she was unsure if he was the titan or duke.

Uneasily he squirmed in his chair. "I know you don't understand it from just one verse, but—"

—but she interrupted him. "Cliff, you've got to have more than that. Me showing up on a horse? You didn't meet me on no horse. And how are we going to end?"

He gasped, exasperated. "I already said, it doesn't matter how it ends. The beginning can be the ending, or our ending the beginning," he argued.

"Ah, no...I don't think I like this idea...you writing a story about me with no ending," she fussed back.

"But it's not going to be about you," he pleaded. "It's going to be about us..." and he took his time conjuring up an old *Dirty Harry-Charlton Heston* look, lowering his voice and dipping one brow. "It's going to be about a never-ending love fest of two people falling hopelessly and endlessly in love…"

"Love fest? …illlll…noooooo…" she dragged out in a giggle. "That don't sound so good to me. That sounds kind of creepy."

"Okay then…what do you suggest?"

"I suggest we know each other before you go writing some book. Have you ever even written a book?"

He had. The book didn't make a big splash, in fact it sold fewer than 5000 copies, the reason both his agent and publisher dropped him. There wasn't much of a market for vampire stories selling so few copies, even if he had a film producer in his back pocket. Too bad the producer ran out of capital and had to back out.

"You looked at it last night…" he winked, elated at the chance to entrap her again. "You didn't notice my name on the cover?" His turn to smile big watching her scramble to think back.

"I was wondering why that book looked so strange," she shrugged, downplaying her surprise.

"You like me? Don't you?"

Again he trapped her, enjoying precious seconds sail by watching her turn tail.

"Cliff, I just don't think them stories sound like love stories to me," she replied.

"I bet you would make a good publishing agent."

She looked at him, wrinkling her nose, which didn't wrinkle very much. "Why you say that?"

"Because…you know what will and won't sell."

"I didn't say it won't sell," she objected. "I said it don't sound like no love story to me. Big difference," she laughed.

Aww, she was good. Playing cat and mouse with him. What a great answer. She obviously knew her way around novels. *Nora Roberts* and *McNaught* were her favorites. He hadn't read them but felt like he had fallen into a sinkhole, dropping out of his thoughts into hers, clumsily clutching onto her belief that strong heroines made better stories. The pacing was better, so she wisely claimed, naming another novelist—*Jane Austen*—whose work he didn't know a herringbone about either.

"How you gonna write a love story and don't know Austen!?!" She was done fooling around with his goofy self. She rolled her eyes about to move on talking about something else.

But Cliff wasn't done. He was like a virgin having his first drink. He wasn't trying to get sloppy drunk and pass out. Like what would be the point? Yet he wanted to keep the buzz going. "Then you should see Austen's writing in our story," he cheesed. "We're just ahead of our time…"

"—But—" —and he cut her off.

"—But, I'm cloaking our story," he cheesed harder.

"Cloak?"

"See, you don't know about that writing style," he boasted, explaining what cloaking meant as she looked at him sideways. She loved *The Time Machine*, but found *Rendezvous with Rama* troubling; the opposite for him. He wasn't as smitten with a story, as he was with detailed writing. So, yeah, she didn't know it all, despite the two of them spending much of the morning batting literature balls back and forth. She liked it breezy. He liked it real.

By the evening this breezy real business turned into him telling her about his unholy Greek myth, the half-written story about the 16th century whore. "My writing flows better when I use the command of early century language," he supplied. "Most people don't really read word for word anyway. They just seem mesmerized by the rhyme of words flowing on paper."

"What?!" Tebby shrieked. "Well, not me," she flatly stated. "I'd get seasick if I saw words moving in a book I was reading."

Cliff had to chuckle. He couldn't help it, hearing her mousey skweet-skweet voice. She sounded like a piccolo. "Tell me something, where are you from?"

She stopped smiling and tilted her head to one side. "Why? Where are you from?"

"Born and raised in Baltimore," he replied.

"Well, I don't know exactly where I was born, but I was raised in New York," she answered.

"Hmmp!" he hummed. "Don't sound like it. Sound like you're from down south... waaaaay down south—"

"—What? I sound countrified to you?"

Well, when she put it like that, she didn't. Though he shrugged and replied, "a little," watching her pencil thin lips stiffen and her beetle bug eyes harden.

"But you sound like the cute kind of country," he added. "You have one of them Dallas drawls...with the sticky feminine honey poured on top," he teased.

"Dallas!" she sneered. "What's so special about the way Dallas folk talk!? And why don't you sound like a country bumpkin!?"

"Dallas females," he corrected. "And I never lived in the country. I'm from Baltimore."

"Oh please," she giggled. "Maryland is south of the divider...below the country bumpkin line," she teased before finishing her point. "Clearly, where you're from has nothing to do with what you sound like!"

"Tebby, let's write our story together," he smiled, reaching across the table and grabbing both her hands. He didn't want to argue, upsetting the tone of her wind chime. He loved her accent, wherever or however she inherited it.

She didn't pull away, but made it clear she wasn't interested in writing their story. "I can't write," she said. "Just because I read books doesn't mean I'm interested in writing them."

"Aww, anybody can write," he said sucking his teeth and releasing her delicate hands. "But if you and I team up, I bet we'll write a best-seller."

"Cliff, you don't need me to write a best-seller. All you got to do is buy some labels from Kinkos."

He burst out laughing. That was a first. Her making him laugh out loud like that. Had he not swallowed when he did, coffee would've been all over the place, to include her face.

"Did your mother name you Tebby, or is that your street name?" he asked.

She snaked her neck and flicked a little sass at him. "Oh, and so now you're making fun of my name too?"

"I love your name," he gushed, reaching across the table to touch her hands again. "I've never heard a name where two syllables turned into a song."

She turned down her eyes and looked away. "Well, my name is Tabitha," she whispered. "My granddaddy gave me that name. Said I reminded him of his mother."

"I knew it was something special behind that name. Your granddaddy must have been a great man."

Abruptly she looked up. "Why do you say that," she asked, the sweet pitch, once more, running along.

"Because any granddaddy who'd name his grand-daughter such a beautiful name has to be great."

"Well, I hated the man. He was a liar, a bully and a punk!"

Wow. Perhaps that explained why she didn't know much about her birth. Odd. Though he didn't follow up with questions. Instead he changed the subject, a skill he was growing adept at when conversing with her.

"So how'd you like that mattress? Did you—"

"—Cliff, why did your sister want us to take off our shoes?"

Great question. "She's a nut," he replied not missing a beat.

"No Cliff...there has to be a reason," she probed.

"All right then, she's a religious nut."

"Cliff, what sign were you born under," Tebby asked as if his answer would explain everything.

"I was born in a month that didn't have a sign. Only an archaic calendar could locate my zodiac coordinates," he teased, testing his humor.

His reply was the ideal deflection. Neither of them needed to go into their whereabouts and thereabouts so soon and so seriously. Easy always won the race.

Tebby batted the remark away. "Cliff, when are you taking me home? It's after 4 o'clock," she sprung on him.

Of course he hadn't noticed the time. He hadn't laid eyes on a clock since he left the house looking for her. But couldn't she have asked anything else? Like, why he was staring so hard, trying to read her mind? Didn't she want to know if he'd seen the mole in the sclera of her left eye, and had counted the ridges on her lower front teeth. Couldn't she have asked if he wanted to take her to Magic Kingdom, and the Golden Temple, and Paris to shop, and Italy to eat, and the Amazon jungle to sleep, and to his bed to kiss her?

"I'm not," he replied applying his best spooky voice. "You're mine. I'm keeping you here with me forever," he chuckled stealing Dracula's curdled laugh.

"Cliff, you better get your buns up and take me back home. I can't stay here forever!"

• • •

Their relationship started out nothing like the others; full of loose scribblings jotted down on 1x2 post it notes lost beneath time, garbage and ammonia. Not one woman he dated, or okay, *slept with*, had he ever come clean with. And not one person, to include people who interviewed him for jobs, or like pastors who by scripture he was supposed to confess his already forgiven sins to, had he not lied to, almost (*pun fully intended*) religiously. He lied all the time, answering questions with erasers and the backspace key, whatever the occasion warranted. Often he didn't recognize himself, showing up in mirrors like uninvited roommates pulled off Craigslist. It might take a surgeon to excavate the man he buried in the annuals of his pain.

That's where he was, in mulling over consummating his relationship with Tebby. Three of him were in the room; his horny self, his desperate self and his lying self.

No doubt about it, he wanted to make love to Tebby. Except his desperate self bogarted the room, beseeching his lying self to help him out. All three knew his desires, and ultimate goal. Despite knowing Tebby less than 24 hours, he'd get rid of all three of his selves if Tebby went home and decided not to return. Like how many times could she call him strange before this became the singular recourse to *divorce a snag?*

Cliff, man…you know you'll be dead in the water if you let her go. That was desperation speaking, of course. *If I were you I'd go outside and flatten all four tires and then get back in here and call every insurance agency on the planet to help you out!*

It was almost irrelevant to point out which self, pitched which flimsy tent, since his third self, his best quadrant, hopped both feet in with the saving act…going back to the days when Merda was out shopping pounds for hounds that would love her…and hate him! *'You can't forget how she took in that supposed pure bred with no papers, fixing to make a killing off the mutt!*

Cliff remembered the incident with clarity. It was his favorite mutt memory, tickled by a humping Afghan. Every day for the rest of his life he would replay Merda getting sick *as a dog* catching one of her un-neutered mutts humping everything in sight; couch pillows, door frames, table legs…and her legs! *Hahaha times ten!* He said not a word, but laughed his boxers off when he heard fatso casually tell her *"…what did you expect? That's what animals do."*

The havoc the hound caused to *his house* was not

a lovely sight for sure, but was an unbeatable inspection when a brotha' from *her church* dropped by to take the humping fake Afghan off her hands, dumping his take on top of fatso's take. The *good* brotha's reply was in response to Merda tearing a page out of her biblical handbook and hitting him square in the back with it. According to the highlights marring up her Bible, that dog needed Jesus. "He humps everything in sight!" she shouted out the door.

Just as Cliff was Clifford Maurice Blanchard, he recorded with his own two eyes, the church brotha' turning around, resembling Coffey out of the Green Mile, looking Merda dead between the eyes as he replied, "it's in the Bible. Look it up. He told all living things… mammals, insects, trees and the air we breathe…to be fruitful and multiply my sista'. Lust is a very natural thing."

WoW. Like Just WOW! A quote straight from the good book she carried around like a rifle. It still didn't stop her from flexing her nostrils, but did cushion his anxiety worrying about his desire to seal the deal with Tebby.

"Can you keep a secret," he asked.

"I don't know," she replied. "Nobody ever asked me to keep a secret before."

"Oh, come on now," Cliff groaned. "You mean to tell me, not even when you were a kid, no one ever asked you to keep a secret!?"

"Cliff, you're the one keeping secrets. That's your specialty."

He begged to differ. "How's that?" So far he'd been upfront. He was single, had no children, and had never been married. What else could he have up his sleeve… *or maybe in his shorts*… that he hadn't shared?

"Well, I still don't understand why you go beggin' with all of this," she differed.

· · ·

A week later Tebby was still there, and Merda up on the roof peeling away cinder and tar with her bare hands. Not literally, but figuratively of course.

She ripped off Parker's left ear, and then tore out Theresa's right ear, before careening through an 11am church service with a prayer that implored a moaning congregation to pray for her brother...and her.

Something had gotten into Cliff. First it was the cross-dressing. Now he robbed a cradle, stopped going to work, and was hiding some poor young girl in his room. She told a very alarmed congregation there was no telling what all else was going on in her mother's house, rest her soul, but something had to be done. *Please pray for her.*

His soul beyond redemption, the church prayed. And called authorities too. A Crisis Intervention woman promised an investigation... like Merda's closest friends, and neighbors, and family who, one by one, dropped by on a host of pretexts trying to catch a glimpse of the cradle Cliff robbed.

All week innocent bystanders, troublemakers, Christians and otherwise interested nosey rumor-makers grazed the front room like someone had died; tacking all kinds of paper products to his door...some official, some phony invitations and greeting cards. Valentine's day was a full three months into all of their futures and yet some-one named Sylvia Greene taped an orange haired baby cupid to the door.

He didn't bother to read any of the notes and cards, official or otherwise. When the AO cleared he'd open the door and in a wide sweeping swipe removed the graffiti, tossing every bit of it in the trash and washed his hands afterwards.

By the end of that first week Mrs. Grant stopped by, for the third or fourth time in one day, determined to draw him out of the room. But he looked over at Tebby, curled up in *her* favorite chair, one leg crossed over the other and reading, and turned on the water to drown out a ruse that couldn't be disguised if she had announced she was from the Sheriff's department.

"Is he in there now," he heard Mrs. Grant whisper in her lovely hoarse voice.

"Yeah...he's back there," Merda cued Mrs. Grant, in her unmusical shrill cackle. "Go ahead," she instigated, "go on back there and knock again."

Mrs. Grant knocked on the door, heavy-handed, startling Tebby.

"So where are you now," he asked Tebby, ignoring the knock to check how far his girl had gotten in his best novel. Peeking over her shoulder he noted the page.

"Cliff," she squealed singing his name in an octave of stanzas. "Would you let me finish... and go see who's at the door."

Wasn't happening. He heard Mrs. Grant behind him, howling his name in her hoarse rattle, "Cliff, come on out here...I made some custard pie...haven't seen you in a month!"

What a nice big flipper. He passed her at least twice before she heard about Tebby. Once he was even with Tebby! Neither time did she flag him down about those custard pies, not wholly unusual. They passed each other frequently, when he was employed, heading to and from work. Sometimes they waved, most times they didn't. The only time she hunted him down was when she made so many pies she had to beg people to take them off her dining room table. Of course he was her leading guinea pig. No one liked her custard pies as much as he did.

Cliff rummaged through cabinets making as much noise as possible, contemplating creating other noises to block out Mrs. Grant trying to draw him out of the room.

This was the beauty of his carved out space. Fortunate him, he had his own kitchen after splitting his parent's 5-bedroom, 3.5 bath ranch style home into two cozy semi duplexes. He would've been even luckier had he thought about creating a separate entrance, but when the house was being renovated Merda wasn't configured in the plan. He was only trying to accommodate Mama and the stream of nurses, and give himself some privacy.

The banging on the door continued. Encouraged by Broom Hilda herself, Mrs. Grant's stubby balled up fist wasn't giving up. "Cliff! Wake up, Cliff... and come get this pie," she yapped, knowing good and well he wasn't sleep.

"Cliff, why you ignoring them people?"

"Because they're spirit-eaters," he said over running water. "Hey, I know! How about we catch a movie after they're gone?"

"To see what?," she smiled, gaily turning a page.

He had nothing, except escaping a witch-hunting spirit-eater who sic'd the entire hood on him, plus a crisis warrior for damsels in distress. He escaped most of them, leaving the house with Tebby when the coast looked clear. Only the crisis warrior caught up to him, but departed the scene when she saw with her own cradle-robbing eyes Tebby hardly was a child on the black sex-trafficking market; not after affably complimenting a gawdy class ring she wore around her neck. People stopped wearing that type jewelry at the turn of the century.

"Do you like romance comedies? I could go for some perspicuous giggling," he chuckled, pulling fajita wraps from the freezer. He decided on making quesadillas; a dish that didn't require leaving their sanctuary.

"No thanks. I'm fine right here," she replied shifting in the chair, gently turning another page.

The knocking stopped and their voices retreated, mobilizing next on the front lawn. Cliff saw them through the blinds. Merda standing in front of Mrs. Grant with her arms folded across her brittle chest where fleshy round breast normally grew. He couldn't hear their chatter but could read her energy like some read lips. "At least he isn't gay," she mouthed, the reason why she had to deal with cocoa nibs on her chest!

"Devil be gone…" Cliff murmured.

Tebby looked up. "What did you say?"

"Oh nothing," he sighed, shaking his head, returning to what he was doing…chopping a fusion of veggies, careful not to chop off a limb.

"Cliff, sometimes you be scaring me," he heard her say through the noise tinkering in his head. "Stop all that talking to yourself," she continued, not taking her eyes off the page she was reading.

He turned the eye off and removed the skillet from the burner. After wiping his hands on a towel he walked over to her and got down on one knee.

"Tebby, there are some mean people in this world who really need to be taught a lesson," he began. "My sister is one of them. You may not see it…I don't think anyone but me actually sees it…but that's why I keep the door locked and try to avoid her."

He paused for effect, deep in thought watching her watch him…through the top of his bowed head. They… or maybe just him…had yet to seal the deal. A whole week gone by built anxiety, giving him a temple-ache. It wasn't that he rolled on the chaise at night, writhing in pain, such as when he was a teen and preferring a warm body to a warm hand. It was a culmination of tinkering toying with his mind. Merda…the house…the meddling…Tebby's essence… and what she thought…his entire altered routine… He had so much on the line.

Down on his knee he looked up, his eyes wet but not tearing. "Miss Lady, I don't want you to think for one second I'm the weird one."

"I don't think you're weird Cliff. You're just not like most men. You're a distinct breed."

That was an observation he hadn't heard. Should he take it as a compliment? While he had her on his side... at least he hoped, and before she changed her mind he asked if she ever wanted to seek revenge on someone. Still on his knee, caressing her slim fingers trying not to concentrate on how sweet she smelled, even so low from her neck, he didn't wait for an answer.

"I'm talking about mean-spirited calculating people who spend every waking second their eyes are open trying to hurt people," he went on. "Have you ever met anyone who had it out for you from the day you were born," he asked looking up.

"So, is that what this is about?" she grinned.

He twisted his head. "Is this what, what is about," he asked confused.

"Is this what this is about?" she asked, leaning over the chair, gleaming wildly as she shoved the book she'd been reading in his face. "This, goof ball!" she laughed.

"Wait...hold still," he said, squinting and grabbing her wrist trying to hold the book still and read the text.

"Your plot is waaayyy too obvious," she laughed. "I already know how it's going to end. Your going to send Grejeckula to live the rest of her life in Helveticas!"

Okay, so he learned from critics the story was kind of thin. But how'd she guess he was writing about Merda? He didn't even realize the twist...until then. He'd swear it happened wholly by accident. He hadn't even adopted the term cloaking when he wrote the book. Man! He was going to have to go back to the drawing board and really scrub the story he was almost finished cloaking.

"So, I guess you're taking her side too?"

"Cliff, I'm not taking no one's side. I just think this would've been better if you'd switched things... making the witches come out as angels."

He wanted to defend the book, except it dawned on him. She was right. Still, he didn't like it. It turned his stomach envisioning Merda as an angel.

CHAPTER...6

Let it go! ...so said the Lord...and Tebby. But honest to goodness he couldn't. Whether others admitted it or not, the mind overruled the heart, or was that the other way around?

The reason Tebby couldn't see his battle scars was because he hadn't pulled out each gritty tale for her to inspect. She didn't know the dirty deeds described in his book, Grejeckula had actually done to him. It wasn't only the beating incident, Merda teased and humiliated him since the day he was born. He grew up believing it was normal to have a hateful sister, and hating her back became as natural as opening his eyes when he woke up. He only realized their dysfunctional relationship when one day he casually told his mother about what Merda had said to his friend. Well, the kid really wasn't a close friend, but they used to walk home together. The boy's name was Todd and he lived in an area known as *across the tracks*. The thing was, both of them were black boys, included in a class of people globally recognized as the underclass. Only Merda, and those like her, considered living in a single family home a huge leap above those living in the projects, the poorest of the poor.

But Todd was a decent kid. Sure he wore the same high-water pants all week and was on the free lunch program, along with his half dozen siblings who were all raised by a grandmother because his mother was dead and his father's whereabouts a vague mystery.

As usual both of them, he and Todd, were walking home when all of a sudden there was Grejeckula draped by some gangster-dressing thug hanging over her like a wet rag. Soon as he saw her, his heart fell between his knees and hit the ground. He didn't know what she was going to do…or say, but knew whatever it was, it was going to be evil. Sure enough she scoffed, "why are you walking with this ragamuffin!?!"

He didn't reply. Merda was nasty. She'd hit him as soon as look at him. One time she pulled down his pants and spanked him in front of his friends, claiming she was punishing him for some nebulous made up deed. Later when he told Mama about the incident, Merda turned the whole story around, claiming he called her a word he had never used in his life. Poor Mama didn't know who to believe. Apparently she could understand someone calling Merda a bitch, simply telling him it wasn't nice to call his sister that word.

Thus with his reality and vocabulary out of whack, he ran in the house and asked Mama what ragamuffin meant, explaining the context in which he heard the word. He got no response. Mama grumbled like usual and left him on the sofa watching TV, where he was when Merda strolled in and Mama asked, *'what you doing calling people ragamuffin?'* On cue she started to lie, except she made the colossal mistake of opening her defense with *'you know damn well that boy…'*

Mama went off. She let loose, slamming her fist dead into Merda's face, socking her so hard a line of snot shot across the room. Merda grabbed her jaw and Mama grabbed her hair, boxing her like a heavyweight champ.

The whole time Mama boxed, with Merda's hair wrapped around her fist like a jump-rope, from behind it looked like Mama was dancing as her backside bounced up and down. All Cliff needed was popcorn, watching Merda flailing around like a ragdoll screaming, 'Mama it's me! Mama it's me!'

Mama had lost her mind. She was so far gone her pupils looked like shooting asteroids. It was Pops who came to their rescue. He ran in the parlor after listening to the screaming for the length of time it took the football game to ...thank heavens for Merda... go to commercial. Otherwise, Mama looked well on her way to murdering her first and only born daughter.

If there'd ever been an occasion to celebrate, that was the moment. Merda continued bossing him around and being her familiar nasty self, but the assaults stopped. Whether she found easier prey, or lost her momentum due to Mama beating some sense into her, the mood in the house got better.

"I know you're gonna frown when I say this," Cliff said to Tebby. "...but I think I have an idea."

"Now whatcha' got cookin' in that mind of yours?"

"I'm going to tell her I'm a spy," he said falling back on the bed, clasping his hands behind his head to gaze up at his amazing ceiling.

"A spy!?! A spy, Cliff? That woman is too smart to be believing you're some kind of spy."

She may have been that smart, but he was that fixed on making sure they had a place to live. He still hadn't told Merda about losing his job, and she was still hot and heavy conspiring with an attorney more crooked than her. As irony had it, greed didn't collude with logic and reason. That would be too civil and humane. Crooks would rather hold up an estate combing every law book in the state trying to plot his demise, totally overlooking the open and shut clause directly in their favor. Served them right...the gluttonous fools.

But Tebby didn't care for him making a bigger fool of his sister. "I don't see why you don't march out there and tell your sister...I lost my job, found another mouth to feed...so now bring it!"

He looked back at her, lying on the bed with her cute little self and sweeter little voice, and chuckled. She may have had a grandfather who lied about what happened to her mother, and grandmother, and why he ran off with her social security benefits, but she didn't have a sister who hated her guts from birth. Like bring it? Bring what? He just wasn't that bringing it type guy.

"Okay, so we have a little teaser here," he chuckled, rolling on top of her though not sure what he wanted to do next with her. She hated being tickled and hadn't yet clued him in as to whether an intimate relationship was suitable. "I got you now," he laughed, making her giggle and squirm until she had rolled herself into a cocoon of covers. He had kissed her and she seemed fine with that show of affection, but he wanted to unravel her, and for the first time make love to her.

They rolled on the bed for a while, until the toying and tussling got intense...of course intentionally on his behalf. Carelessly he touched parts of her body waiting on the first hint of rejection. After the emotion invested into this relationship he didn't know what he'd do if she pushed back.

At one point when they were face to face, laying in a horizontal position, he asked if the mole in her eye was a secret camera recording his every move. He had no real motive for asking, other than being goofy, and stalling, or perhaps subconsciously leery of her age. Though she maintained she was thirty-five, a revelation that made the crisis interventionist even gasp, he still had doubts. Women were crying date rape ad nauseum, what made a camera to his benefit. All he had to do was look into the mole and ask her name, age and if he had her consent. He didn't, but was surprised by what he learned.

"I stabbed myself in the eye," she said. "A dorm-mate found me with a letter opener sticking out of my eye."

He sat bolt upright. "What!?!"

"Oh, it happened years ago," she replied, waving a hand like nothing. "I have some kind of sleep disorder. Doctors said it's a chemical imbalance in my head," she giggled. "But don't worry," she added. "I'll be fine. Isn't like parasomnia can kill ya'."

Hardly funny, not even remotely, even if it explained why she was so hard to rouse in the morning. "Teb, this sounds dangerous. I mean…was it painful?"

"When I woke up it was. But my brain produces a chemical equivalent to anesthesia so I didn't feel much."

"Damn," Cliff muttered. "That's serious! You could have killed yourself!"

"Yeah but… since I was knocked out it really didn't matter."

Say what!? "Teb, you matter to me," he exclaimed. "I can't have you hurting yourself!"

"Cliff, I'll be fine," she giggled. "So long as you don't leave any sharp objects on the nightstand…"

. . .

Before making another move he needed to know Tebby more intimately…beyond inserting himself into her more private spaces, why he partly didn't miss a beat offering her a lift to look in on a woman she hadn't checked on in weeks; ahem…*due to the two weeks shacked up with him.*

It was good timing. A woman Tebby befriended over a decade ago left a message on her phone, yakking about how long ago it had been since she'd seen *hide or hair* of her Teb.

It was a no brainer. Cliff had to meet this very vocal friend Tebby met at a homeless shelter. For as loud and long as she yapped at an automated robot made it highly unlikely she wouldn't unwrap more about her Teb he longed to know. Plus, good men like him didn't let good women like her, who he had every desire to marry one day soon, wait on a corner for a bus. Nope. No way. Wasn't gonna happen. Not when he had a brand new SUV, save for a busted-out/boarded-up back window, parked in the driveway.

Naomi, or No-No as she was affectionately known to most of Southeast DC, lived in a housing project. As legend held it, the woman lived one fabulous famous blockbuster life, launching her legacy when she started hopping up on stages, often unscripted and uninvited. Her debut performance happened when she was sixteen, chasing chitlin circuits seducing musicians. *Fats Domino* was her first. She sat in his lap croaking to *Blueberry Hill*. Pretty much from there, when she was in the audience the crowd went wild, or so she said. Everyone knew the live wire who started showing up, up and down the Eastern seaboard, leaping on stages and interrupting productions to grab 15 minutes of fame.

From the fifties, straight through to current times, No-No played the extra in everything from musicals to plays to big time films. Bag ladies, vagrants, hobos and a bobble head in the crowd, she'd done it all, playing the extra whether solicited or not. And though no one ever saw her in any movie, she proudly backed up her claim to fame by framing a dollar from each film where she was paid, hanging what amounted to roughly a hundred bucks on a living room wall.

Cliff faced that wall, amused by the tawdry frames and notations on the dollar bills; *'Debil in a Blue Mess'* the funniest. *'No way had that bill been autographed by any legitimate film producer,'* he chuckled.

But to appreciate the wall was to know No-No,

a feisty little woman who hustled most of her life, nearly three quarters' of a century.

"Teb," she started in her Southern twang, sounding much like Tebby, "I don't have it in me to be giving Deiga a bath today."

Godeiga was a tenant in the building. Both of them, No-No and Tebby, took turns caring for the woman who weighed close to 500 pounds. They picked up her meds, prepped meals, bathed her and such, since the woman couldn't do those things herself. Cliff tried to fathom it, figuring out how Tebby and Naomi, both weighing a couple hundred pounds soaking wet... and together, managed such a project themselves.

"Don't worry No-No. My friend will help me bathe Deiga," Tebby said.

Instantly Cliff's eyes got to fish-bowling, troubled by the logistics of accomplishing this feat. How on earth did anyone get a 500 pound woman near a tub, forget the manipulation it had to take actually putting that much weight in a tub!

"Who?" No-No asked, peering around Tebby as if he wasn't standing a foot away from a museum of odd laurels, so basically he stood in the center of the room, snickering at a wall.

This was another thing about No-No. Along with missing teeth, and legs that no longer worked, she was partially blind, and couldn't hear so well either.

"Me, Ms. Naomi," Cliff gently replied, bending over to speak in her ear. "I'm Tebby's friend, Clifford."

The little wiry woman leaned so far away two of the wheels on her wheelchair were off the floor. "Who?!? Cliffy?"

"Yes, this is my friend Cliff," Tebby replied.

"Well, tell your Cliffy he don't need to be buzzin' in my ear. Sound like some kind of bumble bee...bzzz... bzzz... buzzin' up my ear," she harked, abruptly looking back up at him. "Is that why they call you Stang?"

Cliff wasn't sure how to answer. This wasn't the run-of-the-mill geriatric woman. She seemed as easily playful as provoked. He decided to test his humor.

"Because my mama didn't like Sting," he laughed.

No-No laughed too, a small tinsel sound rattling her vocals as if thumb tacks were caught in her throat. "How you know what ya' mama did and didn't like? You was just a kid," she yapped, her little golden eyes igniting the dingy room as she swatted at his knee.

"My mama knew you was gonna one day come askin', that's how I know," he teased.

"Stang, I thank you pullin' my leg. You pullin' my leg, ain't you Stang?"

"Ms. Naomi, you ain't got no legs to pull."

"I do too have legs," and she hoisted her dress to expose two pencil sticks sitting Indian style in the chair. "And why you callin' me Ms. Naomi? I'm plain No-No to you! Bet I'm old as you anyway!"

"How old are you Ms. Naomi?"

"I told you I ain't no Ms. Naomi!"

"My apologies ma'—I mean, No-No. How old are you?"

Naomi blushed, which chocolate as she was he could only tell by the way her eyes fluttered. "I'm fifty-nan," she answered on a bashful pretext.

Keeping the small surprise to himself, he smiled and found another distraction to occupy his attention. In a corner of the room, opposite where he stood, loomed a happily stuffed grizzly bear. He noticed it when he walked in, initially assuming it was a lounge chair, how the wall stole his eye. But on second inspection he realized this huge rag doll was standing on its hind legs with its paws extended. He didn't know whether to ask the purpose of the monster, laugh or fill up his phone with camera-ready images to use as cover art for one of his novels.

"What 'chew over there thankin' Mista Stang," No-No yapped, reaching over and swatting at him again.

"You fixin' on stealing my bear Mista Stang?"

Struggle as he did, trying to stifle a laugh, he patted her hand. "Don't you worry ma'am…that bear will not be leaving this house…at least not with me."

"Ma'am!!!" she shrieked. "Aww, ain't no way I'ma let a man old as you call me ma'am!" She looked over at Tebby walking in and out of the room gathering things she needed to bathe Godeiga. "You hear your Cliffy in here callin' me these dirty names Teb?"

"No No-No, I didn't hear him. What's he callin' you?" And before No-No replied, Tebby leaned over and pecked her on the jaw. "We've got to go now No-No. I left some fruit and cold-cuts in the frig, and will try to stop back in a few days."

"Try!" Naomi shrieked, abandoning the flirting with Cliff to give Tebby the up down. "So that's how you gonna do me? You find a sweet ole' thang," she scoffed, also giving Cliff the up down before continuing her rant, accusing Tebby of 'just turning her back on her No-No.'

"Oh No-No, you know I love you," Tebby giggled. "I wouldn't be here if I didn't."

"But I bet you debated on it though," No-No griped, pulling on her arms as if she felt a chill. "Leaving me in here with some ole' nasty dried up fruits and cold cuts," she muttered in feigned anger.

Tebby ignored her. "Just make sure you lock that top lock after we leave," she reminded her, backing out of the door and bumping into Cliff.

"Don't pay her no mind," she said after they stepped in the hallway. "Like they say, she is a live wire, but she's really sweet too."

But he was paying No-No a lot of mind, especially when she opened the door and shrieked, "don't let that gal drown that pretty boy and flood this building! And check his pockets. I bet' not be missin' any money off my wall!"

Cliff laughed after she slammed the door. "I'm sure

glad that wheelchair has her on lockdown," he said shaking his head.

"Don't hold your breath on it," Tebby replied. "She can do things in that chair inventors never intended to be done."

"Well, I kind of feel bad leaving her here like this," he said as they stepped on the elevator headed down to Godeiga's second floor apartment. "Feels like I'm taking you away from her."

"Oh...she'll be okay," Tebby quickly replied. "Trust me. No-No is well-known and has plenty of friends in this part of town. Sometimes I think she's working with Washington. Everybody around here has been robbed, except her!"

• • •

After the visit with No-No he was sure kismet energy brought them together. The coma-like deep sleeping patterns was disconcerting, but negligible in the grand scheme of finding good company...and knowing Hopkins, where Mama was taken excellent care of, was nearby. He met a bunch of phenomenal physicians over the course of her care. Small potatoes. Any one of them could help his soul mate. The brighter picture was meeting a beautiful human being so worthy of walking his last mile seeing to it she got well...and stayed well. Divine intervention he settled on believing, the same cosmic force that sat him bolt upright in bed that night.

"I really think my *spy* will work," he said, smiling like he was reading his horoscope promising him years of good fortune. "There's a ton of spies in the area. No one will really know, and I can always tell her I'll have to kill her if she talks," he beamed. "She won't have a choice. She'll have to believe me."

"Cliff, I don't know about that," Tebby sighed. She had a better idea. "Why don't you just tell her the truth? You know you can always stay with me."

"How about I don't tell her the truth and you stay with me?"

One manly lesson his father left him with was that a man never asked for, nor accepted money in any form or fashion from a woman. Not ever. For no reason. A man who supported his woman or family robbing banks was a better man than one who laid around milking money from a woman. They were the lowest scum on the face of earth his father said.

He could never live with Tebby. Even if he was fond of mice and roaches, his upbringing wouldn't allow it. Already he designated himself the sole provider. In fact, he didn't even want SSI and disability funds associated with any address they might ultimately share. He would squirrel away every bit of savings he had left before he'd resort to a third hand. And if all failed, he'd sell relics his father left behind, treasures Merda hadn't gotten her paws on because she had no idea there were paintings in the garage worth over $150,000.

Rolled up in a dusty rug were paintings his father brought back from Africa and got into a heated dispute with Mama about. He recalled the trip, the paintings and the subsequent fight. Merda needed money...like what else was new...apparently badly. This was shortly before she had run down to Florida barefoot. Mama wanted to help. Pops didn't. But Mama was insistent and usually got her way. So Pops, which he learned later, burglarized the house and told Mama the insurance company denied the claim, when in fact Mutual Omaha paid $15,000 and Pop kept the artwork (not included in the claim). Merda never got the money and Mama never knew about the paintings rolled up in a rug and stashed in the garage. Yeah, Pops didn't play with his dollars.

"Why don't you want to stay with me? You think

your place is better than mine?"

"Not at all," he replied. And that was the truth. Even if her place inside looked dimmer and seemed draftier he would pack up and move in with her, just to be together. A dimpled mattress, cold cement floors, or the cluster of loud smelly dumpsters lined up beneath her window wasn't enough to turn him off. Material things were nice, and sometimes important, but he treasured them living under one roof more.

"I don't know how you can ask that given the way we met," he added.

"Yeah, but pretending to be homeless is different from actually being homeless, Cliff!"

"Not really," he argued. "Poverty is a state of mind."

"Un huh, yeah right! Run that by me in February," she countered. "Besides, poverty and homelessness are not the same thing smarty pants!"

All right! He got it. She was right. "Look, I just can't let her run me…run us… out of this home. I've worked too hard, and she—"

"—I know, Cliff. Your sister has been a thorn in your tush since you were born," she said as if she was tired of hearing how rotten Merda was. "But two wrongs won't make this right."

Oh, good grief. Like how many times had he heard that one. He didn't say it, but a right and a wrong didn't solve issues either.

They stayed quiet for a while, his head dancing around bringing it. Although Merda stopped calling him Satan didn't mean she wouldn't beat the Satan out of him if he tried to bring it like Satan. He would have to kill her for sure to keep from breaking another one of his father's rules. *'Never put your hands on a woman, son.'*

"You know Cliff," Tebby started, softly stroking his hair and looking into his eyes. "The more you want, the less you'll have."

Oh, goodness, not again. This was the same line his father used to explain why he duped Mama about the art. Of course Pops reversed the argument, despite the premise remaining intact. He said *'the more they kept giving Merda, the more she kept asking.'* Haha. His argument when Merda called asking rarely veering. *The buck had to stop somewhere.*

"What are you smiling about," Tebby asked.

"How beautiful and right you are," he smiled.

• • •

His mind worked like a revolving door. The thoughts kept coming, something like commuters going through turnstiles at rush hour. Pushing the Merda debate aside he pulled out his slickest pick-up line yet, for the woman he had already picked up, but had yet to bed down. It took extra grease to come upon the line because Tebby was different than the average woman he wouldn't have bothered to ask how she felt about premarital sex. Like, why would he care? If they returned for more, great, and if they didn't, even better. A soul mate was different. He couldn't mess up and risk her not returning.

Tebby laughed when he asked about premarital sex though. "Cliff, I'm not marrying you! Marriage is for people who want children."

Had she not been teasing him with a coy smile he would've been crushed. Flattened like Road Runner. "You mean to tell me you don't want little clones?"

"Not in this lifetime," she replied, talking like she had made up her mind a long time ago.

Truthfully, children had never been on his agenda either. A couple of times he checked his healthcare plan, to see if he had any prenatal coverage, and once looked into a passport, preparing to flee the country after a real

Godzilla told him he impregnated her. But no offsprings ever materialized…thank heavens…given the myriad of child-support horror stories filling jails across the nation.

"Not even adoption," he asked Tebby concerned.

"Hmmm…" she hummed, rolling over on her back to stare at the ceiling. With the humanitarian efforts she supported, she hadn't thought about that one.

"It's a lot of children out here in need of loving homes," he goaded, raising up on an elbow to admire her features. She had the prettiest heart shaped lips. And they, of course, were soft as butter at room temperature.

"Maybe," she said, quickly adding, "but I wouldn't want to raise them in this house!"

"Why not?" he idiotically asked.

"I wouldn't dare bring a child into this toxic house!"

Oh yeah. He forgot. "But let's say I got rid of her? What if—"

"—Now you're really talking cray-cray. I definitely would not bring nobody in here, not even myself if you kill your sister."

"Well, I wouldn't kill her," he sheepishly said. Like gee whiz. He talked a good game but without those acting lessons he was as harmless as the vagabond he gave up on. "I'm just going to get her to leave…like voluntarily," he said shirking his eyes.

Tebby laughed. "For some reason I don't see that ever happening. You remind me of men who say they're leaving their wife but never do."

He frowned and tilted his head. "You had a man that did that to you?"

"No, but when I was in college I knew a lot of girls who had married boyfriends that played them hard!"

"Oh, so you think I'm playing you?" Their talk had turned a serious corner. Tebby no longer looked like the giggly school girl with the sensitive spirit. She looked raw, like the age she claimed to be.

"Look Cliff, you don't have to go through all of this. We can have all the sex you want, but I don't want to be dealing with no extra drama. I've had enough trouble in my life. I just don't want any more."

His eyes opened so wide it looked like a torpedo was headed straight for him. He didn't know whether to continue pleading his case or kick off his shorts. "Tebby, I'm not playing you," he said growing up some himself. "One thing my father taught me was to treat women right and take good care of the one I loved."

"Well, your sister is a woman. Did he say anything about treating her right?"

"Naw…he didn't mention her. We both hated her!"

"I'm serious Cliff," she sighed. "We have enough to make bills without having to stay here."

"And I'm serious too," he said in a similar tone. "It doesn't matter where we stay, so long as I get to take care of you."

"All right now," she warned. "If you don't do the right thing with that sister of yours, or if I hear anything more about that spy, it's over. I'll be done!"

. . .

His mirage was gone. Thanksgiving was a day away, so he dropped her off at No-No's apartment where every year they made dinner to feed those unable to cook. He started to ask if he could help but thought 'don't be such a Pepe Le Pew!'

The short of it was, they had been underneath each other for three weeks, no breaks. The longest separation was when they used the bathroom…and turned in at night. That being, save for the last night. Before he dropped her off at No-No's they really enjoyed themselves. So, it was only right that they catch their breath. He even hoped to get some writing done, since he accomplished nothing while she was there. The file sizes of each manuscript was the same as the night she arrived.

He returned home, pulling onto the driveway to see who but Merda guarding the front door looking like a bronzed statue...of a Buffalo soldier. All missing was her posse ...and the year!

Pretending as if he hadn't noticed her standing there he played with the headlights, testing the high beams for a few minutes, in increments long enough to force her to raise an arm to shield her eyes.

Satisfied trouble was on the horizon when she didn't move, filling the entire doorframe dressed in a furry bathrobe with a high collar, he stopped to inspect a bush he never paid attention to before. It was the same bush in the last photo his parents had taken together...some 20-30 years ago.

Just before he got to the steps where Merda stood with her arms now folded across her barreled torso he bent down to make sure one of the pebbles that came from the flower bed wasn't in fact a dime. He might need it once he got to the precinct, provided it still cost a dime to use the telephone. He hadn't used a public telephone in so long he'd forgotten. He actually thought prisoners were allowed one FREE phone call.

Out of distractions to entertain he briskly headed up the steps, taking one at a time, where he bumped into her, intentionally of course. "Oh, hey...I didn't see you standing there," he said acting surprised. Had he been on Broadway he would have been up for a Tony award.

"Clifford Blanchard," she spat as he slid by without touching her. "I never thought I'd live to see the day of you acting as if you've lost your mind!"

He kept walking, letting her snap at his neck like he did every time he met her in this mood. This was a well rehearsed theme between them. Even with only the light from the TV illuminating the room, he knew exactly how many steps it took getting to the archway where he would turn the corner and march to his room door.

"Do you have any idea what this is doing to Mama and Dada?" she hissed, pronouncing each syllable with several s's.

He hastened his step, feeling in the dark for the key that would unlock his room door.

"You laying up in that room with that child," she continued, breathing like a rhinoceros over his shoulder, and putting special emphasis on child as if Tebby was two. "You ought to be ashamed of yourself...acting like you haven't been taught no better! But I'ma tell you like this. It's gonna cost ya! It's going to cost you big time brotha!" And she wasn't calling him brotha' in no kind of affectionate manner either.

He had almost gotten by Parker, when one step past the laser that lined up the remote resting in Parker's lap perfectly with the television, she herald at his back, "...and brotha, believe me when I say this, if you think for a second I'm gonna let some white broad take all Mama and Dada slaved for, you got another thought coming!"

White broad!?! That was one he never expected. He spun around and hissed back. "Merda, she is as black as you and I! And since when did Christians start talking like racists?"

Maybe he was colorblind, but in case he wasn't, then Tebby wasn't much fairer in complexion than either of them. Tebby, in fact, had more honey in her sauce than the loafer stuffed in his mother's lounge chair.

The room was dark, save for the flashes of light coming from the television, so he couldn't see much of Merda's face. The most he could make out was the white of her eyes spinning around her pupils. Kind of like the Damned Children from the 60's Damned movie.

"I'm no racist," she spat. "And don't you dare try to turn my words into a holy war! Just you wait! Let her get tired and she'll run right down to that precinct with her lily-white looks and turn your old simple behind in for rape! Then tell me who's the racist!"

If a calendar had been nearby he would've checked it for the year. "So what if she does," he spat back. "You think it hurts more if a white woman beats me down to dust, than a black woman shooting me in the dirt?"

She couldn't answer. She wanted to. She even tried to. But she had no words to.

"...Besides, I'm protecting that woman. She's in a witness protection program," he blurted.

And that did it. That one line, which came out so effortlessly and naturally, sealed the deal. All the tapioca out there he unlocked his room door and head swinging low, lumpy drooped shoulders, and empty chest cavity he entered his room and gently closed the door. Just like that, that slip of tongue took the wind right out of his sail.

Mama told him a long time ago though, *'God don't make NO mistakes.'* "Sometimes you're going to wonder *'why me'* and beg God to change your circumstances, and blame Him when he doesn't, but remember this son," she said pointing up. "He don't make no mistakes."

Mama was right too. At least partially. When Merda was busy lying on him and physically abusing him, he got down right angry with God. A loving God wouldn't let Merda get away with murder, and make him suffer. Mama also said one day he would understand the reason for each trial and tribulation, through a reward equal to his distress. Well, 52 years had passed and he had nothing to show for what his sister put him through.

But sitting on the bed wearing remorse twice the duty of a burqa, it occurred to him, he would murder Merda, as God was his witness, if he lost Tebby over this.

CHAPTER...7

𝒯𝒽𝑒 𝒮𝓅𝓎. True to her character she fell face first flat into the spy novel. Ignoring Parker's concentrated look lining the remote with the TV's radar she started with him first.

"Do you believe that...that he's working with secret service!?!"

Parker said nothing. He was channel surfing, looking for his brand of entertainment...perhaps a real spy thriller. He knew nothing about real work; national, federal, local or otherwise. He hadn't seen a job since quitting high-school. Frustrated with the slug, she moved on.

She called everyone. Verizon had to be opening her own billing department for all the calls she placed. Cliff imagined the conversations; something like when he nearly walked in on her church committee meeting. He was almost in sight when he heard her hushing the group of worshippers. "Sssh...don't let this get out."

He stopped on the dime. She would've left them hanging if he showed his face, and he wanted to hear. The gossip could've been about him, or better, about her.

"You know why Pearl put her daughter out?"

One of the committee members tried to answer but got it wrong. She echoed a g-rated censored for publication version. He stretched his ear around the corner to get the untainted x-rated version... the version Merda whispered, though she really didn't have to. There was no one in the house but the women she was telling the secret to, all with mouths bigger than hers.

It took a minute but he finally caught on to the story, '...Pearl caught her daughter in the bedroom with another girl.' By evening that same day, the secret was no longer a secret. Everyone who knew anyone that attended the scholarship meeting knew to shun Pearl's daughter.

Surely it was the same way she handled his secret, despite the abject repercussions that she could be killed if she opened her mouth. Just one more person who couldn't keep their mouth shut to save their life.

As it came to be, the next day, Thanksgiving Eve, the entire clergy board from Cedar Baptist, plus half the neighborhood and close family and friends, traipsed in and out, prepping for the throwdown Thanksgiving dinner Merda planned to host in her fabulous inherited home. *Show out!*

No doubt she began working on the dinner upon Tebby's arrival. This was her big chance to air her smelly laundry, letting her small world know how wrong her brother was, and how rightfully she deserved the house.

At first he was going to stay locked up in the room, working on damage control. He had exactly two days to walk back the spy lie. That's how long Tebby was going to be away. Except Theresa got to banging on the door.

"Cliff, come on out here," she shouted through the door. "Don't be shamed...I ain't seen you all month!"

That was a hunk of bull. There were times when he hadn't seen Theresa all year...sometimes he hadn't seen her in years...precisely why he opened the door.

He actually like Theresa. She was an alright woman. Aside from Merda, she was one of his first sitters. She got him his first real date...for the prom. And his first real drink, and cigarette, and reefer, and 'head job' too... friendship stuff. So when he said he liked Theresa and thought she was alright, he really meant it. She hadn't done half the things Merda had done to him. In fact, she often looked over him, protecting him from the wicked witch that tormented so much of his early life.

"Aww yeah...he's shining up a storm," she grinned with the onion brown eyes...the white part...and a mouth full of teeth jammed pack behind powdered donuts.

"Give your big sis a hug," she said in a musty husky cigarette voice, causing him to recoil, and not due to the scent or crusty ashy lips, but because it sounded like an order to kiss Merda, his only biological sister who he would kiss, only AFTER locking lips with a hyena, or any grisly creature that might chew off his face FIRST.

He hung around in the common areas of the house for a few minutes...dragging in tables and chairs from the shed and answering shady questions.

That was the thing about these Christians helping Merda chop greens and bake sweet potato pies. They were so in debt to their borrowed niceness that coming right out with it was like pulling a trillion dollars out of a bank account with a zero balance. Shady Christians he called them.

Most suspected he was seeing a young runaway, likely in her late teens, even if this still didn't sit well with shady Christians who believed a fifty-two year old man baptized by their church should behave better. But then too, this was Cliff they were assessing. A man who at fifty-two had never married, had no children, and still lived in his parent's house. He wasn't right to start with. Plus, he was a writer. It all fit, and was coming together, especially after getting wind about *the spy.*

"Cliff, so where do you work nowadays," asked an undercover Christian herself, who he'd seen before but couldn't recall her name.

122 · A Piece of Peace

The question was funny, in a paradoxical way. The doorway he tried passing through...with two chairs... neither foldable, was only 4 feet wide. He and the chairs, if he moved sideways, was roughly a couple of feet. The undercover Christian however, no matter which way she turned, was all of 4 feet...in every direction! There was no way, with this plus-size woman blocking his egress, was he escaping this paradox.

He told her he worked for secret service and if he said any more he'd have to erase her. Of course he was kidding, though not everyone was taking this spy thing as a laughing matter. Parker sat in Mama's lounge chair giving him a look that reminded him of Hagerstown. You lying bastard. Save your worthless soul and shut up now. But most of the prep cooks weren't as gullible as Merda. They knew better. Little Iola had a husband who worked in Quantico. Shelly worked in Bethesda, and the big gal blocking his path worked at Langley, for the agency, in its Information department! All of these government workers knew better. No one in their right mind walked around calling themselves a spy, and refrained from work-related comments during socials. They likewise knew not to address the matter with Merda either. In an egregious way it made the buzz more satisfying. People laughing in Merda's face behind her back seemed so fair.

This wasn't the scenario for Merda, or Theresa who returned from a cigarette break picking up where the undercover shady Christians left off.

"So, tell me a secret Cliff," she grinned up in his face, smelling like a mystery and looking like a picture where he ran out of guesses. In her favor, she wasn't either a Christian or shady. Though she visited churches a few times a year, and every Easter, and knew the Bible about as well as any of them, she walked in her truth calling a spade a spade. The woman really had a heart of gold.

Working against her however, she knew too much. Few things got by her. She knew people very well...

too well...even people she didn't know well at all.

Like Bin Laden. She knew more about what that man was thinking and planning than the jihad warrior knew himself. McNabb was another one. She knew what he wanted to say but didn't say to the press about going to Washington. Name anyone, say anything, she knew all the big conspiracies, like who in Washington had been creeping beneath desks and sneaking into briefcases to see who was calling, touching and sleeping with who. Nothing got by her, except one thing. What she didn't know, otherwise she wouldn't have been smiling as broadly, or as much, was how unnerving he found it seeing her mouth peeled back so far showing so many teeth. Inside her mouth looked like an orchestra. No one tooth was the same size, and each tooth had a different situation going on. First off, she had three rows of teeth; one twisted sideways... some long...others short... even less conspicuous than all the colors in her mouth. How could anyone who had that kind of jamboree junking up their mouth find the nerve to poke fun at him?

"I don't know any secrets," he replied turning away.

"Not even an itty-bitty secret?" she pried.

And here was the real kicker, not that it revealed much of anything, but Theresa married a man who retired from the CIA... Alvin...or 'ole Al behind his back...a white man. The thing about 'ole Al was also behind his back it was rumored he had ties with the Klu Klux Klan. Yep, the good 'ole KKK, and Theresa, with her brown skin and extra junky mouth didn't seem to suspect this. No, when she wasn't grinning in everyone else's business, she was busy ranting about why Obama needed to be in office, which was something else she didn't know that everyone else suspected. 'Ole Al was a staunch Republican. How's that for how much Theresa knew?

"No, Terry, not even an itty-bitty secret," he glumly muttered, making his last trip to the shed. He was done.

"Now where ya' going Inspector Gadget," Theresa ribbed, "you know before this weekend is over we're gonna get a secret out of you!"

And the very next day that's what everyone sought to do. Merda invited at least fifty people over for dinner, so he ended up telling the story fifty times, sometimes likely, in fifty different ways.

The crowd worked him hard too. A round woman walked up to him, a woman he soon learned was Mrs. Grant's baby daughter, and plopped on the couch next to him grinning evocatively, with a plate perilously close to spilling over, balanced on her stomach. She wanted to know how she could get a job, "where he worked at."

"Who are you," he asked returning her mannerisms.

She leaned away. "You don't remember me? I'm Carrie's daughter!"

She really wasn't supposed to answer that. Even if he had remembered the elder chunky face coming up for air out of the larger cloned face.

He lost his appetite looking in her plate. Some took time placing food on their plates, trying to avoid certain foods from touching. Not her. It was difficult to tell what buried what. It looked like one large colorful mountain on her plate.

"Yeah Cliff, how much they pay for that kind of work anyway!?!" Squealed another woman standing in front of Mrs. Grant's baby daughter.

"Me and a friend of mine just went in to take the test to be a guard at the CIA...they was talkin' about starting us...if we pass the test, at forty-five."

There, that was the right word. *If.* Even if she passed every written, oral, and psychological test given, there was no way she was passing the physical...not with all that gumbo strapped around her waist.

Normally he didn't berate large women. After all, he had rounded off over the years, plus, one of the largest women there had to be his Aunt Idell, the sole reason he even left his room that morning. Otherwise, these other people, many he assumed were neighbors or church family, could ride off into a deep dark sunset and, as large as they were, he'd never miss one of them.

Other than an occasional wave across the street to a figure he only waved at because it waved at him first, he never said two words to these people, other than Mrs. Grant with the custard pies. As these neighbors died off and their children grew up...and out, he split 99% of his time between the bedroom and work...of course when he worked. Long and short of it was, neighbors became strangers. Most times, had it not been for the technology advances installing a GPS in his vehicle, he may have forgotten his address as he often didn't even recognize the neighborhood.

The anger festering inside him he soon realized grew from this familiar niggerish jaw-breaking crowding him in. The forty-five thou number blossomed and swelled into an ungodly awful figure.

A chocolate girl standing near the CIA possible had better information. Her brother was a SPO. They started him at seventy-five, and now he was about to retire... "yep, he been there over...umm..." and she looked up at the ceiling to count back, lashes flickering and fluttering as she counted, "...umm, yeah...over thirty years now," she rattled, tearing a piece of ham apart with her greasy fingers and throwing it to the back of her mouth. YUCK!

The thing was, chocolate girl wasn't fat at all. Her hair was a little peppery, knotted up on her head as if no one would look past the scoops of chiseled jello shaking behind her hips and not realize she was missing a cute face. But why was he looking her up and down, seething inside about her boxed toes she bunched into a pair of pointy-toe shoes?

"If you make it in, you got to be able to swim," so said chocolate girl.

'Please, muscle mama would sink like a rock,' he grimly noted as another taller and older woman leaned into the dialogue.

"My daughter is a SPO. She didn't have to know how to swim," raised the older woman matching every word to a fantastic beat of the most wickedly flapping eyelashes he'd ever seen. These lashes were about three inches long, and very, very dark and thick. Altogether he'd say they weighed a couple of pounds each. So each word she said, and he counted about ten so far, one lash would go up and then down, followed by the other. They didn't flutter at the same time, which was good considering how stuffy it was getting in the corner.

And that's when it happened. Jamison, Mama's baby brother, the family rogue, barged between the ladies resting his chin on chocolate girl's shoulder. "So Cliffy, where's this sweet young thang I hear you been back there shackin' up with?"

Any other day he would have let Jamison slide with this type question. But trapped in a corner, hot, irate, and most annoyed by Jamison's greasy look too, things went further than he would have liked.

First off, he and Jamison had this love-hate thing going on. He loved Jamison when he was penning his colorful antics to the characters in his stories, but hated being in his company. For one, he had one of those juicy mouths. When he talked, because he was missing a few side and bottom teeth, coupled by a drinking problem, he spat…a lot.

At the point of explosion, though no one knew it, not by how coolly he told Jamison he wasn't shacking up, his energy started rising above them all, about to pull out and bring together a large tambourine!

"He ain't shacking," chocolate girl informed Jamison leaning away.

"Yeah, he a spy," Mrs. Grant's baby daughter sort of argued in a giggle.

"Okay...okay...so then if you a spy, then what's the code?" Jamison drooled on chocolate girl's shoulder.

Enough. If Jamison thought he was a comedian, then he had a really short memory. It wasn't long ago, as he was sharing time with mopping floors, cleaning toilets and emptying trash cans for companies that never once invited his kind to their Christmas parties, he would recall that stand-up comedy gig where he blew up the stage. He was so bad, loving his poop and fart jokes so much that the club owner pulled the plug, embarrassing all who had come to hear him cut up, as it turned out, on Parker.

He stayed on Parker, asking when was the last time he got out the chair, betting he hadn't washed in weeks, sniffing the air to insinuate he hadn't brushed his teeth either. He wasn't even marginally funny, laughing at his own jokes and having the nerve to ask the audience if they got it? Hell yeah, they got it. But did he get it?

You're a janitor Jamison! A clean-up man working in one of the stinkiest fields a person can have. Here's twenty sticks of gum for you. The stuff coming out your mouth stinks!'

Hanging on for dear life, reaching for the balls to tell this motley crew he was in love with Tebby and wicked Merda could have the damn house, those words never taxied down the runway...or pushed back from the terminal. The words merely hung on the tip of his tongue as his favorite chunky Aunt Idell barged between the huddle, rocking side to side, panting and swatting at Jamison to move aside, before easing, or more like squeezing herself on the sofa beside him.

"Ah," she wheezed as the worth of her weight sank into the sofa. "Go on with ya'lls nonsense. I just wanna sit beside my nephew for a while," she smiled, patting his leg.

Cliff smiled too. *'Who wouldn't want a loveable cushion to saddle up beside?'* The slither of turkey he held up slid nicely across his tongue.

Not only was Aunt Idell his favorite warm and cuddly, he admired her vocabulary. She could whip a sailor and win a presidential debate, at the same time, with her tongue. Aunt Idell, as it turned out, was his tambourine.

"Nan, Cliffy finally got him a sweet young thang he been keepin' in here, tryin' to have us believin' he protecting her! Yeah right," he laughed in his deep Sam Jackson voice. "Tell the truth," he teased Cliff. "…how much work you be gettin' done at night?"

Valid question. But two things. Jamison was extra and then some, but one thing he wasn't, and that was a fool. Even if he didn't know, he knew. That's because he never talked from his head, but spoke from his heart. And one thing the heart never did, and that was lie, which was the other thing.

For thirty minutes Cliff had been aching to make his peace and call it a night. But each time he tried, someone cut him off. He could've been mistaken, since he was more heavenly grounded than heavenly bounded, but it felt like God's hand trying to cover his mouth.

All he heard was, *"Sex, sex, sex! That's all that's on the brain nowadays!"* Followed by sailor talking Aunt Idell echoing, "…and purgatory, purgatory, purgatory. Ain't y'all sick of hearing that mess too? Guess not," she chuckled, wheezing a little as she laughed. "I guess y'all cool wid' it since the Bible y'all DON'T read promotes so much anarchy!"

And man, did this remark not kill the buzz of giving. This remark kicked the meaning of Thanksgiving out of the house and SLAMMED the door SHUT! No need to know who said what because after all was said and done, he definitely saw himself in need of a gun!

"How can you say such an evil thing? God is—"

"—Evil!?! Evil brought your tail in this world!"

Gasp! And there stormed off the fan.

"You big fat bitch, don't you be talkin' to my Ainty like that!"

"Whoa…whoa…" and that was Jamison stepping in. "Ain't gonna be none of 'dat!"

Jamison did what he could, until Theresa and Merda joined the anarchy. Again, forget who said what because it mattered none.

"We need prayer in this house right now!"

"No! What we need in here is some truth…this one got they hand in the collection plate… the other one in the pastor's lap…and that one over there ain't doin' no betta than any of us!" Of course that was Aunt Idell, Mother of No Mercy. She lived the best years of her life. She was now free to speak her mind.

"She goin straight to hell! Straight to hell! I ain't hanging around here. I got to go!"

"Well go! Git! Pastor got enough ho's!" Aunt Idell howled, tickled hot. Laughing loud, she was on a happy roll. She was just getting started.

"Oooool, who she callin' a ho?"

"You," Aunt Idell replied, concerned none about the possibility of an 80 year old woman getting roughed up. Didn't even register in her mind.

"Idell, stop it! You stop it right now—"

"—No! Let her fat ass talk. Karma coming for her!"

"Hey, hey, what I say about talkin' like that—"

"—aww Jamison, you need to go sit down somewhere. I bet it was you who got all this mess started anyway!"

"But how y'all gonna let her sit over there talkin' about our pastor like that?"

"What you worried about Pastor for? Pastor ain't worried about you! All Pastor concerned about is you emptying that purse in the plate on Sunday, be it good money or drug money," Aunt Idell cracked up laughing.

"Oh Lord, where's my coat…and my purse? I got to get out of here!"

"And you go on and get out of here too," Aunt Idell carried on, belly rolling and gyrating, looking like she was struggling to straddle a yoga ball. "But you best call John before you go home," she lopped on, catching a tear with the back of her hand.

A small dark object shot across the room, coming fast in their direction. His and Aunt Idell's. It was dark and rock hard, about the size of a bird, but shot through the window like a bullet. He moved just in time, shielding Aunt Idell to keep her out of harms' way.

A scuffled ensued. Nothing to include either him or Aunt Idell, given how the both of them were wrapped around each other. He couldn't see much, not with his head tucked between his aunt's two pillows. He heard lots though. There was tussling and grunting and an onslaught of cursing. When it was over and the smoke cleared, the damage was evident.

One card table leaned on two legs. The contents once on the table all slid to the floor. A picture hanging on the wall lopsided had obviously lost a nail, and glass had shattered, splitting Merda and fatso's image in a dozen pieces. The dining table too, once festively dressed with candles and much of his mother's fine crystal and China, looked like a heap of mismatched food and broken glass.

Distraught and beside herself with grief she of course blamed him. "How could you let this happen," she sobbed. "You totally ruined dinner."

Him? How exactly did he cause this fiasco? Did not he tell her knock-kneed hard-head self NOT to open her big mouth!?! He didn't dare utter this but expressed it in a shrug. 'There was always next year. Maybe next time she wouldn't invite so many hostile Christians. Weren't they supposed to be loving and patient and kind?'

Apparently not. *'Oh, that's right. His bad. He got it backwards. Those closest to temptation and furthest from God had to be in a church building to be plugged in. Love and all that saintly stuff didn't cross over.'*

In all fairness, Pastor Edmonds seemed like a good man. Despite Aunt Idell's harsh accusations, his mission seemed fairly familiar. Let the record speak for itself, he did let Merda play in his vault. Corrupt ministers would never let that fly, unless of course, they were in cahoots, a conspiracy he'd have to change his world purview to accept.

So he wasn't in agreement with all of what Aunt Idell said. What he enjoyed was *his tambourine* getting the attention off the spy. Even as Merda ranted, sobbing and picking up broken glass, the spy was the last thing on her mind. And oh! He was on her mind. Just not the spy.

. . .

Once the glass was swept up, trash hauled off, and the window boarded up, Merda tallied up the damage and true to character got to assigning blame. Top on her list was him. He shouldn't have gotten Jamison worked up. He knew how he was. And he should have stopped Aunt Idell. He knew how she was too. Because of him the last of Mama's memories was gone.

What a retarded reality. Fortunately, to the gods which he owed much he remembered another limerick Mama hummed frequently. *'Only stupid tries to argue with stupid, stupid!'*

He wanted to though. Mama meant far more than broken dishes. In fact, he'd rather have Mama in his life, than a bunch of pottery from a land he had no affiliation whatsoever.

"And where are you going with that," she asked as he headed out the back door with a gallon sized bottle of unopened ammonia.

He paused long enough to glance over his shoulder before rolling his eyes and going about his business. His attitude said, try to stop me! She knew how Jamison and Aunt Idell were too. She shouldn't have invited them.

And to settle all matters, he told her he'd have to kill her if she told anyone about his spy work. But did she listen? No, she told everyone, which despite all, wasn't what got Jamison going. Her blabbing about his robbing a cradle started that brawl. It was all her fault. Every bit of it. And no he wasn't replacing the broken dishes.

"Cliff, before you leave here I hope you understand that woman is not welcome here."

The pieces were coming together. This had to be why God covered his mouth and what Mama meant when she used to say 'God makes no mistakes.' Going by what he witnessed only Aunt Idell could frame what never occurred to him to say. Her timing was perfect too. She set the stage for him to stand up to Merda and put her in her place once and for all. For too long he overlooked her, ignored her, excused her, avoided her. It was time to, as Tebby put it, bring it!

"You may have forgotten, but this is my house too! So you know what you can do with your hope," he seethed, his teeth clinched and jaws tight.

Her reaction wasn't expected. Merda could be Idell plus Theresa, dialed up past that whooping Mama put on her if pushed. She didn't always go around flaunting this part of her character, at least not anymore, the fake she inherited honestly, but there were times when she lost it and basically acted like a nut. With Mama's dishes broken and Thanksgiving in the toilet, he expected the nutty reaction.

"But we live here together," she pleaded. "You have to be respectful of everyone here...not just you Clifford Maurice Blanchard!"

He clenched his fist. Her voice started nice, slow and peachy repentant, but ended in a snarl that promised by the time this exchange was done his expectations would likely be met.

"How would you like it if I brought a gang member in here to live with us," she continued pleading. "Like, what if the gang member was after that woman," she suggested, betraying a look in her eyes that went from plea to glee. "See," she said, apparently catching his eye jerk. "See how we have to respect our home? You should have never accepted that job without first talking to me."

Okay, so she had a point, but only if Tebby had been in a witness protection program. But since there was no witness, thus no protection program, she had no point. She could invite all the gang-bangers she could scrounge up. She was the only one who didn't have a deadbolt on her bedroom door.

He didn't pause to breathe. "Merda, let me tell you something. Until you become a real Christian, I will never consult you on anything! I told your big mouth not to tell anyone about my assignment, and now look at the mess you conjured up!"

The Exorcist came to mind watching her turn from tan, to red, to bright red, to where did she go? The peacock feathers on her head shot upward. Her eyeballs popped out. And her jaw fell, leaving her tongue flapping about. "How dare you! How dare you!" she snarled at a pitch so high her words were chewed up and swallowed. 'Until she became a real Christian'!?

"How dare you blame that catastrophe on me! I worked all week on that meal brotha'! While you—"

—And he was gone. In one giant stride he was out the door, sliding into his SUV. She didn't come after him because remember…her knock-kneed self couldn't run. The most she could do was stand behind a glass storm door looking like a giraffe choking on Bazooka bubble gum… dressed for church.

. . .

And still, there was no telling how Tebby might react if she learned he'd done *exactly the one thing* they discussed he not do.

With no destination in mind, as Tebby was spending another night with No-No, he drove around looking for somewhere to park and think. Too bad Mrs. Grant's pies, or none of the desserts for that matter, were spared. But thank goodness he at least got to taste the food before the tragedy. Hopefully everyone else did too because spiritual busybodies might be a lot of things, but one thing they weren't, was bad cooks. The turkey, collards with the right amount of vinegar, and cheesy mac-n-cheese and stuffing stuffed with cranberries made the whole meal pop! Women with stretchmarks and arms that wobbled, and loved laughing in the kitchen, even at his expense, knew how to put their foot in food (no pun intended). After that delicious meal he craved sweets, why he pulled up on Shopper's parking lot. He loved their donuts.

Taking his sweet time selecting the freshest pastries, since the early morning batch were gone by this time, he returned to his vehicle where he sat... eyes closed, head rested back, chewing gently letting the springy sweet dough and syrupy glaze mix in his mouth. Except for the holiday tragedy, and short story he started working on the minute the spy lie left his mouth, his life at the moment was perfect. He wasn't bruised. Had no money problems. Wasn't hungry. And, sitting on brand new wheels (save for the busted out window), he could park in a driveway attached to a fully paid off home. He was living the American Dream. At 52. *Free of IV tubes and trudging into concrete buildings filled with ham-fisted cold-hearted bosses, backstabbers, a sluggish clock and banal mind-numbing work, HE WAS IN LOVE!* People dwelled in churches, on their knees, buying lotto tickets to have what he had. No way was he letting a knock-kneed bird take his piece of peace away.

Reaching for his cellphone to check in with Tebby, a startling knock on his window stopped him. *Now what?* He looked over to find a grinning wide and waving green-eyed woman bouncing a little blue-eyed blonde-haired child on her hip.

"Sir, I've been watching you and thought I'd ask if you might want to join my family for dinner."

Somebody was in the festive spirit, even if he looked down checking his cardigan for holes, rips, tears, spills, or damage invoking this sympathy. But his wardrobe was fine. He escaped the ghetto affair unscathed. Grotto would let him in without handing him a loaner jacket.

"It's okay if you have other plans," continued the blushing woman. "I just got a sense your Thanksgiving was probably ruined."

He chuckled. Bucket list check. Be darned, he just met his first real Ms. Cleo. "I appreciate the offer Miss," he gushed, before sighing a million mile away sigh. "Yeah, the holidays can be tough for some of us…and hey," he chuckled, perking up. "I apologize if you were at that one I just left. We usually try to send my sister *away* around this time of year…you know, to Greece… Burberry Farms… or Mars…" he teased.

The woman laughed and they chatted for a few minutes. Seeing him dressed as nicely and sitting alone in the car munching on the donut toggled her sixth sense. "Don't worry, we've all been there," she said cheering him on, her flushed cheeks nonetheless quarreling with a wheat colored 55 degree day. "Go family!" she teased, bouncing off with the kid on one hip and a box of Sugar Smacks sticking out of a bag.

He watched her hop into to a white Mercedes, and imagined her rolling off to a home in far better shape than the one he ducked out of. Typical. Miserable surroundings rarely brought out the best in people, what motivated him to turn the ignition and get moving. Next thing he'd know, a lava lips guard would show up and sweep him and his busted up back window off the lot.

The sun setting, gracefully bowing out, allowing a chestnut sky to take its place, he made his way over to a

Pier where he sat unmolested watching vacationers, non-cooks, and a mix of folks celebrating the holiday in unorthodox ways. To his left were skateboarders taking pleasure weaving in and out of pedestrian traffic at 20 mph, missing collisions by the hairs. Up ahead another unorthodox cluster convened. They were shoeless and their pants legs rolled up, strolling towards water thirty degrees chillier than temps dropping as day advance to night. One tool was completely nude, save for a pair of swim trunks!

On his right was a blur of activity, mostly sellers and buyers huddled around food carts and plain card tables exchanging dollars for…and all be darn if he didn't spot Rasta man! What were the chances!? The fake jewelry seller had rolled his operations clear across town.

At this point he just wanted to kill time; put distance between the absolute and resolute, loosely characterized as what happened and was about to happen, or straight to the point, how Tebby might react if, or when she got wind of the spy lie. His American Dream was skating on thin ice, and he knew it as he hustled over to Roscoe, his mind spinning in the old familiar turnstile fashion.

Desperate for conversation as he hustled over to the hustler dressed unceremoniously in the Dreds, fatigue jacket, and partially gloved hands he talked to himself, aching to know why he wanted to be stiffed…again!? Like what was going to be his opening? *'Hey my man, I got 60g's in my savings. Do you want it?'*

And that's when the Shoppers' empath, his jest and the 24/7 hustler made sense. He wanted to send Merda off on a getaway, or at least a nice long nap.

"Hey Rosc my man," he greeted his friend hunched over fake jewels and accessories.

Roscoe spun around. He didn't seem to recognize him but reciprocated with a warm pitch he would have delivered exactly the same way to anyone willing to stop and give his knockoffs the time of day.

"How've you been, my friend," he replied, shaking

his hand using two scratchy, partly gloved hands with eight fingers and two thumbs poking out. "I see you ran into some new money," he said standing back to admire him glowing in the sheepskin Shearling coat, matching hat, and cashmere scarf loosely tied around his neck.

"All man, it's nothing," he chuckled, sort of brushing off the compliment. "Just tryin' to keep warm."

"Looks like Jack Frost won't be bumping into you," replied jive talking Roscoe. "—Hey, I got something for you," he went on, wasting no time strolling to the other end of the table. "Just got some new pieces in…flown in last week," he boasted.

Cliff looked at a table filled with much of the same fake junk he remembered from his last visit. He started to admire another bangle, but recalled the last bracelet not making it to the coffee shop where he met Tebby. He looked down and the bangle was gone.

"Psst…down here," Roscoe nodded and grinned, jerking his head towards the real deals under the table.

Cliff noticed it before, *the spaces between Roscoe's teeth*…top and bottom. His smile kind of reminded him of a piano, and something his father used to say. "Don't trust a person with more than one gap between their teeth. *'One gap was a person with great wisdom. But more than one gap spelled a con-artist.'"*

'And so here comes the 60g con…' Cliff muttered, peeking beneath the table where Roscoe held up the table skirt. He smiled when he saw it, boxes reminding him of the 70's when Rasta men were called black Panthers. They used the same cardboard boxes to hustle the same velvet pictures.

"Man! Where'd you find these," he asked juiced up. He never bought one of these portraits but Jamison had. His *no-bedroom* shack was covered with wall paneling and identical evocative nude paintings. The artwork was so dark that he could have put a hazmat flood light in his crib and the room would've remained blackened.

"...Look my friend," Roscoe leaned in whispering, elbowing him, on his way for the grand steal. "I can't give you the frame, but I can give you any one of these pieces for 60 bucks!"

"That's all," Cliff replied shocked, not surprised.

"That's all my man," Roscoe cheesed. "We gotta look out for each other," he lathered on. "If we don't, who will!?"

"Hey...*say* Rosc man," Cliff interrupted, since they seemed to be hitting it off. "Do you know where I can find some..." and rather than say it, he demonstrated, bringing his hand to his mouth like how he remembered seeing Jamison do it when he was looking for weed.

Roscoe looked at him, hard, reading his mind but struggling to read his intentions. "Say my friend, this is all Rosc got here," and he dropped the cloth and started dusting over his wares.

"Hey Rosc man, it's me...remember...you got me for twenty last time. I know I look different, but I'm not the police."

Roscoe turned around, not losing one stride in his skit, "for you my man, let me show you these silk ties I just brought back from the jungle."

At first Cliff thought Roscoe was going to continue ignoring him. He even started walking away, when Roscoe caught him by the arm.

"Hey, hey where you going my friend," Roscoe said, sounding the way the Temptations feet in rhythm slid across stages. "Rosc got something here for er'one."

Roscoe pressed the fattest, ugliest necktie he'd ever seen in his hand. "Go on...look at it," gleamed the joyful broker. "For you, it's only sixty-f-a-v-e dollas'..." he laughed Jamison style.

It took a minute to catch on, before seeing a tag hanging onto the garment. He looked up, wanting to ask if he at least had a prettier tie but thought not to push it. "Now, is this the really good stuff," he asked instead.

"'Cause I'ma need to be out of it for a while," he cheesed like the goofball he naturally was.

"Absolutely," Roscoe replied, doing the bounce all hustlers did after making a hustle; snatching a used bag from a DIY shopping rack to load the laced necktie. "My friend, when you put on this tie and er'body see it…you, my friend, and er'body lookin' at you, gonna think you flying!"

"Great," Cliff replied skeptical. Merda had been on earth creating hell for over 60 years, and so far nothing had taken her down. She was like a Jurassic dinosaur. "You accept credit?"

"Of course I do my friend," Roscoe sang. "But I have to charge twenty extra singles…you know, to make sure the cabbage blings through," whistled the gapped tooth con-artist, cheesing like ever the professional.

• • •

"Cliff, have you done any writing while I was gone?"

No he hadn't. Between missing her and dealing with Merda and Thanksgiving, how could he? But to answer her question, "I've started working on another piece."

"Another piece? Cliff, you're too distracted. You've got to make up your mind or you'll never get published again," Tebby fussed.

True. Though, the least of his worries. He had a very angry sister stewing over a foiled Thanksgiving dinner, at home tapping her foot and pivoting…waiting to slide the whole house right from underneath him. He also still hadn't concocted the story for why she was so angry. Far as Tebby knew, it was *Grejeckula being Grejeckula*, the evil wicked witch of Satan's rise to rule, which was besides the real concern; the crumbled plastic shopping bag in the back seat, full of a nameless substance that could land them in a slammer for only God knew, depending on the weight, how long.

"I'm in no hurry," he coolly replied. "Sometimes you gotta press pause on life and enjoy the moment."

"Cliff, where are you taking me?"

"Out."

"Out where?"

"Out to eat."

"But why? You didn't save any leftovers? I thought your sister and her friends made all this food?"

"I've been eating leftovers for two days," he quickly replied. And this was no lie. In fact, he hadn't lied to Tebby at all. He just failed to disclose the full truth.

"Well, I was looking forward to tasting some of that ham and mac-n-cheese you described," she said. "We didn't get to pick up a ham this year and No-No burned the mac-n-cheese."

"Yeah, well... the last I saw of that ham and mac-n-cheese, Grejeckula was dragging it out of the house in large dark green hefty trash bags."

"All of it," Tebby asked shocked. "That's insane!"

Tell him about it. He couldn't believe they cooked enough food to fill a hefty trash bag. "So, how did things go for you?"

"Well, we fed over 7000 people," she replied. "But it's such a shame someone would throw away good food like that, when there are so many hungry people in the world."

He snatched around and grinned. "Wanna kill her?"

"Cliff," she whined. "No I don't want to kill your sister, and I already told you, you need to stop talking about her like that."

"Then you might be happy to know where we're headed," he smiled. "I'm taking us to meet with a pastor who's going to help me squash the beef I've been having with my sister."

"Seriously," Tebby replied, looking at him wide eye. "What kind of pastor is this? I thought only head shrinks dealt with kooky minds."

"Hey. Hey. Hey," Cliff chuckled. "I thought we were going to stop calling me a weirdo."

"Alright, you know I'm teasing," she giggled. "But why am I going? What am I going to say?"

"First of all, you're not going to tell the pastor I'm a kook," he teased. "And secondly, I love you, and want you to trust me...and to let the pastor know you feel the same...you know... that I'm nice, levelheaded, and all that jazz..."

"—Cliff, I can't lie to no man wearing a collar."

"Are you saying I'm not nice and levelheaded?"

"No, I'm saying if I'm asked about you, I won't lie!"

"How about we do this," he suggested. "How about you sit there and look like your pretty self."

"You mean... even if he's talking to me and asking me questions?"

"Yes," Cliff replied. "Just smile and nod, and let me do the talking since I'm the one that needs help. Besides, knowing these pastors nowadays, he'll probably think you're mute."

"Cliff, what is wrong with you? That man will know I'm not a mute!"

"How?"

"Because I'll be talking!"

Cliff shook his head and laughed. Fortunately Pastor Edmonds wasn't able to meet him and the sweet lovely Tebby. He hadn't made a proper appointment, and the pastor had to deal with someone more needy than him.

They left the church and enjoyed a quiet, and pricey dinner in Logan's Circle, returning to Tebby's shoebox apartment. It was wrong, but he concocted the excuse he was low on gas and too full on Romarin to risk driving 45 minutes it took to get to his home. Plus, Merda was there,

and like who wanted to spoil an otherwise pleasant after-
noon arguing about an aborted Thanksgiving and the lie
that founded it?

Besides, this was his chance to prove he didn't
mind laying perfectly still staring up at a water stained
ceiling on a lumpy floating mattress that wasn't a water-
bed. He clasped his hands behind his head and smiled.
Literally he laid beside the ideal human being, albeit in
a drafty room with not enough electrical outlets, rusty
plumbing, rotting wood, creaky floors, and too, on a frail
mattress. Outside, the building offered a more pristine version. Anyone passing by wouldn't doubt the building met
all safety codes. Images of it in fact, made it to the cover of
foodie magazines; once captured in a standalone photo,
and once spotlighted among a polite row of neighboring
buildings. The restaurant itself served millions, though
those millions had no idea while wining and dining on
Sauvignon Blanc wines and farm raised tilapia, indigent
residents lived above the swanky dining room setting mice
traps and bathing in rusty water.

Figuratively Cliff was on cloud nine however, up
until the following morning when he awoke and found
Tebby curled up beside him, tucked in like a little kitten,
in one of her comas.

As instructed he peeled back the covers. Supposedly, cool air aroused her senses. But a few minutes later
and nothing happened. She lay as motionless as the first
time he found her in this condition. This was not ideal.
Mama would've never accepted this work-around. Far as
she was concerned, poor diets produced frail people. In
her mind, the reason vegetarians looked so pale and had
circles and bags around their eyes, and brittle bones, was
because they weren't filled with her soup. And while the
medical board failed to compensate, or even thank her for
her efforts, she staked claim in healing many flu congested
children.

When minutes passed and Tebby hadn't budged

he swung his legs off the bed, carefully sliding into his shoes, hoping a furry pest not on the lease wasn't using his loafers to keep warm. As much as he wanted to, he couldn't live in this place, and neither did he want his Tebby living here. Bless the people who had a hand in helping put a roof over her head, and so what he had no medical license, but he had enough common sense to know drafty dumps like this was where he'd open his diagnostic lab to draw blood and run tests.

He called a woman who helped him when Mama got sick; Rita Flynn. It had been months since they last spoke but she recognized his voice. "It's so good to hear from you," she said so lemony he could see the pearls around her neck and knew she was gassing him.

Avoiding pointless personal tributaries he glibly updated her on his whatabouts, grazing over his relationship with Tebby to explain her symptoms in more detail. All he wanted Rita to know was he cared as much for Tebby as he had Mama, and of course wanted to see her stay well.

But Rita blew more gas at him, responding in a way a platonic acquaintance ambushed with this type info might. *'Take her to a doctor, or call 911.'*

"Oh, she's seeing a doctor," *he assumed*. "I'm only asking for my edification," he explained. Damn. Some people, no matter how civil or cordial or high up on totem poles, couldn't hide their close association with morons.

The reason he called her was because she did things for his mother that friends, or casual acquaintances wouldn't, or could. She wasn't in the medical field but researched Mama's conditions, broke down medical jargon, advised her on which meds were more or less effective, hooked her up with the best physicians…and basically was Mama's rock in her last days.

But apparently she was Mama's friend, not his. In fact, she had the nerve to ask how Merda was doing, given they all hooked up through church. All the same, it pissed him off so much that he replied, without taking a breath, "oh, she's the same old hate. I know one thing, I would have her hair follicles tested before I let her near any child I loved!"

He wasn't joking, though he chuckled, trying to play off his *serious as a heart attack* jab that he realized, sooner rather than later, was going to have a detrimental impact on some of Merda's philanthropic work. Rita, who hired Merda, was employed by the schoolboard.

Surprised, Rita gasped. "Oh Cliff, stop it. You can't be serious!"

And yes he did. He had the unmitigated gull to add, in a dead serious cold as ice tone no less, "Merda needed help!"

This was the real strange thing however. He stood by the drafty window, his back facing the bed where Tebby lay, looking at a mural of Jesus painted on a building. The mirage's hands, neatly clasped together in prayer fashion and eyes closed and head bowed, wore a smirk when he squinted, and a blurry smile when he opened his eyes. The smile modeled peace, and the smirk…sin. Either way, and far as he was concerned, since he had trouble differentiating, whatever came to be wasn't his fault. Yep, he blamed it on the One who made no mistakes…and also according to Mama and the Bible she often cited… the Creator of heaven and earth Who breathed life into ALL that was and came to be. That's right. He blamed God.

Even *Mama said it. Only God, and not the devil* would permit such a sequence of events, *so believing God created him, the devil, and the devil's identical twin*. It's why she never kicked Merda out of her heart.

"Ugh!" he muttered disgusted, turning around to see Tebby sitting up in bed.

"Who were you talking to," she whispered.

"Myself," he sheepishly mumbled. "You know how I am…always working on a script…"

"Cliff, I saw you talking on the phone," she replied

groggily. "Don't tell me there's more than two of you in this world."

He could've left the remark there. She didn't sound choleric or jealous or suspicious even. She sounded too tired to care, grabbing her robe off a door hook to drag down the hall where she shared a bathroom with two other residents on the floor.

Except he stopped her and told her. "I want to marry you," he said. "But first I'm taking you to see a doctor."

CHAPTER...8

Oh Lord. And here goes it. He walked in the house, right by Parker, hand in hand with Tebby trailing close behind. It was Sunday, mid-afternoon when he knew Merda was in church, likely praying for someone who wished she didn't pray as hard; like anyone seeking peace and prosperity, and a morsel of sanity...such as he. Truce was not a word in her graffitied glossary. When she got down on her knees and brought them ostrich claws together, squeezing her rat-like eyes good and tight, it was to hope he'd give in and let her have the house. Philanthropic as she pretended to be, she was no servant of goodwill. Back-sliders, the wayward, and those with no chance of resurrection she rallied around. Golden parachutes she thanked God for creating. Had it not been for these bonafide losers, keeping her buoyed in the air, she'd have no purpose selling the misery she kept, on a nonexistent salvation.

"It's cold in here," Tebby noticed right away, and this was coming from a woman who lived in a drafty, chilly apartment.

He started to put his hand over a vent when he noticed one of his clocks sluggishly flashing. He turned the light switch in his library and found no light. That's when he looked back at the clock on the nightstand. It went to battery mode when power was lost, but dimly lit and sluggishly flashing meant the clock was losing its battery life, which further meant power to his room had been lost for some time.

"Wait right here, I'll be right back."

Sure enough the circuit breaker had tripped. He doubted it had been a fluke seeing Parker in the front room blithely watching TV. He flipped the breakers, all switches sourcing power to his room, and stormed to the kitchen. That was his last straw. She had to pay. This would fix her evil knock-kneed behind he muttered to himself, pulling from his pocket the tag Roscoe had given him.

Inside the fridge, like an old bad crack habit, chilled an opened can of her favorite drink...her beloved diet Pepsi. He opened the packet, his hand stiff as a straight-jacket, recalling the many times and people she bragged to about her Pepsi crack habit, how she only drank a half can a day as if that made her better than those who chugged down a whole can. Carefully he emptied the entire packet into the can, a good ten grams he estimated, as his friend Roscoe had been particularly generous. When he peeked in the tiny packet, ensuring every trace of white powder was invisible to the naked eye, he smiled. If one pinky of a sniff could make a man fly, as Roscoe hinted, then the whole pack would send a giant bird like Merda into orbit...hopefully forever!

"What happened," Tebby asked rubbing her arms and blowing in her hands when he returned to the room.

"Don't worry," he said flipping on light switches and moving to a closet to pull out a space heater. "In a few short minutes it'll be nice and toasty warm in here," he smiled, quickly turning on the stove and opening the oven door. Because he kept his room door closed, air and heat didn't circulate naturally. Usually this wasn't much of a problem. Portable units cooled and warmed the room, provided the power wasn't cut off!

"Come here," he said, pulling Tebby into his arms. She was cold to the touch, and shivering. "Just give it a minute," he whispered, vigorously rubbing her back and arms. "Would you like me to make you a cup of tea?"

"No, it's okay," she replied, her lower lip trembling and turning blue. "I just think I need to get a little more sleep," she added.

Ensuring her warmth wasn't disturbed he helped her in bed and covered her with an electric blanket. By the time she (and the room) warmed up, he would have a nice hot bowl of Tortellini soup ready for nursing her back to health, like Mama healed her many patients. In no time she would be fine...while he focused on the underlying menace disturbing his peace.

He kept an eye on Tebby as he prepared the soup, checking to make sure her cheeks were warming up and her tiny nostrils flaring just enough to let him know she was breathing normally.

The broth had just started to boil; the onions, carrots tomatoes and celery bouncing like children splashing in water, when he heard a car door slam. He looked at his watch; 2:30pm, hours ahead of the usual time when the inferno crusader unplugged from Jesus.

He parted the blinds and there she was, draped in fake fur up to her cheeks, wearing a brim wide enough to hold a watermelon arrangement. She eyed his car dutifully, her upper lip meeting one of her nostrils and her color changing to the tone and texture of an albino alligator. The war was about to begin.

Sure enough the room went dark. The lights, his PC, and the stove all lost power. All be damned, an hour of intense labor on his next novel lost. Precious thoughts he'd never recoup. And the time and energy he put into heating a room that shouldn't have been cold in the first place, along with the possibility of the soup... and Tebby turning to a block of ice took him to the furthest reaches of inhumanity.

Breathing like a dragon he yanked open his door and stormed to the circuit box. She left her corner too, raising up off the sofa still dressed in her church costume; heels, nylons, fake fur, jewels and all. "I already told you not to bring that woman back here," she growled, coming at him like a bull eyeing its target.

He spun around, halting her charge, partly due to nearly breaking her ankle as no one who'd been walking for nearly seven decades, and was knock-kneed to boot, was narcissistic enough to dare try running in 4-inch heels balancing a watermelon on its head!

"What gives you the right to be so damn wicked," he shouted back. "That woman is sick in there!"

He turned around, leaving her hobbling behind him and shouting, "Clifford Blanchard, you disgust me! But not today brotha'! Not on the Lords' day am I lettin' evil in this house," she hissed, reaching him as he reached for the circuit box.

"Move," he hurled, batting away her long flickering ostrich claws decorated by a ring on each finger; and by no means refined rings either. These were huge vulgar clusters, the same size as her knuckles.

"No," she grunted, trying to keep him from opening the box. Only her meanness was no match against his muscle. He gripped the ostrich claws, about to squeeze and twist until her knuckles and jewels formed one mold. All that stopped him was a closed fist connecting and stinging the side of his face. He felt each chiseled stone stabbing into his temple. So instead of breaking her claws, with both hands he went for her neck. Except, because she was a foot taller, he ended up grabbing her by her fake furry collar and shaking her to the point that the watermelon flipped forward, landing on his head. If this had been a movie, he, at this point would be falling backwards laughing. But this was not fiction. He was in a blinded all hands on deck dogged struggle, holding onto a whole lot of bear imagining this was how he'd take down a grizzly.

It was the second time he heard her scream. Instead of *'Mama it's me,'* it was "Parker, help! Parker, come help me," she shrieked in a feverish pitch that sounded like a spinster quarreling in the abyss of her own inferno.

Parker rushed to the scene, the oddest part of the entire ordeal. That man hadn't moved as fast since the purchase of the wheelchair, a scooter he never parted ways with when there existed the possibility of a public audition. But there he was, all six feet of a slumped over figure, catapulted out of Mama's chair by a nightmarish scream.

"Let my dogs in here," she barked at Parker staring at both of them as if wondering what two strangers were doing in his garage.

"Gooo," she screamed, her cries halted by nosey Mr. Joe (Mrs. Grant's husband) banging on the garage door.

Cliff was already on the way to his room. Wasn't no way, with that kind of wail, sounding like Pearl Bailey on a bullhorn, bringing neighbors out of their homes on an otherwise divine day, one of the holiest of the week, Sunday, that his evil behind wasn't on the way to jail. What a mess, given the worst part was, he hadn't even killed her yet!

The sobering picture was seeing Tebby still in the coma-like sleep. She hadn't heard a thing, and in this one instance he was glad she hadn't. She warned him about this, and like Pops dogmatically believed, 'good women like her were always right!' This was one goofy spy about to go down.

He looked out the window to see a dozen flashing lights rolling up to the house triple-homicide fashion... accelerating his feet to get moving. He needed to figure out his next move, and quickly. Should he call Jamison? —*Surely he'd have some useful advice, having been in this sort of situation countless times.* Maybe if he called Aunt Idell, she could talk some sense into Merda? —*A long iffy stretch, given Idell needed time...lots of time...like days worth of time just to pull socks over her swelled feet.* Lawyering up would be quicker—*about as quick as police turning him and his room into a crime scene, guaranteeing his love novel was over...in more ways than one.*

In the end he ended up pacing the room, not calling anyone. In a last ditch effort he tried to wake Tebby, to get her friend No-No's phone number, but was stopped by an authoritative knock at his triple padlocked door.

In the parlor stood a barrel-leg pot belly nasally tone police officer blocking Parker's view to the TV. Notepad open and writing lazily the cop asked him questions as if he had been responding to domestic disputes since the day he joined the force...some 200 Pantheon years ago!

Cliff sat on the sofa, on the opposite end from where Merda sat. He didn't even want to look at her, except the blue can caught his eye. He did a double take, almost blurting *'shit'* out loud.

While auxiliary officers milled around the room touching things with their eyeballs, he watched her nursing her favorite diet Pepsi... pursing her skinny red lips and hooking them wrinkled ribbons over the can, with an extended pinky partly hidden by a Target rock *(likely with a piece of his skin hanging off it)* looking so satisfied and full of herself.

Disgusted he scoffed. It was impossible to ascertain the level of hate held for this one person, so much so that he earnestly prayed for her. *Please don't get greedy now. Take nice and slow sips.*

Last thing he needed was her passing out. There was no telling how worse things might get if that Pepsi fell under suspicion and was checked for one thing, all to discover another thing.

Ordinarily these things didn't happen to everyday decent souls *like him*; a man who kept to himself, wrote novels, paid his bills... on time and in full, spoke when spoken to, and responsibly secured his trash before putting it on the curb every Tuesday.

And yet, there he sat, head in his hands rubbing his eyes, every so often peeking over at Merda portentously nursing that Pepsi; a diet Pepsi to be clearer. She even swished the can in her hand, making sure all of the ingredients…the acids and additives and preservatives and uncut super tainted and contaminated high-grade contraband was good and mixed. She was so certain it wasn't her, the stringent judge of hellish matters that was headed to jail, but rather her brother, the semi-tax paying lover of staying in his lane.

The pot belly officer moved from Parker to Merda for questioning. Cliff tapped his foot meanwhile, getting anxious about Tebby sleeping in the room. Normally she woke up and carried on about her day, like no harm, no foul. But this day she hadn't been feeling well, taking a turn for the worse when she walked in his ice cube bedroom, every bit of thanks to the wicked witch.

Fully expecting to end up in the cuffs in any minute, seeing one of Grejeckula's nails flipped up, like an open car hood, and possible eyelash stuck in the peacock spray of feathers dusting her head, he started looking for the best advocate to look after Tebby. None of the cops milling around looked particularly helpful, like Parker who had returned to Mama's chair, channel surfing. His best bet was Theresa, elbowing her way into the house to make sure she hadn't lost her sister or brother from another mother and father.

Merda must've spotted her at the same time he had. It was the only rationalization that explained why just as he was about to solicit Theresa's help, telling the cops to go on and take him in, that the felonious worshipper, eager to display her version of praise dancing, beat him to the draw.

She surprised the old pot belly veteran, who sprang back as she leaped off the sofa reciting to the top of her soft-boiled lungs verses everyone assumed came from the Bible.

"Not my Jesus! My Jesus said set my burdens down and he will take them," she wailed extending her arms and shaking her head, and moving her feet (out of the heels) in a step dance cadence.

Pot Belly looked at her with his nose hitched up as if watching her pull out her intestines...didn't matter which end...waving them in an unsafe and threatening manner. "Ma'am...calm down—" ordered Pot Belly, with the law on his side, proven by his reaching for the radio clipped to his collar and urgently speaking into it.

The milling around officers came to his aid, strongly urging Merda to take a chill pill. "Sit down and keep your hands where we can see them," ordered one cop, hand over pepper spray.

But Merda was paying none of them no mind. It was Sunday and she had an audience, and was in a praying egomaniac mood.

"Hallelujah! Praise Him!" she called out, her eyes closed and hearing turned off. She had been in church four days straight, tried, tested, and left unhealed and now unplugged, reeling from Thanksgiving's leftovers. "Because YOU said so," she cried. "I know thy Will, will be done! Won't he!?! Yes Lawd, nobody but You will! May not come when we want, but will ALWAYS be on time," she chanted.

Officers didn't seem to quite know what to make of her act. For a minute it seemed like they were going to ask him what to do, as asking Parker was a lost cause, staring at the TV as if they were discussing who should give Merda a ride back to church.

Reinforcement came quickly. After all, the back-up didn't have far to travel, not lined up right outside the door and milling around in doubles and triples on the front lawn. They stormed the parlor like DEA, and this time Cliff was less worried and more amused.

"Ma'am...Ma'am...I need you to extend your arms out to the side," a young female officer tried to bark. Her and Merda sounded like they were in competition to secure the remaining solo soprano spot on 'Guess Who's Screaming Now?'

One thing was palpable. Merda's hands were raised, but not to be cuffed. Dancing in small Seminole circles, moaning, crying, and calling on God, Cliff looked away; the real ugly part forthcoming.

A patchwork of blue swooped around and drove her head first into the sofa. Merda's little peacock feathers disappeared, along with the top half of her, leaving her knock-kneed bird legs kicking and clucking like a wild turkey on a chopping block.

This got Parker's attention. Seeing a near seventy year old praying woman who'd just returned home from a day of worship getting arrested in designer clothes and top quality fake rocks had to be better than whatever was on TV. The remote fell from his lap as he leaned forward, eyes opened wider than his mouth, he stared. Like, where was her Jesus in this epic yarn?

• • •

It was a no brainer. He spent no time debating his next move, whether to follow police transporting the prayer warrior who wanted his head on a pogo stick to jail, or transporting the love of his life to the hospital.

Tebby was breathing but still sleep. He blew on her face, fanned her, and removed the covers but she was hard to rouse.

"Come on Teb, I want you to drink this," he said pulling her into his arms. Her head flopped on his shoulder and soup drooled down her chin, but her eyes were open and she was upright.

It didn't take much formulating a plan at this point. He wrapped Tebby in the blanket and lifted her off the bed, bumping into Theresa who came barreling in his room. "Come on Cliff, she'll probably get bail when—" —and she looked down at the faint figure wrapped in the blanket. "Oh God, Cliff! Who's child is this!?"

"She's not a child," he replied walking around her. "Close my door please. I'll deal with Merda after I get back from the hospital."

Theresa did much better than simply close his room door. She helped him help Tebby into his SUV. "I'll sit in the back with her," she offered, eager to see this young thing that had been the root of so much gossip and friction.

"Aww…Cliff, she's not a baby," Theresa sighed when Tebby tried to smile. "But she is a young one," she added admonishingly.

Cliff ignored Theresa, skipping a few stop signs and running one light.

"Alright now," Theresa called from the back. "I'm not trying to end up in jail too. Like, how are we gonna get bailed out if all of us are locked up!?"

"Woman, quit your yapping," Cliff replied, glancing in the rearview mirror, mostly checking on Tebby. She looked like the Virgin Mary draped in his Egyptian 600 count cotton bedspread. Normally she wasn't as pale, and her eyes not as watery, nor lips as soft pink, but given the given this was a woman worthy of breaking a few laws to ensure she stayed the apple of his eye.

"You probably should've called an ambulance," he heard Theresa yapping. "We'll probably be stuck in ER all night…provided you get to the hospital before we get stopped!"

But that didn't happen. Well, not exactly. Tebby was admitted right away, deeply disconcerting by the look on medics faces and how quickly they moved around doing but not saying. He asked a half dozen times if she would be okay, and a half dozen times he was told, in so many medicinal words, "sir, we're running tests! Now, who are you? Are you the husband?"

Basically they wanted him to step aside and go sit down somewhere...especially if he was just a friend, and not the husband! That's what really hurt. He'd give his last breath to say Tebby was his *until death did them apart,* signing every sheet of paper he was asked to sign, to claim full financial responsibility for whatever it cost to fix her... which he ultimately did anyway.

They left the hospital, him and Theresa, and after a chatty 20-minute drive arrived at the precinct where they could hear an unholy suspect in one of the back rooms sounding like a Neanderthal trying to escape out of one of Nostradamus's 'end of times' tomes.

"I see it! I see it! And my Jesus see it too!" warned the medieval warrior. Ostensibly she had been echoing versions of this observation since she arrived, going by the tried and tested look on a dreary-eyed clerk's face.

"Do you mind signing here," sighed the displeased keeper of books and records, looking up at Cliff, pen in hand, expecting a quiet signature with no commentary.

"Well, what am I signing," Cliff asked. "Will I get a refund if she disappears, or like dies before she gets her day in court?"

The clerk looked up at him, totally unamused. "Sir, it's a $25 processing fee," she flatly replied, as the hoary banjo played uninterrupted in the background...wailing about red rivers, Hercules, and her constitutional rights.

Cliff, trying to get the clerk to lighten up, started to ask if they had a layaway plan, but saw the bookkeeper was in no laughing mood, plus there still was the matter of Tebby. One more abject sound out of him and he, the whining banjo, and powdered doughnuts might all have their day in court...in a not so speedy fashion.

Merda came out of the back looking like every one of Nostradamus's predictions had occurred. The 40 straight days of rain and floods had happened. Jesus had come and gone. And the fire in Hell had burned out, where only she arose from the ashes.

"These buzzards tryin' to kill me," she huffed. "But I got news for y'all! The God I serve is a mighty God! I promise you He gon' sho' nuff fix it! Mark my word," she promised through tears.

"Come on Mary. Let's get out of here and go home," Theresa said, draping an arm around her. And like two drunks supporting the other they slow poked their way out of the precinct.

Merda got in the car and took one up and down look at the covered window, and went right back to fussing. "Got me out here ridin' with Judas," she bemoaned, using the headrest of the passenger seat to rock back and forth, attempting to get the momentum needed to hoist herself out of the car. Theresa stopped her, wrapping her arms around her, promising everything was going to be all right.

He kept his mouth shut and his head low, in case she decided to use his face as the momentum needed to lift out of the seat and clobber him upside the head. For that reason he also kept his head turned to his left. Listening to Theresa pampering her with the 'Oh Mary' and 'we're going to get to the bottom of this' and 'Jesus will fix it' was screwing up his face, cartwheeling his eyeballs back and forth across the bridge of his nose and twisting his lips in the form of a smirk. Shucks, if that was the case, they could've walked home. The Potomac River wasn't but a stones' throw from the jail, and a hop and a skip (in Jesus miles) to the front door.

"Mama and Dada got to be turning in the ground," she wailed on, sobbing like the modified Pepsi was working on her, though nowhere near the flying trip Rosco promised. Her knock-kneed behind was supposed to be knocked out...on Pluto, not crowing in his ear about a busted out window and whatnot!

"Unck, man, I need your help…"

"Aww…come on now Cliff, it's almost two in the morning," Jamison growled into the phone. "Me and my old lady are here in bed!"

"Unck, you know I wouldn't have called if it wasn't important." Jamison had to believe him. No one in the family who knew his uncle's bad habits ever called him for favors, especially not in the dead of night when his repayment fees were often steepest. One of them could need a ride to the doctors' and he be the only one in the vicinity with transportation, and still an ambulance ride at a whopping $1000 fare was cheaper than asking him for a favor. It took only once to learn the hard way, a story so horrific that the mere mention of his name made the family shake their heads no.

But this was different. Tebby was really ill, and Cliff really in love. An edgy emergency room doctor said she wasn't in good shape, which translated to hanging onto life by a thread as thin as angel hair. He needed help, or a second opinion, translating once again to needing a ride to the hotel complex where No-No lived.

"Cliffy mannnn…ugh!" That 'ugh' was a good 'ugh!' He might have to pay for it dearly…but for the moment he was desperate.

Only Jamison could get him in and out of Rainman at that time of night, and just what were the chances of anything being opened where he could *swing by* and leave the car running while he robbed the place?

Jamison pulled up in the driveway, motor running and engine sputtering, with him inside looking around as if someone was after him.

"Ugh, unck," he stammered, leaning into a souped

up undercover cop cruiser rushed into a chop shop and hurriedly repainted after being hustled off an auction block, "I was thinking, maybe we can take my car…"

"Cliffy…if you don't git in 'dis here car man!"

There was no time to argue, but he never prayed harder than the forty minutes it took them to get over to Rainman. If police pulled them over, and there was every chance this could happen, and he got arrested, as what happened to Aunt Idell on the last favor anyone ever asked of him, he'd surely die a tragic death.

"I cain't believe you got me out this time of night caught up in yo' spy business," Jamison huffed, plainly excited to have been chosen for the run.

Cliff kept quiet. He was a many praying men on this car ride, thinking only of Tebby lying in a cold bed, in a colder room, kept alive by ice-cold machines.

"Cliffy man…you got yo' skid on you?"

Skid? He looked down and around, and patted his pockets. What was a skid?

"Man, where's your gat!?! Yo' damn nan!?! Yo' grip! Yo' blessin' man!?!," he argued as if a major part of this trip was going to include the both of them hanging out of a window each, 1920s cops and robbers style.

Cliff looked over at Jamison, concerned. He thought he had his. It was one of the main reasons he called him. Otherwise he could have gone to Rainman alone.

"You know I don't carry weapons…"

"What!?!" Jamison nearly leaped through the ceiling. "You got to be kiddin' me right!?! In yo' line of work? I cain't believe you ain't packin' no heat." He shook his head and settled back. No one went to Rainman in the dead of night minus a gun. And preferably two. Not even if they were a tenant. It was something no one did. And if they did, they didn't live to talk about it.

Something amused Jamison and got him smiling. "Man…what the hell is you up to?"

"What do you mean?" Though he knew well enough what he meant.

"I mean what the hell is you up to that you got me riding out this way at two in the morning?"

Tebby's image came back in focus. He could see her lying there, amid white sterility; the bedding, and walls, and drip tubes, and her small russet face blending into an offset haze of unspoken peace. He wanted her back. He wanted to hear her. Hear her nimble voice and petite laugh and see her eyes light up his world.

"It's this woman—" he started explaining before Jamison cut him off.

"—Cliffy man!," his uncle yelped. "You got me goin' over here for some poo-na!?!"

"No! No...it's this wo—"

And there was Jamison again, cutting him off. "—I know! I heard that," and he mocked, "...it's this woman you want to see. But damn Cliffy...couldn't this wait!?! It's two in the morning! You don't know nothin' bout chokin' the lizard man!?!"

"Unck! With all due respect, please!"

"Unck...*with all due respect*..." Jamison mocked again, though jovially. He always got like that when he thought he was teaching Cliff something new. His eyes would lift and brighten, and spit would start sprouting, almost like a water fountain.

Everyone he knew, except Merda maybe, saw him as a clean-cut straight type. He didn't run the streets like Jamison and many of the men Merda worshipped next to Jesus, boasting and bragging about sexual conquests, or how many bars they closed down and ultimately put out of business. That wasn't none of Cliff, and none of his type fun.

"This must be one hell of leg! Cause I ain't never heard of some poo-na that good!?!"

"Unck! This is not what this is about...so please!" This was the main reason he kept Jamison at a distance.

"My friend is in the hospital... dying okay..." and he let that sentiment hang in the air for a minute. "...I'm picking up her friend to take her to the hospital."

"Just pull in here," he told Jamison, pulling up to No-No's building, a tall red brick structure during the day; a mean brownish pile of rubble in the night. "She stays on the ninth floor...9-G."

"Man Cliff...I didn't know you got down like this," said one piped down Jamison. "Man...you done gone out and got you a hood rat!"

"No Unck, she's not a hood rat, and she doesn't stay here. This is where her friend stays," he replied, making eye contact to help Jamison get his drift. "...And her friend isn't a hood rat either."

He hoped Jamison got the hint. No-No was a no-no to rile. It was time to get serious because night crawlers casing the hotel in this hour didn't take well to humor ... good or bad... which speaking of surly, one leg out of the car and look at who strolled over.

—Gadoor. A man he had a run-in with the day he first visited Rainman with Tebby.

"Mannuuun..." Gadoor started in his hood drawl, a street accent matching Jamison's. "Where you been," he asked strolling stooped over in a crooked limping gait, the result of street shrapnel catching him in the thigh.

"I ain't seent you in a bit," he said looking around them, as if they knew one another, but straining to get a look inside the car.

"Got sumfin for me...got sumfin I can hold...what 'chew carryin' in here," Gadoor leered, barreling into him, his chest pressed against his arm the same way he'd done the first time they met. The other time it was a lot warmer out that day. All he had beneath his arm then was a jacket. And it's all that fell to the ground when Gadoor went to check him.

"Aww...you ain't got nothin'," Gadoor sneered that other time, stepping on his jacket and limping away.

Gadoor's twin partner Lucky did him the same way. "Whoa...whoa...whoa my man...where we gon wif 'dis," and he pulled on his jacket, also realizing it was just a jacket. "Aww man...you ain't nothing," Lucky had sneered too. "What 'chew doin' sneaking around here like 'dis for?"

Gadoor and Lucky were two of the most notorious menaces casing Rainman, aided by dozens of clones just as intimidating. He asked Tebby how she handled going to Rainman amid all the terrorizing agents. He couldn't imagine a woman as meek and frail getting by those characters.

"No-No will be fine," Tebby told him, which still didn't answer his question. No-No was in a wheel-chair. How could a woman more fragile than her keep those villains from hurting her too? Those were some of the unanswered questions Tebby left him with.

"Look at you," Gadoor went on, acting glad to see him, patting him down anyway. "Look like you found some money!"

"We're here to pick up No-No," he said brushing by him, Jamison on his heels paying Gadoor just enough attention not to have to introduce himself too.

"Aww mannun...No-No probably in there washing clothes or sumfin'...you know 'dat, baby!," he chuckled, limping and strolling away at the same time.

They got inside, he and Jamison, where he learned something new about his uncle. He didn't know Jamison feared riding elevators.

"Unck, you're kidding right?" How could a stick-up man with a nine in each pocket, who'd been hauled off to jail as many times as Gadoor and Lucky combined, be afraid of anything? "What, your nine scared too?"

Jamison looked at him, holding the stairwell door open, eyeing him inhospitably. "Ha, ha, ha, ha" he dryly laughed, "but I think you're forgitten who called who."

Like Gadoor said, No-No was up, but she wasn't up washing clothes. At two in the morning she was in there playing Bid Whist. A mean crusty-voice barked through the door. "Yeah! Who is it!" And a hostile eyeball filled the peephole, doing donuts around a circular opening missing its magnifying glass. Behind the eyeball, out of view, they heard No-No ask who was at the door.

"Some knuckleheads lookin' for a No-No," replied mean-eyed crusty, cracking the door open and hooking a soupy eight-ball eyeball over the chain.

"Well, let 'em in here," No-No chirped like her old afternoon self.

They stepped inside, with the angry man hovering over them as No-No's face dropped when she looked up. She stared at him, and then eyed Jamison, before asking in almost a whisper, "where's Tebby?"

"Tebby's in the hospital No-No. She needs you."

Just like that the card game was over. "Git my hat and my coat," she ordered the mean-eyed soupy eight-ball eyeball. "...And git my fixadent too!"

· · ·

He couldn't have dreamt up No-No, even if he wanted to. She was so polar opposite his lovely Tebby, and yet he could see how the two connected.

The huffy staff that started eyeing him suspiciously embraced No-No as if she was the First Lady of the United States. Well, and then again, it did take No-No introducing herself. Initially the staff said it was against hospital rules to visit patients after 8pm, which by this time it was three in the morning, but No-No insisted. She told the nurse she was the best spiritual healer in the world, she could both cure and strike people down. "Now, get out my way Shirley and go git the doctor!"

Cliff was sure security, instead of a doctor, was on the way, except thirty minutes later she wheeled into the waiting room speaking in her naturally loud screechy voice. "Stang, you stay nearby here?"

"Not too far away," he cautiously replied, not sure if the question represented a good or bad sign. "About 15 to 20 minutes away," he added.

"That's close enough. Take me to your place so I can sprucen up."

"But how's Tebby?"

"She'll be fine," No-No slung over her shoulder, wheeling down the hallway like an Olympian racer. "I talked to the doctor. This ain't the first time Teb got chugged up like that," she said, spinning around after pressing the elevator button. "She just gotta get some of that mucus out of her. After I sprucen up you can bring me back here so we can get her out of here. Teb hates hospitals."

He felt ten pounds lighter on that slither of news. A little chugged up he could handle. On the other hand, No-No's abrasive nature colliding with the real thorn at the place where she wanted to sprucen up, posed the real problem. Could he even get her wheelchair in the door?

They got back to the car where Jamison lay stretched across the back seat, four in the morning. Surely he was tired. But did this matter to No-No?

She flipped out a Chuck Norris chuck-stick she kept tucked in her chair, and banged it against the side panel of Jamison's chopped shop car. "Open up Timmy!," she yapped in what to her probably sounded like a bark, but came out more like a scratchy squeak. "This is the law," she turned around laughing at Cliff. "...See, I bet that'll raise him up," which sure enough it did. Jamison sat bolt upright.

"Git this door open Timmy! This the law!" she added for extra fun, yapping as she hurled herself in the car, reminding them on the proper way to handle her chair, how to drive, what she had a taste for, the last time she had been alone with two strange men, and who she would get to come after them if anything happened to her that night. She yapped like this, through a 20 minute order... or ordeal...at an all-night burger joint, plus a stop at a 24-hour CVS to pick up super glue *(one of her wigs kept coming loose)*. All the way to his house she yapped.

CHAPTER 185

CHAPTER...9

𝒯𝒽𝑒 𝒯𝒽𝒾𝓃𝑔 𝒜𝒷𝑜𝓊𝓉 𝒩𝑜-𝒩𝑜, he couldn't slip her in the house, quietly and undetected like he did Tebby. By the time they got to the house it was almost five in the morning and No-No was wide awake. Just as he feared she came right in the house banging her chair into doors and walls, talking at the tip top of her voice like she'd done from the time they left Rainman Hotel.

"What 'chew doin' living in a place all dis big. Stang, this place too big for one little man like you!"

Her shrivelly crackly voice, but chillingly loud, woke Merda right up. She burst out of her room... barren face, no accessories, and head wrapped in a yard's worth of curtain type fabric... braced against the doorframe. Cliff jumped. No-No didn't. No-No barely batted an eye at the undressed ostrich pecking for a fight.

At the time Merda plowed into view, one of the handlebars on No-No's chair had gotten caught on an edge of the hallway doorframe. Head down and curtly smacking switches, she was steering the chair in reverse, turning the wheel in rough hand yanking movements when Merda made her presence clear. She stood in the doorway a cold solid minute watching the maneuvering before No-No looked up.

"Hey honey, did I wake you up? No-No sorry about that. Shugga, go on back to bed. I'll catch up wif' you in a bit, after I git some rest!" And she jerked on the wheel, turning the corner, bumping into a wall, and backing up, accidentally clipping one of Merda's ostrich toenails sticking out of her slipper. "Watch ya'self," she yelled, before continuing into Cliff's suite of a room where he held his door wide open ...grinning, cheesy Chessy cat wide at this point. This was no Tebby he brought home this time. *This was what could be referred to as not only Tebby's best friend, but man's best friend!*

"Stang, why ain't you tell me you was stayin' in here with ya' mama," she asked an octave lower. "How you gonna hanky pank with ya' mama in the house?"

He ignored her, quietly pulling towels from the linen closet and laying them on the bed. "No-No, would you like to wear one of my night shirts?"

"Now why I want to wear your things when I got my own things," and she reached around and pulled out the pad he had mistaken for a pillow, the same pillow that kept falling off the chair and she kept snatching up off the ground and stuffing right back where it kept falling from. "I'ma house on wheels," she laughed. "Just let me use your washroom and you go on and git you some rest too. Teb don't need to be lookin' at some bush-wacked man."

"Well, the bed is all yours. I'm—"

"—and yeah, just don't you be comin' out here tryin' no funny business crawling up in it either! You see this here stick," and she shook her Chuck Norris cane at him, "...I'll use it!"

· · ·

Roughly six hours later he woke up to a strange silence. He heard the regular afternoon noises; the usual muffled outside racket...car doors closing, engines going, hedge clippers clapping, alongside Fester's clatter, or whoever Fatso was watching on TV. But he had fallen to sleep in the middle of World War IV, expecting to wake up in an Apocalypse. There shouldn't have been so much light in the room, nor should he have heard the fatso switching butt cheeks, getting more cozy in Mama's chair! No-No no doubt had gotten loose.

He sprang up instantly, tumbling off the chaise and landing on his hands and knees. His room door stood wide open, and like he feared, No-No was gone. That old woman sure 'nuff had rolled out!

Hungover from a long moving holiday he scrambled to his feet and rushed by undone deadbolts and a door swung raggedly wide open, and staggered to the parlor where he came to an abrupt stop. 'Good heavens, Mother Satan, *meet the birth mother of Satan,*' he muttered.

"Well, good afternoon Stang!" No-No screamed in her serrated grating timbre, its pitch determined by who loved her, and how much.

"Whole day just about gone now Stang! You missed it! A whole day!" she sang-shouted, pushing back from the table and turning towards him.

"Yo' sista' done made me up some toast and eggs and grits, and some good 'ole thick-cut slices of ham," she laughed, showing off her little chiclet teeth...*thank goodness she had them in*. "We in here like the U S of A Army Stang!" she cackled, the only one in the room with her head throwed back and generously laughing.

Parker sat in his designated spot, less than a foot away from the wheelchair that left a tire mark on his arm-rest, while Merda stared at the table, facing a sea of papers. "We got more done by 6am, than the whole world Stang!" she cracked herself up laughing, her voice hanging in the air long after she stopped talking.

"Stang, you know what these coo-coo bugs trying to do to yo' sista'," he heard behind him, as he stumbled dazed into the kitchen. She kept talking, her shrill slicing voice slaughtering any possibility of making sense of her babble. The only picture he had clearly in frame was the spotless clean sink he faced. Yeah, that was a habit of the sterilized freak, he ruefully scoffed. She drained the hot water tank, doubling the energy bill since her and fatso got there, drowning the kitchen in bleach like he soaked trash cans in ammonia.

"Did you hear me Stang," No-No shouted from the dining room.

"Ugh, yeah I heard you," he dutifully huffed, not eager to hear her repeat herself. "I think half of Waldorf, and all of Annapolis heard you," he grimly chuckled from the kitchen.

"What!? You tryna' make fun of me, saying I'm loud talking Stang," she shouted back, her voice rounding a corner to reach his face stuck in the fridge.

"No, No-No, I'd never make fun of you," he obliged her with. Nothing was in the fridge, or kitchen that he wanted. He was just buying time to re-face the crowd of distractions he just witnessed.

"You better not be making fun of me Stang...not by the way you was carrying on last night," she cracked up laughing.

"Stang, you know what we need to get for you?"

"No, No-No," he replied, once more, obligated.

"We need to get a muzzle for you," she went on teasing. "...One of them kinds that grizzlies wear," she laughed her loudest yet.

He tried to tip out of the kitchen and slip around the corner, headed to his room, but of course No-No broke his stride.

"Stang, where you creepin' off too," she yelled. "And what 'chew got in that napkin?"

Merda looked up, of course she did. It was instinctive. That was her kitchen he just came out of. Except her eyes weren't narrowed like usual. And the darts that used to be on her forehead had softened…a lot…looking more like question marks. Her spotty complexion had evened out too, turning her from halfway yellow, to a chapped brown. Obviously, No-No had gotten next to her.

"I gotta make a few phone calls—" he mumbled, a lame lie that hardly cleared No-No's head.

"That ain't the question I asked you," she screamed, skipping on by that retort to move on to the next. "'Dees coo-coo bugs trying to hem yo' sista up! You need to sit down at dis here table and hear this mess…and 'den we got to git Teb out that hell hole!"

At the moment his back faced them, daring to move, posed like a caricature frozen in frame. Caught like Ned, a nobody who had a habit of lying, he had no comeback on the tip of his tongue to explain there was nothing in the napkin, unless his covered up concern counted as something. But No-No would regain the use of her legs before he ever sat down at any table where Merda sat.

"Ump," he muttered into the napkin, pretending to be chewing. "Give me a sec," he continued mumbling, dashing to his room where there was no fire to put out.

No-No wheeled after him. "Stang, what in the devil done got in you? Why you running around here like you scared or something'!?"

"Look No-No," he started in a low reasoning voice. "There are some things you don't know about me and my sister…"

"Stang, I don't need to know all y'all's secrets," she replied in her natural voice. "That's between y'all! I'm talking about the law fixin' to pop yo' sista' on some trumped up bogus drug charges!"

Wait. Come again? *Had Merda already been popped on a drug test?* Well, Hallelujah! And don't blame him. That test couldn't have had anything to do with suggesting her hair follicles get checked ...before letting her get near children. Besides, he did pay her out-processing fee. He could've just as well left her dealing with a bereaved clerk aching to clock out ...or clock somebody. Merda was not a first time offender!

"Yo' sista' being framed," No-No explained. "I thank somebody out to get her."

Now, that was no mystery. Everyone who knew her constricted high ba'hind, cheeks squoze together like two bricks, was after her. One day No-No herself might join the state long line, the length of the East coast, 'out to get her'. Too bad she hadn't already been got!

Hence, Cliff expressed none of that out loud. Instead he listened to No-No let loose her legal knowledge. "But I know the law," she exclaimed. "They can't pin any 'ole test on her," she argued, waving a crooked finger at him as if he was responsible. "Dem tests got to be done by a certified testing center. Can't just anyone take dat test! It got to have an official seal. I know! Dey tried to pull the same thing on a friend of mines. Dey had to let him go!"

Turned out, after hearing No-No's closing argument, Rita had stopped by *(on the day of the showdown)* after he dropped Theresa and Merda off at the house. Evidently, she either witnessed or heard about Merda in handcuffs and connected the dots to his helpful tip about the hair follicle. Dang it, *Rita had to be on her p's & q's* if that was why she bee-lined it to the school, collected Merda's paraphernalia, and dumped the junk off, along with demanding a clean drug test before she'd let her put her claws on a nair' 'nother child. Good! Like Mama used to say, *'one child saved was better than none.'*

"Woman, how did you figure all this stuff out," he

teased, acting relieved that someone had found the one needle in a haystack to cure all social ills. "You need to be a detective," he laughed.

"Stang, this ain't no joke," she shouted. "They could put yo' sista in the can!"

"Oh, No-No, I doubt it," he glibly chuckled. "That's one broad who got about nine lives! Trust me! I—"

"—Stang, what's wrong wif' you!? Yo' sister ain't no cat! We need to stick together. Don't you know if we don't stick together they'll git us all!?!"

He couldn't tell how serious No-No was about equal rights, or getting justice for Merda. She seemed pretty scatterbrained herself. But he lightened up a little, just to get her to lower her voice. With his room door still wide open, and Merda he was sure, all ears listening to every word, he didn't want her having access to any more ammo than she already had.

"Look, I ain't never learned to read and write, but you need to go in there and look at some of them papers that lady left yo' sista' wif," she said. "I thank yo' sista' too upset to be dealing with all that stuff right now!"

"How about if I ask a friend of a friend to call her and work this out," he offered. He had just the person in mind. Nobody.

"Well alright," she said as he schlepped off, headed to his sanctuary. "Just make it snappy wif' yo' slow poke self! We ain't got all day to play. We got to git back over to the hospital and git Teb!"

•••

Though her raucous voice alone could sear iron, he got a kick out of that loose little live wire. She wheeled out of his bathroom dressed like she was headed to the Oscars. Red carpet, Look Out! Here comes the project's oldest and most celebrated scooter bound street-war decorated fashionista…wearing Lost & Found's signature apparel, socket to famous last words.

Had he not feared the repercussion he would've bust out laughing when he turned around and saw that curly wig cocked to the side, decked by water lilies and pebbly plastic gooseberries hanging off the side.

"What 'chew standin' there lookin' at," she snapped. Apparently his ceiling to floor bathroom mirror told on her. Marilyn Monroe's mole was above her lip, not below it on her chin, and the designer never intended that hat be worn after, or before Easter Sunday!

"You done already held us up with ya' sleepin' and hidin' out in that room," No-No railed on. "What was you doing in there, all that time anyway!?"

"Well ma'am you told me—"

—WHACK! She hit him with the Chuck Norris cane. "What I tell you about callin' me that word!?"

He looked at her, and then the chair. Tebby was so right. The wheelbarrow she sat in held mystical powers not discernable to the naked eye. Close up it was an ordinary black mobile scooter. Seat, back cushion, large rubber wheels, arm rests, there was no place to harbor all the contraband she had pulled out in less than eight hours. And most titillating was how she rigged the chair to collapse like an umbrella and work like a crutch. To see this woman in motion was like watching a circus in a one second magic act.

"Right this way princess!" he chuckled, brandishing a hand to gesture ladies first.

WHACK! That time she swung her purse. "What I tell you about gettin' fresh! You only got one princess, and that's my Teb!"

She got that right! Though he almost flew over the handlebars when he mistakenly tried to guide the chair through the narrow hallway, to avoid scarring the wall… more.

"And don't be treatin' me like no invalid either," she yapped. "I might be sittin', but I ain't no cripple! Keep ya' paws off this here chair! I got this! Now move out my way and git the door!"

As she bossed him around, manhandling the scooter, he watched handle bars transforming into Chuck Norris weapons, and the entire chair becoming a kitchenette, and trade booth, and he looked the other way when it seemed possible the contraption also served as a porta-potty. Without the chair the woman was a loose cannon. With the chair she was an unvetted arsenal!

He let her go at that point, mashing the gas button with one of her mini sausage thumbs, hurling towards his SUV the same way she raced across the hospital parking lot. When she came upon a set of steps, driving at it like an obstinate debater refusing to believe a ten foot fall could cause instantaneous death, he started to run after her but was cautioned by one of Mama's stern warnings, *'a hard head will make a soft behind!'* Actually, it would've been jerkish to heed Mama's threat at a time like this, except doing the right thing was out of his hands.

Before reaching the steps, and he made his best effort to catch up to the chair quickly, No-No took on a hill of steps, hitting a lever that jerked the chair in a backward lean, and skipped down six steps, in three tiers like a gold medalist gymnast. HE-LARRY-OUS! The wig and gooseberries flip-flopped and bounced in test dummy style. He doubled over. That woman was a comedy and tragedy in production.

Clearly, she did not need his help, as clearly Tebby was elated to see her, and just as eager to get out of the hospital. "They say they want to keep me a few more days...to see a hematologist... but—"

"—Oh no Teb! We came to git you outta here today," No-No shrieked. "These white jackets been in these labs fooling around wif' you for years...making your arms look like an addict! They could end up pokin' a big giant hole in you so big, you disappear! Did they give you the juice yet?"

Tebby nodded, unperturbed by that invasive screech of No-No's, garnished with the blunt edge that sent the less direct scrambling for exits, such as the nurses who scattered out of the room.

And yet, going by the glow she evidently had drank the juice, intravenously fed into her scarred up arms. And still, she looked ravishing, as good as new.

"Well, I'm bringing you home with me," Cliff spoke up, standing at the foot of the bed, careful not to set off the bell-clapper's alarms. "I can take you to Hopkins," he declared, as No-No busied herself at the head of the bed bumping into walls and medical equipment trying to sample pudding and crackers abandoned on the food tray. She didn't appear to be paying him a lick of mind.

"I know the doctors in that hospital," he was saying to the pleasant but expressionless figure staring back at him, before the bell got to clapping again.

"Well why didn't you take her to yo' hospital in the first place," No-No shouted, spitting out a chewed up cracker in her hand, along with her dentures. "Ugh! Dey must've got 'dees crackers from the dollar store! Ain't got a drop of salt on 'em!"

While No-No maneuvered the scooter out of the tight space, taking down Tebby's heart monitor when she hit the motor—extra hard—, pulling wires hooked on the back of the chair, he finished explaining his plan. "You're going to be fine," he smiled. "Because I'm going to make sure you get the best care—"

"—You mean like that care you givin' yo' sista'!" shouted the bell-clapper, using hand sanitizer to wipe off her teeth as nurses rushed in the room.

"Y'all might as well leave that stuff on the floor," she told the nurses, who downgraded the emergency when they realized what caused the mess. They even ignored her polishing her dentures with hand sanitizer.

"How you gone' care for somebody else when you can't even care for your own!?" she shouted over heads and butts cleaning up the mess.

He didn't dignify the question with a reply. Instead he mollified Tebby, asking what she had a taste for and if she wanted to try his homemade sticky buns...when the bell got to clapping again, hitting him in the back with, "Stang, why you call yo' sista' that name?"

Despite as loud...and clear...as the question was, stinging him in all four of his ears...his forehead, his hippocampus, and both lobes directly beside his sideburns, he still misheard her. *Was there another name for sticky buns?* Starbucks called them cinnamon rolls. And Mama called them honey buns. Maybe No-No had a *surlier* name? She probably called them sweet pockets, or *suga* pokers, like Pops did when he was getting fresh with Mama.

"You know what that name sounds like?" he heard her ask.

Of course he knew exactly what she was talking about, and the particular name in question. "I guess it just stuck," he shrugged. "I've been calling her *Merda* since I started talking," he mumbled, 100% annoyed the question came up. "Back then it was hard to pronounce Meredith."

"Stang, you know how to say Mary-death," No-No shouted, almost causing him to burst out laughing for one of the manyeth times since being in her wake.

"You a grown up now Stang," she cried on. "You got to stop callin' her that name. Sounds like you callin' yo' sista' murder!"

"Oh, I don't think she minds," he replied. "She calls me Satan."

"See! 'xactly what I mean," she shrieked, turning to Tebby. "It don't bother you none, him callin' his sista' a name like that?"

Tebby's heels, and not the petite gas pedals at the bottom of her legs hidden beneath a blanket, but the sparkles in her eyes looked dug in. If she had something to say, it stayed a guarded secret, neither here nor there. "No-No, you not meddlin' are you," she sighed.

"I ain't meddlin' nothin'. Stang jus' too grown to be callin' somebody that. I don't like it is all," and No-No turned away, pursing the ruby red dash between her chin and nose, really peeved about the matter.

The room grew silent, save for one nurse's snicker. It wasn't an audible noise she made, but the smile on her face was loud...too loud to explain what was so funny about informing them that a doctor was on the way to sign off on Tebby's release. Fortunately No-No's sight wasn't so great.

"Stang, you know what an eye for an eye does," she asked. "It leaves the whole world blind," she answered herself. "And I'ma tell you something else it does," she continued. "It'll steal yo' joy! You keep that bitterness in ya' heart and you'll die an old bitter loner 'cause the last thing I'ma let you do, is take my Teb down with you!"

...

It was the jolt that sent him to Pastor Edmonds. Tebby left the hospital, deciding to recuperate in No-No's ideal version of moral choices and ethical habits, rather than surrounded by plush amenities, in an albeit hostile habitat. To be honest, he understood. He had done little to fix the relationship between him and the aberrant vice wicked-fying his ambience. There was no telling what Grejeckula might do next. In hours they could be right back where they started. *In the abyss of a nightmare.*

It was around dinnertime when he arrived at the pastor's home prepared to lay his burdens down, hoping the gesture would be like one small step for mankind, and one giant leap for the starry-eyed wistfully in love. The

First Lady was just setting the table when he showed up.

"Oh, I don't want to interrupt you guys dinner," he started, cut off by the pastor who boasted he was a 24/7 servant of God.

"We haven't eaten a meal alone in 17 years," the 24/7 servant gloated. "In fact, that's what that stack of plates at the end of the table are for."

Cliff looked right, to the end of an 8-foot table where First Lady dropped a hill of plates, the dishes clanking to the table reminiscent of dishwashers dreaming of the day when they could throw their apron at the boss's face and find employment more equivalent their worth.

"Go on, have a seat," the pastor said, gesturing to one of seven chairs vacant at a table that seated eight. He, of course, sat in the eighth chair...directly across from the chair he pointed to...smack dab in the middle of the table; a rather odd choice Cliff noted. Usually the man of the house sat at the head of the table, the number one spot. At least Pops always did. He said it denoted who wore the pants and paid the bills...and was King of the Castle. He further instructed doubters to read *their* Bible...Proverbs all the way through, in any version of *their* religious tomes. In other words, *'don't let him have to tell somebody to get the hell up out of his chair and not sit in it again!'*

"You're in luck," chuckled the pastor, heavy voiced and big hearted. "We're having surf and turf tonight. My wife makes the best pot roast, and there's not too much you can do to mess up lobster!"

Cliff doubted it. He had had plenty of tough lobster before. He also remembered something Mama said a lot. *'Inhospitable cooks, cook inhospitable food.'* It's exactly what Dottie looked like...inhospitable. Despite a pretty face and slam-banging body, for a 36-year old snatched right out of a cradle *(Merda's words)*, she wore the mask of a Pocahontas stuck in a 17-year old loveless union. But he acted like he hadn't noticed a thing. After all, he wasn't there to eat.

"The wash room is over there by the stairs," First Lady tersely snapped, dropping a plate in front of him and turning on her heels to march into the kitchen where she remained. The woman had attitude galore. He had seen her once or twice before, when Mama, and later Merda herself invited a group of their church buddies over to the house. Her expression never veered. Cold. Angry. She had an arms folded pissed off look, as if bidding time for the day when she would finally get her much deserved wings and crown, and assume the throne.

He returned to the table, after turning on and off the spigot, and checking the mirror to ensure no boogers were visible, to find the pastor leaned over the table, with a huge rack of beef facing him, fixing both of their plates. Now THAT was really odd.

"Oh, buffet-style huh," he jostled, making light of Dottie leaving them high and dry. That was guy talk, the way he heard men begrudgingly speak of the balls and chains they ended up married to.

But Pastor Edmonds wasn't playing ball. Ignoring the air quotes he explained, "oh, Dottie won't be joining us, though make no mistake about it, she is a major for Cedar!" That part he was clear on. "She just likes to give some of these meetings a little privacy…" and to Cliff's surprise, as if they were hanging over a bar drinking the 24/7 servant admitted, "…provided no single woman with her skirt hiked up her back is trying to sit at her table!"

What the…! He didn't know the pastor all that well. Though he had been to the house when Mama was alive, far more times than his basinet baby breath wife not even born when he was chased out of the Lord's House by that feral beating, the church had swapped ministers a dozen times since. Edmonds took over after Pastor Barnes, who Mama loved, left the church. Barnes was an old times preacher. He knew everybody in *his house*, making a point to visit his regular tithers, showing up at their homes after service. The men didn't like him so much, inviting himself to eat up what little food was in the house and checking out their wives and daughters. And Cliff liked the guy even less than the men. Barnes was just too countrified, kicking off his funky shoes at the dinner table and digging in his nose when it seemed to itch, preaching about right and wrong, something like his sister, and those in her gossiping camp was downright disturbing. He sided with Pops. That pastor belonged outside under an acacia tree, not like the better mannered Edmonds who he preferred to give the benefit of the doubt.

Unlike Barnes, Pastor Edmonds never claimed to be Jesus, or God, or any deity above his ordained title, proven by his full disclosure of his wife's *rightfully so* jealousies. Though shocked by the feral confession, the man wasn't a put on, so heavenly decreed that he ignored the sleazy habits of pretentious women lusting over him. He stood up for his old lady, announcing loud enough for her to hear, *in the event she needed to run the dishwasher or throw a load of clothes in the washing machine*, "she's my rock! My rib!"

Okay, so that was a bit much, and he definitely took offense to him boasting about her philanthropic work. "One day I came in here and thought she turned our home into a homeless shelter," he went on, flaunting a huge rack of pearly white teeth.

While he shelled out kudos for his wife, with her ear stuck to the wall, Cliff sat glued to the chair wrestling his tongue to be still. Whoever serviced the pastor's teeth, deserved a Nobel Peace Prize! Without doubt it had to be a man who'd been in his mouth because no woman would waste so much porcelain on one mouth when photoshopping had been invented.

"It took months to find them people a place to live," the amused 24/7 servant bellowed on.

Cliff's jaws started coiling so tight he could barely chew. Dottie might've been flattered, but the homeless wouldn't have been, and neither sinners *like him* seeking salvation. But he was on point about one striking detail. The pot roast and lobster was so succulent and moist he didn't need to chew. Rich dark gravy rolled over a hill of creamy white mashed potatoes and pooled around a roast and lobster he could cut with a spoon. That was all there was to savor about that meal.

And still, he wasn't ready to hang the minister by his toenails. The man just wasn't making a great impression talking with them hamburger patty lips and cleaning his plate with the cigar sausage fingers. In 60 seconds tails, entails, gravy and all were sopped up and inhaled through his rhino nostrils, and gone.

"Damn," Cliff muttered to himself (of course), what the pastor mistook for another type of disappointment.

"If you'd like, I can have Dottie make you a doggie bag," he said, nodding towards his empty plate.

There it was again; *'have Dottie make him'*. Wow! And *his mistake*. Maybe the dude did think he was God! That was another thing Mama got right. *'Assumptions made asses out of both of them.' (Ass-u-me)*.

"No thanks," he replied. "But thanks for the meal. It hit the spot," he said.

"Well, I know you didn't come here for the meal," the pastor chuckled, elbow on the table and rubbing his fingers together, as if he expected a tip. Maannn…Mama would've slapped the mess out of him. Don't ask him why but elbows on tables was the ultimate sin in the Blanchard household.

Buuurrp. "Oo, excuse me," Cliff replied thumping his chest with his fist. Belching like that was okay. It was the greatest compliment to the cook, though reaching for his coat hanging on the back of the chair could be viewed as rude.

At this point he decided to interview other pastors, preferably a minister who had no interest in getting up in the pulpit on *Sunday morning*, and broadcasting his business at the 11am service.

"Actually, I gotta run," Cliff replied, interrupted in his feigned haste to get going by the pastor clearing his throat.

"You know your sister called this morning," he said as Cliff had one arm completely in one sleeve. "Seems that someone is trying to set her up."

Trying? It's not how he'd describe it. He was trying to get a tub of lard out of Mama's chair and completely rub out the ostrich, or at least get her back to the zoo.

"She's a warrior for the church too," he heard as arm two slid in the other sleeve.

Cliff shirked his eyes and hoisted the coat over his shoulders. "Yeah, she knows her Jesus," he muttered.

"Ugh, Cliff, have a seat," the minister stiffly sighed, resembling Winnie-the-Pooh as he removed a soiled 12-inch tablecloth from around his neck. "I know you came here to get something off your chest," he said. "So sit. Let me see how I can help you."

If the pastor was really paying attention he would've also known to let this one charity case get away. That ship had sailed... and sunk.

"Cliff, your sister has her faults like any of us," the pastor lectured on anyway, rising from his seat with his head bowed, like the look Pops used to give him before apologizing about one of life's less hygienic secrets he had to lay on him. And that was the other thing. The pastor wasn't much older. They could've gone to school together, which wasn't no way he'd let a man with so little wisdom lecture him.

"We're all flawed by designed," the pastor preached at his back. "But she has a big heart...and a good reason for wanting to sell her mother's house."

That one line brought Cliff's determined stroll to an abrupt and sensational pause. Before he had a feeling he might be wasting his time. Now he knew. God wasn't bull-jiving around. He spun around and let Aunt Idell go.

First of all, it was NOT her mother's house. It was

THEIR parent's home! *Like what kind of minister hijacked a sinner's confession anyway!?*

Pastor Edmonds caught all that attitude, and like he'd done with his wife, he ignored it. "I know. I know," he said as if he had already read Merda's long rap sheet. "But the Lord expects us to give," he went on. "And he expects us to forgive too..."

"No, I didn't know that," Cliff replied, his tone chillier than ice. Braced for a fight all he had left to do was throw up his hands.

"I suppose you don't know why Meredith wants to sell the house?"

"I suppose for the same reason anyone holding a winning lotto ticket would," he quipped with heaps of irony tangled in his tone.

"Cliff, she wants to help a family move into a home, so they don't have to live in their car," he sighed looking at him like *don't you get it!*

But while the pastor waited on a reaction, wearing a face that mirrored a mudslide, Cliff stood unmoved, feet soldered to the floor daring the minister to *make his day*.

"Cliff, she has HD...Huntington's," he said, as if a pissed off bull about to deface its nemesis really gave a damn. "...With Parker's health...and her health, plus their age...and your age," he stutter-muttered on, "she believes the house is naturally more suited for a young growing family who can run up and down stairs, and do yard work, *and you know...* basically keep the house up."

'What in a backwards black sun was this holy fool talking about!?!' Maybe the minister had the wrong sister? After all, unlike Barnes who rolled around town visiting a few dozen members, Edmonds ministered to over 10,000 lost souls a month. *'Yeah, this dude had to have someone else in mind* with all the upkeep he put into Mama and Pops house!'

"—So, is it contagious?" Cliff blurted. *Why not?* since they were talking about different people anyway!

"I mean this HD thing," he clarified softening his tone, in case he was wrong. Probably wasn't the minister's fault he bought such a pathetic lie. Merda hoodwinked people with extra wide nostrils all the time.

"No, HD is not contagious," sighed the 24/7 servant shaking his head and chuckling. "But it is debilitating..."

"So, is it something you die from?" Cliff asked with a semi-straight face, the extent of his pity. Afterall, it was neither vessels harboring the hypocrisy he loathed most. It was the open sham, the audacity to regard him as less than human.

"Okay," the pastor gushed, breathing noisily. "Why don't you tell me what's going on between you and your sister."

The pastor wasn't ready for that conversation. And even if he was, Cliff didn't have the lung capacity to go back that far. It would've been easier explaining Adam and Eve, text he knew nothing about, than going back to Merda's creation!

"Look, I've been trying to get an appointment with you to speak about getting married," Cliff coolly replied, exhausted by the word tango. "...But based on what I'm hearing; sounds like I might need advice on where we'll stay...preferably somewhere without a steering wheel and backseat," he chuckled, showing all his teeth ...and the tips of his tonsils too.

"Oh, un huh, yes...I see," Pastor Edmonds stuttered, wistfully nodding as he stared into the floor. "I think I heard about *this girl*," he replied with emphasis on *this girl*. "Umm...tell me about her," he asked looking up, head tilted, smirking with a licentious glint in his eye. "How long have you two been...umm... *dating?*"

And so they were talking about the same ostrich. Through clenched teeth Cliff replied, "a few months," and waited for the next ball, suddenly realizing he was dealing with a pitcher he'd like to take a swing at.

"...And are you two expecting to be married in the church?"

'No, just one of us,' Cliff snarled, beneath his breath of course. At this point, it was clear. Neither of them were escaping this spar as they came. "Actually, I want to get married in the home where I was raised," he said out loud. "...You know...the home where I currently live." If he was trying to get into hell he would have added *'the home I spent over $100,000 remodeling'*...that had no stairs...nor basement...and a manageable yard he paid kids $20 to mow the grass and $100 to shovel snow!

When he got back to the conversation he realized the pastor was still judging his relationship with Tebby.

"That's not long," the pastor quietly offered, a wheel turning so loud in his head he looked to be cranking out a hairline. "But...umm, let me ask this," he continued, his huge forehead receding as he talked. "I'm not exactly sure what's going on between you and your sister, but definitely sense conflict between you and I. Have I done or said anything to offend you?"

"Look dude..." Cliff sighed, and yes he called the 24/7 servant dude, but quickly apologized and corrected his mistake. "I shouldn't be taking out my frustrations on you," he wryly chuckled. "My sister and I...*for lack of a better way of phrasing it*...do not see eye to eye. She wants me dead, and I see her dead."

It was the pastor's turn to *'WoW!'* The blow knocked him backwards, and like that he was baldheaded again. "...I didn't realize that," he replied rubbing his brow raised where his hairline used to be. "We're certainly going to pray for you two," he said before cheering out of the blue. "But, hey! None of us are perfect, right? Flawed by design He says. The good news is, that can be fixed," he celebrated. "Whatever this beef is, no matter how big, God will work it out. Trust me on that brotha'! God will work it out!"

Cliff must've looked like he had wandered into a

forest because he was lost, Lost, LOST! Was this the best the 24/7 servant, who studied spiritual materials only God knew how many years, had?

"Well then, I guess I'll be crossing my fingers and waiting on it," he replied, reaching for the doorknob, stopped by the pastor placing his hand over his. Time stamp it. Because Cliff sure did. Pastor touched him first!

"Look brotha', I feel you're a good man," he leaned into his ear and whispered, smelling like roast beef, lobster, and that hill of mashed potatoes. Basically he smelled like feet, armpits and soiled diapers.

"...But you see...being a good person isn't going to get you in," the 24/7 minister preached at him like his old pal Roscoe sold street wares. "...Just like punishing people on your short list isn't going to bring you peace on earth, either. That's God's job, brotha'," he concluded with an extra exclamation.

"Hey, look, thanks," Cliff replied stepping outside and inhaling the best gulp of air he'd inhaled in roughly 39 minutes and 7 seconds. "...And please thank the wife for me. The meal was really good."

"Cliff, let it go brotha'! You gotta forgive her and let it go," the pastor called out as he hoofed it to his vehicle, mad enough to turn back to test the man's transitioning theory.

CHAPTER...10

Down On His Knees is where he needed to be, praying for his sister. Mama always said, *'what comes around, goes around,'* and Merda was getting her just due sitting on the other side of Rita's desk... smoldering.

"But I just came here to give you one last chance to change your mind," she said swelled of moxie...and diet Pepsi. "This is a clear case of class discrimination," she claimed to a career woman who knew the Board of Education's policies and rules like the back of her hand.

"Discrimination of what," Rita asked, brow raised. She was a serious business woman...a no nonsense *Judge Judy* type who ran a tight ship. She had no time for long-winded tales, and zero interest in her service to the Lord. After consulting a number of sources, police annuals and a few of her church buddies chiefly, she reached the conclusion, Merda had to go.

"Well then, guess you'll be hearing from my attorney if this is how you feel," Merda shot back. "People with blemishes in their past have rights too."

Blemishes in her past? Was that how she described the huge gaps in her address history?

Rita knew better than to respond. Not only had she done her homework, but the toxicology report had come back, along with disturbing details of Merda's very recent nutty blemish. Not a court in the country would force a responsible facility catering to children to retain a loose noodle claiming it was clean and saved. *Sell that story to Mueller's macaroni!*

"I'ma tell you like this," Merda spat in closure, "My mama always said watcha' back! Because what comes around goes around!"

And so seal that chapter! Wasn't no coming back from a threat like that, though Cliff knew none of this, why he needed to be down on his knees. There was an addendum to Mama's wisdom he flat out ignored, since he wasn't in a gang. *An eye for an eye leaving everyone blind'* was necessary advice for people like Merda when she was running around with thugs settling scores. It was like 13 to 14 of them when they were at their baddest. By the time she hauled tail for Florida, after the comeuppance had gone around and around 'blinding everybody' (her group and a hundred other rival badasses), only one badass was left...and he was in no shape to defend any turf.

But now here Cliff was, oblivious about the havoc spiraling from the bitter fued with his sister. From his little square peg, factoring in the ancient crud Merda called an attorney...successfully holding up the probate decision, along with a number of others taking her side...excluding Rita, but including Pastor Edmonds, it looked like any day he might return home to find his life scattered over the yard and front door padlocked. The beef between Rita and Merda was like way out there in the boondocks.

After a week gone by, his soul beat up and spirit knocked down, plus missing Tebby terribly and still no probate decision, he took his chances and drove to Rainman... alone, albeit in broad daylight. Meeting Gadoor was almost a relief. He started to hand the guy the keys to his SUV, *telling him to park the car around back!*

Except Gadoor surprised him, tossing him a box and blowing a kiss. "Merry Christmas," hooted the limping glassy-eyed projects' OG.

Cliff looked in his hands, impulsively about to drop the box. All that stopped him was fearing an explosion when the box hit the ground. A gift from Gadoor was hardly on his wish list. But tossing the gift in Rainman's lobby wasn't an option either. Last thing he needed was Gadoor finding his gift sitting on a Burger King bag and hassling him about it on future trips to his new mailbox!

So he held onto the box and made it up to the 9th floor with only one other brush. A man with a knife stuck in his back raced by, chased by a female it sort of looked like, dressed in a Bambi robe wielding a hammer. Promptly he stepped aside, counting his third strike, like folklore counted death in waves of three. *'No decision from the probate courts. Gadoor's gift. And now the knife in the back!'* If his luck hadn't run out, then the track was running out of field.

The girls were up. Tebby reclined in one of No-No's fat armed chairs covered by an orange popcorn spread, and No-No sat in a high-chair at the sink washing greens. One of her male friends, a yellow-eyed character on his way out let him in.

"You scared to go home, ain't cha' Stang," laughed No-No.

That would be sort of incorrect, though he admitted nothing. "I'd much rather get beat up over there than in here," he teased, leaning over and pecking Tebby on the forehead, with his hand holding the gift behind his back.

"Well, bring yo'self over here so I can put ya' butt to work," she yapped back.

Cliff eased over to the table scattered with whole chickens, slabs of ribs, plus hot sauce by the gallons and buckets of chitterlings. He slid Gadoor's gift in one free space at the edge of the table and pulled off his coat.

"What's that," No-No yapped, missing nothing...

even with her back facing him and an agglomerate of food bleeding over much of the table. "You gonna' tell me you bought Teb a gift and not me!"

Why she reached that conclusion, greasy as the box looked with finger paws tattooed over all six sides, was a wild guess. "No, No-No, I'd never do that," he replied, sounding tired as the bucket of intestines smelled, so reminiscent of the pastor's breath.

"Well, whatcha' got in there, Stang," she quacked. "Is that all yo' sista let you pack," she laughed loud.

"No, No-No," he sighed rolling up his sleeves. "I think one of your neighbors decided to play Santa this year," he sarcastically replied.

"What!? Who," she shouted, abruptly turning off the water and freezing, sort of like waiting on cue to react.

"Ya' boy," he chuckled. "The coat collector."

"Gay-door," she shouted. And before he answered she lowered the high-chair and hopped in her scooter, wheeling over to the table at her fastest speed yet.

"A house just got robbed over 'deer where all them im'potent people live," she explained, more worried than he'd ever seen her. She grabbed the box and ripped it apart. Note to himself: Don't bother wrapping her gifts.

When she finished pulling the box apart, its four corners were no longer obvious. Had the *foreign currency* not been secured by a rubber-band, money would have showered the kitchen like confetti.

"That boy dumb as a bucket of rocks," she tisked. "His mama oughta' be shamed raisin' such a fool! Don't nobody 'round here know anything 'bout them games beuda'crats play!"

Like a baller No-No tossed the bundled currency in one of many trash bags crowding her dark kitchen. "You know anything 'bout them games beuda'crats play," she jovially asked scooting back to the high-chair.

"I sure don't," he replied, leaping over to the trash bag in a giant stride and scooping up the bundle. No-No had no idea the paper she tossed wasn't playing cards. By his estimation, fanning through hundreds of bills, she almost spoiled 100,000 British notes.

"Stang! Leave that mess right where I put it! 'Dat's stolen contraband you messin' wif'," she shouted. "If the po-lees catch you wif' the beuda'crats stuff, they can put you in the can!"

"But Miss No-No—"

"—What 'chew call me!?!"

"I apologize Miss—I mean, No-No I apologize but Gadoor gave this to me, and I was taught it's not right to throw away gifts, no matter where they came from."

"Teb! You hear ya' Cliffy in here sassing me again," she yelled over his head, dumping bundles of sopping wet collards into a bubbling vat tall as her. It was a mess at that sink. In addition to water running over her wrists and down to her elbows, she had scissors, rubber bands, cloves of spastically peeled garlic, grocer tags and a sink full of inedible effects mixed in with greens she dumped in that vat. Streams of steam shot up at the ceiling so forcefully that puffs of clouds ricochet back at the pot with the same viciousness. It was a scary sight for sure, especially when he looked up and saw the smoke detector pulled apart by someone with a similar skill as the way No-No unwrapped gifts. That kitchen looked, in a nutshell, more horrific than scientific or appetizing.

And yet, sweet faced Tebby sat, a safe 6 or 7 feet away, with her back facing the commotion calmly sipping tea. "What y'all in there fussing about now," she asked uncommitted to No-No's clatter.

"Stang in here tryna' git hisself locked up...telling me about right and wrong," No-No fussed. "Stang! When's the last time you been in a church?"

"A few weeks ago," he replied assuredly. "Tebby and I went together."

"Teb, you went to church with Stang," she hollered over his head again.

"Not yet," Tebby replied. She'd forgotten the time they'd technically been in church.

"Stang, why you lying to me," No-No argued. "Did ya' folks tell you anything about what happens when you lie!?"

"I'm not lying," he chuckled, reminding Tebby about their visit to meet the pastor. "You remember when that chump was hiding out in his office trying to pretend like he was busy," he laughed.

"Stang, I told you about callin' people names! You not supposed to talk about pastors like that! You can walk outside and get struck down!"

"Naa…that's only when you leave the TV on when it's lightening and raining," he teased.

"You better stop cuttin' the fool," No-No yapped back. "Besides, you know good and well I ain't talkin' 'bout stickin' yo' nose in no church! You need to sit yo' buns in a church befo' you wind up in a box like the one you tryin' to sneak outta here!"

"But how's church going to help me? I thought God was everywhere," he said holding a pound of intestines in each hand.

"I see why yo' sista' havin' problems wif' you," No-No grumbled, the lowest he'd ever heard her speak.

"But Tebby doesn't go to church," he protested like a bratty kid whining over a toy he was playing with first.

"This ain't about Teb," she fired back, elevating her voice to its normal pitch. "This about you, Stang! You got a bad heart!"

"My heart is good," he insisted. "I treat people the way I want to be treated."

"You know good and well that ain't what I'm talkin' about, Stang!"

"No, No-No, what are you talking about?"

"I'm talkin' 'bout that axe grindin' heart you walkin' around here wif'! What's gonna happen if Teb make you angry?"

And she went on fussing, carrying on about a man she knew who graduated from being the man every girl wanted, to a monster no woman wanted. "See, er'body talk that love stuff, but don't have no idea what love is," she argued. "Love'll kill ya' Stang! Didja' know that!?!"

Before he realized it he was wiping his eyes in the corner of his arms, and it wasn't due to the bucket of intestines flickering waste in his face.

"...Aww Stang," she sighed catching him yucking a little bit. "I know you think you love my Teb," her voice a soft crackly whisper. "You jus' need to fix yo' situation wif yo' sista...so you can love my Teb right."

How he let his emotions get the best of him was another wild guess. He had just been through so much in the past few months. In one of the worthless classes he'd taken at Linthicum it was said that major life events increased the odds of suffering a stroke...or worse. Well, he lost a job, a loved one, and was apt to lose his home. He was a heart attack in line waiting.

But he manned up, fixing his face and posture. Last thing he wanted was to have Tebby concerned she might be marrying a punk. "Welp, if it helps any, I am trying to do like you told me," he muttered. "I stopped calling her..." and he sighed deeply, resisting to utter a name he visualized on a purgatory ledger.

"Un hun... you still slippin', ain't 'cha Stang," she chided. "What's the name of yo' sistsa's church?"

"Cedar," he sighed noisily.

"What you say Stang!? Easta'!? Ain't no—"

"—I said Cedar...Cedar Baptist," he replied like he had his chest stuck out.

"All right now," she continued fussing, gaily albeit. "You betta' not be lying 'cause I'll get me a ride and go right over there and ask her myself!"

194 · A Piece of Peace

He pulled up to the driveway, without Tebby, noticing right away it was going to be a long week. Grejeckula's car was parked in the driveway, a compact Duster she'd been gifted, straddling the conceived dividing line they observed since her arrival; a blatant declaration of war.

Sitting in the dark, as usual, was fatso, Mama's chair, and the gooey remote. Parker didn't budge as he walked by, contraband tucked under his arm secured in a Ziploc bag. The bum looked neither up or down, left nor right, staring laser focused straight through the TV.

On to his bedroom he continued, taking his sweet time to find the right key to unlock his room door. For this war to end, he hoped on her appearance, ready to duke it out again. He was prepared to give up right away, both hands and arms shooting straight up. His word against hers. She knew far more rogues than him. And Rita was not an ally in her corner. Her only hope was No-No, who didn't even know the currency existed.

But she failed to materialize. The concentrated effort he put into jangling the keys and turning each tumbler with magnificent force did not help. He had unlocked, relocked and tossed the Ziploc bag on his nightstand before she knocked on the door.

"Who is it," he asked, knowing good and well who was knocking.

"It's me, brother," she replied in a wimpy voice. She must not have looked outside. Two of his tires had rolled over the flower bed and were currently crushing all of her junipers. Any neighbor passing by would know they were at it again.

"What's up? What you want," he asked with an ear pressed against the door. He'd seen EMTs do this when checking for a heartbeat. Sounded like blood pumping through her veins at Dracula's speed. All he needed to do was stick his neck out and the war was on. Instead he used the pause to grab the Ziploc bag and stash it under the mattress.

"Brother, we need to talk," she finally said, sounding her usual full of it contrite. This had been a 52-year long war. She, too, probably was a hair trigger away from giving in and pulling the pin.

He opened the door, acting put out, so rehearsed in hating her. And she, as well rehearsed in hating him, yet foggy about the calamity she passed every day sitting in Mama's chair spat, "You look like hell!"

No comment. He gave her the messy smile; the grin Mama, and them miserable KAWs at Linthicum taught him. No one was ever accused of being rude or dismissive for imparting this grin, though its assertion clear. She could 'go kick rocks!' Bottom line; something else Mama and the miserable KAWs taught him, 'loose lips sank ships!'

"Them friends of yours called over here asking about my church," she said snaking her ostrich neck, looking around his room and not finding the contraband. "They also think you need Jesus!"

The grin hadn't left his face. He stood there with his lips stretched the width of his face, showing not a single tooth, and looking clear through her eyes to the back of her head.

"Brother, you're going to have to sit down with me and discuss the house," she continued, her eyes darting around the room looking wildly for the smoking gun, indeed securely tucked beneath the mattress.

Still no reaction from him, though he made a mental note of her mug. He hadn't realized it before but the beige patch on the side of her head looked like an outline of Texas. It wasn't as big, of course, but was situated alongside her left temple, which remarkably resembled an Apple ear bud dangling from her ear.

"NARC!" he muttered, snarling just a little.

"What!? What did you say!?!"

"I said HARK," he clarified, semi-straight face.

She leaned back and twisted her head as if probing her own sanity. "Is that all you have to say?"

"Well, if you've got any baking soda in your fridge I can pay you fifty notes," he added.

"What's wrong with you," she snarled checking him out head to toe. Obviously she didn't have experience conversing with robots. She was used to people reacting off her slights, authorizing her to suit up and go into character. Maybe if she found the switch that turned him back into Cliff they could get this war over and done.

But God was on His JOB. He had to be. There was no other rhyme or reason for why that dialogue played out as it did. She backed out of the room as if his face was the holy cross and avoided him, even ignoring his SUV crushing her junipers.

Sunday morning he woke up early and resealed the back window, then shaved, showered, and gassed up his SUV. Nobody could tell him God didn't have a wicked sense of humor as he hightailed it over to the hotel smiling at the mockeries of life.

Standing outside Rainman, on the corner of Bootleg Justice and Making Ends Meet, were children ripping and running around a couple of rappers playing secular music through blowout your eardrum speakers. In the way far background, largely due to her being so tiny, was the love of his life dressed ever so conservatively, and the kick in his pants buried in what amounted to having to do a double take to describe.

At first glance it looked like an ad-hoc yard sale and carnival in motion. He spotted Tebby right away, but it took growing his eyes to find No-No sitting in the wheelchair swathed in pearls, feathers, crochet wraps, and that hat; an aluminum homemade creation fancied-dancied up by utensils found in most kitchens. She, *literally*, had thrown the kitchen sink at that hat. If she had to cook a meal then and there, she'd be ready! Holy Cannoli!

"Look at Stang!," she shouted at the back of his head, loud enough to sever an eardrum. "Don't even look like the same Stang," she announced settling in the back seat.

The compliment made him blush, even if flattery from a woman wearing pots and pans and three-prong antennas on her head warranted a second opinion.

"Well, I thought we were headed to church," he teased. "Had you told me we was going to the Grammys I would've pulled on my red carpet suit."

No-No ignored the insult, and blushed too, though it was hard to see with the cheese-grater veil covering most of her face. She almost looked like Mad Max, save for one minor detail. Her mask was upside down. But she thought she had it going on, was the stuff, fluffing up parsley dangling off both sides of the tin can she probably was going to use later on to sprucen up her next meal.

For 23.9 miles her thinly sliced tomato lips smiled, all the way to the 11am worship service where he rolled up to the church. A robust watchdog servant marched up to the vehicle motioning for him to roll down the window. "Sir, parking is in the rear. Pull up to the corner," he said pointing. "The guy with the yellow armband will guide you in."

"Well, my passenger needs assistance. I have to get her chair out of the back," he replied.

The watchdog peeked in the backseat, where No-No was conked out, head laid back with the Mad Max grill partially covering her face and the tomatoes slices still smiling.

"Pop the trunk," barked the watchdog, disappearing and reappearing in his rearview mirror. In seconds the liftgate flew up and he had the wheelchair on the ground and open. But man! Had No-No seen the way he yanked on that chair, no different from the way she handled flipping it open herself, she all the same might've lost her religion. What kept things civil was her raising that aluminum hat and seeing people and hats converging on the church like someone at the Pope level had died.

"Stang, where you going," she yapped, excited to be in company of so many jubilees. Kind of like being on her own little personal magic carpet.

"I'll meet y'all inside," he shouted out the window, chuckling as he rolled off, though hardly missing her last words.

"You betta' not be lying Stang! I betta' find you in that church or you and Teb are over!"

. . .

That wasn't going to happen, at least not with his input. He loved Tebby *to the moon and back*, and wouldn't have been at church at all had his intentions been anything less. But watchdog #2 liked to have messed things up, directing him to a corner of the lot where his little SUV wouldn't see asphalt before the moon lit up the beltway, or 10,000 prayer warriors had been heard, whichever came first.

He explained the situation to the man in the yellow armband. "I'm disabled," he said, rephrasing what he meant when the yellow band watchdog scrunched up his face. "My passenger don't have legs," he threw out the window, realizing those weren't the best choice of words either. The watchdog looked at him as if he was about to snap his fingers and produce Jesus, sparing him of having to park at all. Once Jesus got there and did His thing, he could just go. Like Scram! Vamoose and be gone!

"If you gotta leave, somebody'll let you out," the yellow band dog barked.

Not good. Barking watchdogs didn't bubbly up his spirit, especially knowing these were Merda's brothers in

Christ, all blood ancestors of Pastor Edmond's school of principles. Begrudgingly he loosely followed yellow band's hand signals, kissing fenders and narrowly clipping sideview mirrors, just to amuse himself watching the watchdog frantically waving and dancing. When the dog cupped his hands over his head, the step before clutching his chest and falling to his knees, Cliff turned off the engine and hopped out the car grinning. "Bro', you're a miracle worker," he said digging in his pocket. "Let me give you a lil' change—"

"—That won't be necessary," replied yellow band, glaring at him like he would a nut job.

But Cliff wasn't laughing as hearty after exiting the junkyard overcrowded with Crowne Victorias, thumb dot two seater Geos and busted up SUVs missing back windows like his. For roughly half a mile he walked to the church stewing, passing big black stretch Lincoln Town Cars, and hearses, and basically run of the mill cars regular tithers drove.

A trio of deaconesses greeted him at the door. "You must be with them," one said pointing to Tebby, and the ever animated No-No regaling a quartet of deaconesses with the unpeeled tomatoes flapping recklessly. Among the quartet was the ostrich, what slowed his edgy stride, especially when he saw her clutching her go-to weapon the way gangsters protected their turf.

He had every right to question God! Like why?! In the days leading up to this Sunday she had avoided him. They hadn't said two words to each other, though the feud was hardly over. One morning she taped a note to his door that read like an eviction notice. *'We need to see your W2s by the 5th of next month!'*

Was this the reason the probate court was dragging their mallet in bringing down the gavel? And exactly *who was WE?* Be damned if he was giving her and her juke-leg lawyer anything! Last he heard (*or rather read*) was in the very least he might have to split the proceeds

of the value of the house. Well, he had that covered. Half
the value of the house was stashed between his mattress.
Again, his word against hers. First she'd have to scrounge
up enough doe...and sympathy...before her word would
be heard, which given how the courts dragged bringing
out mallets, good luck with that!

All he had to do was get through this exercise. That
was going to be the real test, as the first pop quiz turned
out to be a breeze when her god on her side, she spotted
him and fled inside the sanctuary.

"This is a big 'ole church," No-No alerted everyone, likely for the umpteenth time before he joined the
group. "Looks like a museum in here," she noted, exag-
gerating none. Once upon a time Cedar was a wooden
2-room/1-building with an outhouse built over a creek.
But the 200-square foot crate morphed into a massive dy-
nasty of marble and mirrors. Just as Aunt Idell described,
tens of thousands of dollars had been wrangled from
working everyday folk, pimps...hoes...moms and pops
alike, all hoping to secure first class entrance into a place
they'd never seen, only heard about. The bottom of many
bins had been scraped to cobble together and pump their
absolute last into the ever famous building fund, irrefut-
ably not squandered.

"Yep, it takes a lot to convince everybody this is
the place that'll get you in," he chuckled loud enough for
only No-No to hear him.

"Behave Stang," she shouted, her racket favorably
swallowed by higher spirits dominating the pasture. For
one, there was the aluminum hat with the antennas. And
two, the smiling deacons were busier trying to figure out
how to get her and the chair out of the vestibule and into
the sanctuary without touching either.

"We know you ain't been to church in a while,
but your soul 'bout to be redeemed," No-No carried on,
bumping into knees and snaring nylons.

The service started on time, and it had to because

as explained in announcements, this was lo and behold, the anniversary service! So yeah, 'good luck getting out of here anytime soon...sucker!'

His mood dipped, and pressure rose. Scientist said the adult body didn't do well beyond 103 temps, yet his forehead looked like a pork chop frying in its own fat. To say he wasn't feeling it was like saying he could walk on water. First of all, where was the water? And second, where was Jesus? He hadn't felt as hostile about being in one place since leaving Linthicum and seeing fatso living in Mama's chair.

"What you grumbling 'bout," No-No said, elbowing him in the side. "You betta' not cut up," she warned for as many times as he heard the phrase 'praise the Lord.'

Irked wasn't even a proper narrative for how high his pressure rose as he scooted in the pew between his kick in the butt and love of his life. The both of them, on either side, was like a ginormous oxymoron pyrometer; canceling out the other in keeping him seated. It wasn't until the choir got going, involuntarily moving parts of his body that hadn't stirred since he out sung Pearl, that the demons started escaping.

"The ghost got her," No-No said leaning into him, speaking of a lady up front jumping around. "That's how you know when the holy ghost dealing wif' the devil," she proclaimed.

But that woman wasn't the only one the holy ghost slipped inside. People popped up out of pews all around them, one after the other. Church hadn't even gotten started and it looked like a Jiffy popcorn convention. Puppets bounced all over the place. Cliff looked up to see folk folded over a banister in the senate seating arena. One lady had a leg over the railing and both arms flailing. If that railing gave, and or if that woman fell, hundreds of angels would get to test their wings, a sight that despite the spiritual illusion was not exactly a coveted image sitting directly beneath its creaking floors. Nonetheless and all-the-same the holy ghost had come for Cliff too. He got to rocking and snaking (*bad word*) his neck, putting his whole back, nape to backside, into motion.

"Look at Cliffy," No-No laughed clapping her hands and rocking too, them antennas bobbing in rhythm with the woman banging on an organ. Grinning ear to ear and eyes flickering like flashbulbs she beamed watching him on his journey to *claim victory* over the impossible.

But then, as Jesus was taking him back down that long ugly road, some 52 psyche scarring years ago, she leaned into him again. "You see yo' sista' up there," she asked. "That woman blocking my view."

He ignored No-No though. Like who could miss the ostrich standing in the back row, third from the left, with the bright gold peacock feathers poking him in the eyes!? But God's grace upon him, he soldiered on. With the professor at the mic and in spite of the thorns, he prayed. He prayed No-No would shut up and let this good time last. If God was real He would let nothing steal this joy; not the woman blocking their view...or the leg coming over the railing, nor No-No's instigating, and neither the singing ostrich noisily swinging, clapping with those masculine gluttonous wrinkled claws like her Jesus really woke her up that morning! All in her favor was him loving Tebby more.

Suddenly the music stopped, as if the electricity had been severed. Of course he nailed down Grejeckula's whereabouts first. It wasn't a crap shot that she could've left the choir, not that her voice would've been missed, and been at the circuit box trying to kill Satan's fun. But nope. There she was, peacock towering over the vocally blessed; her upper half glittering like firecrackers and rinky-dink opinionators inspecting him. Disturbing!

It seemed to take forever for the pastor to grace the congregation, though much of this eternity was seized by announcements; a reading drive for children under two and adults over 90 was happening in a few days. About

200 parishioners were sick and shut in, requiring five minutes of silence. First-time visitors were greeted, and introduced...where Cliff caught another one of No-No's elbows. Yes, she forced him to stand, and the three of them, along with 99 others introduced themselves. Tebby was so sweet, and a brave orator, telling a flock of hypothetical Christian believers she was raised non-denominational. And she volunteered this information right before the bell-clapper, to Cliff's distress and bone-chilling disgust, thanked the ostrich for inviting them to her church. But at least he was spared from speaking. No-No clapped for so long it took the organist, be it an accident or on purpose, to strike a key drowning her out. It was funny too, because it confused the choir. Some stood, others looked around, cueing the announcer to explain the gaffe, certainly not a part of the program.

And then...a good group of minutes after the praise dancers did their thing too... the 24/7 servant emerged. For a minute it seemed as if Jesus, or someone walking on water, or God Himself was being hustled in from the rear. But it was just the 24/7 servant who didn't simply appear at the mic. No, he rose from his throne dressed in all white and let his popularity descend upon the pulpit. It took a minute for his infamy to settle. He was a whole lot of man, who had done a whole lot for his regular tithers. For 17 years he fed the homeless, and as shared in the announcements was the lead pilot behind the reading initiative for children under two and adults over 90. Plus, he was about to help one man out of his home, to help a whole family out of their car. This was a deity requiring a proper entrance, in the same way theatres operated velvet curtains revealing productions on the Casablanca level. A great soothsayer like this didn't just walk up to a microphone and start talking. Besides, this was a communion reunion anniversary worshipping service.

Cliff took one look at the man draped in sheaths of sterile cloths, and closed his eyes... and prayed. *'Please don't ask me to contribute one red cent to the building fund, the choir robes, the dancing mimes' face paint, or collection plate.* Your plate is full and your damn cup over-runneth!'

He opened his eyes and found the pastor glaring at him. So, he prayed harder. *'And God help everyone in this building if a neighbor, other than my sweet Tebby or the tarot smacking, yakking, elbowing bell-clapper touches me for any god-forsaken reason!'*

The pastor adjusted the mic and leaned in, his large ego echoing before he said a word. "I'm taking y'all back to *the Story of Joseph…*" he declared in a crusty early morning voice people made when gargling mouthwash. Whether telling this story had been the original plan, was only made clear when he abruptly changed lanes, suddenly decrying in a boisterous thundering pitch he was going off topic.

But y'all!? What preacher, *except the one who eulogized one of his cousins…describing her as bat crazy…* plugged y'all in his vocabulary? Nonetheless he grabbed Tebby's hand and prayed his hardest. *'Hope you got the wheel God! 'Cause this y'all is all out!'*

"I'm going off topic today," shouted the pastor.

Cliff jumped, jerking back so forcefully the entire pew shook. No-No laughed. "Bet that woke you up, huh Stang!?!"

No. It really pissed him off. He clenched his fists and glared back at the pastor. He never liked sermons to begin with. Too contradictory. 'If he was supposed to thank God for giving him a job, why couldn't he blame the same God for taking away his job?' Pastors never covered that one, like the idiocy of him moving into his car, in place of a family moving out of theirs!

And so yeah, it could be concluded he was dealing unspecified consecration issues when the pastor, glaring at him and seemingly no one else, announced he was telling the story about a kid asking what God looked like!

"The child told his father, if God was real and he wanted him to believe in Him, then he had to tell him what God looked like."

The congregation gasped, and so did Cliff, surely for very different reasons.

"Stang, look at how the pastor looking at you," No-No reminded him, and not so discreetly either.

"But see, the father told the child God looked like a cloud," continued the pastor. "He told the kid to just look up in the sky and he'd see God," so the allegory dragged, from the coffers of the 24/7 servant elaborating on clouds and thunder and before long, easily excising twenty-thirty minutes plucking a lot of Cliff's nose hairs going through an entire lineage to blame all those who had lied to this poor child.

Finally, and thank heavens, perhaps largely owing to No-No, the pastor took his scrutiny off Cliff to wrap up his message. "Papa," so bellowed the pastor in the voice of a juvenile. "I've asked everyone what God looks like and no one has given me a straight answer yet. You are my last hope. But I'm warning you, if you don't tell me the truth about what God looks like, then I shall have no choice but to go seek Him out for myself."

The End. That was it. Pastor Edmonds closed the big fat book on the lectern and returned his attention back to Cliff, glaring at him through dark seedy eyes.

"Someone in here might be questioning God... thinking logic and their degrees, and them fine Ivy League schools that cost a fortune overrules what is in the Bible. But let me tell you this," he bellowed, slamming his fist on the pulpit.

"Go on and act like a kid," he said bumping his head up and down, shooting Cliff a look reminiscent of big bad 70's Superfly dudes who used to dress in similar white robes, (*their's actually fur coats*), riding around the city in fantastic showboating Cadillacs. "Yeah, go ahead..." he argued, banging his fist on the lectern again.

Many jumped, shaken by the bang, and what sounded like the pastor putting an unhinged dent in the building fund. But Cliff was unphased, despite the foreboding prospect he could've just rolled his eyes and yawned at God.

Next thing he knew, the choir was back on their feet belting out many of his favorite gospels. 'Thank ya' Jesus' and 'Jesus gonna' work it out' and many 'Kirk Franklin' type feet stompers. The music played for a good forty minutes to get through communion. But Cliff wasn't complaining, especially when a guy, who by the sound of his velvety voice, got to testifying singing another old soul cleanser, a 'Mahalia' mock up, 'How I Got Over!'

By the time the choir got around to this song he was back in his seat and immersed in himself, worked over by that man's voice...and the lyrics, plus the organ, and the choir! For the second time, in such a close span of time, his emotions got the best of him in that yucking sort of way. He heard Pops voice. 'Remember what I told you son,' he recalled loud and clear. 'You do not want to get too close to God.'

Unlike Mama, Pops rarely attended church, and DID NOT TITHE, but he KNEW GOD, and one off-brand day when Cliff got to asking why he didn't regularly attend church, his father TOLD HIS TRUTH.

"Son, the reason those people stay in church is because they like the idea of God," he explained before warning him about getting too close. "You never want to see His face," he added, a caveat Cliff never shook. It clarified so much; such as why Merda clung to church, and perhaps Mama too.

Nothing ever seemed to really get better for either of them. Merda stayed running afoul with the law and look at how Mama left earth. As a matter of fact, the only one who seemed at internal peace was Pops.

Cliff, himself, was always stitched between the two sides, not knowing what to believe. He, in many ways resembled the kid in the story, what really ticked him off! After Pops raised the hairs on his back with that chilling warning, of course too, buttressed by Merda whipping the daylights out of him, he put his faith in his own beliefs... stuff he had witnessed with eyes he trusted.

"The church doors are open, won't you come... won't you come..." he heard echoing around him as the bell-clapper poked her boney elbow in his side.

"Don't be shamed Stang! Go on and let Jesus deal wif' that devil!"

. . .

But he was ashamed, though he admitted nothing! Like who wouldn't get caught up hearing 'Precious Lord', and a man testifying about getting over? To the contrary, it was all the witnesses that bothered him. Shucks, in his own sanctuary he cried openly. When he killed off a much beloved character in one of his books, he cried, and cried even harder when life threw spikes in his path and he had to kill an entire book! But crying wasn't half as embarrassing as standing in an imposing Cathedral, listening to a bell-clapper shrieking, "look at you Stang! "You a whole new man!"

'Yeah, okay...' he winced looking for the exit, holding Tebby's hand.

"Where you going," the bell-clapper shrieked again, rolling in a direction behind a crowd with robes draped over their arms. "Come on," she waved with one hand and mashing the motor with the other, going full speed, at over 110 mph if she was on the expressway, straight for the stairs!

That's what really embarrassed him. He sprang into action, letting go of Tebby's hand and jumping in front of the scooter.

"What's wrong wif' you Stang," she shrieked as he lost his balance, and his right shoe, reaching for the hand-rail to break his fall.

No one got hurt but he surely ended up with a lot of egg on his face seeing a half dozen hands reaching down to help him back into his shoe.

"Son, are you all right," asked a Hershey kiss toned man holding a big black Bible.

"Ooo Lord," gasped a stout pink woman clutching a string of pearls and an even bigger Bible, hers was white.

And then there was No-No. "See Stang! Jesus saved you! He gotcha' now! Even if you try to kill ya'self he ain't lettin' you git away," she laughed.

Of course he wasn't trying to kill himself, but rather stop her from killing someone rolling down the steps. But the commotion did spare him more embarrassment. She got to slapping buttons, jerking the chair back and forth, rolling over toes and bumping into knees, going for that famous backward lean when the pink lady stopped the minstrel show.

"Sir, are you sure you're okay and don't want to go to the hospital?"

"Naw...I'm fine," he replied, again more humili-ated than hurt.

"Well, we do have an elevator! I suggest using it," ordered the pink lady.

"Come on Stang," No-No shouted. "Let's get your clumsy butt on that elevator. You gonna cause us not to git good seats!"

Good seats? Get good seats to where, for why, for what? He thought they were taking a shortcut to the junk-yard where he'd been forced to park in the nosebleed sect-ion. It wasn't until No-No, and the aromas perfuming the elevator got to talking that he realized the ordeal wasn't over.

"That smell like 'cue," No-No yapped. "I know my 'cue," she boasted, loud as usual, the only voice commandeering the six-by-six square foot of space. "At my church they usually serve fried bird and tata' salad," she offered, unphased that five faces, excluding Tebby and himself of course, who hopped on the elevator to ensure its newest tithers made it down one flight, all displayed identical messy smiles.

How No-No knew dinner was included with the service belied the point of how she concluded they were invited. "Stang, now that you walkin' wif' Jesus they gone' feed us good," she turned and explained.

The elevator doors opened to an underground world more glamorous and larger than the vestibule. The old Cedar Baptist musty breath mess hall turned card tables, folding chairs and dated wood paneling into glass chandeliers, mirrors and long vineyard tables covered by fine linen.

"Stang, yo' sista' in a rich church," shouted the bell-clapper, six feet across the table. "We wouldn't dare serve 'cue on all white tablecloths!"

He lowered his head and whispered in Tebby's ear, "how's the food?" Mama also raised him not to speak with a mouth full of food, a rule obviously nowhere in No-No's etiquette handbook.

Tebby giggled and dipped her head, coquettishly answering his benign questions only meant to deflect the side glances No-No's yapping was getting.

"Stang, why you ignoring me? And what ya'll over there whisperin' about?"

He was obligated to respond. There was no telling what she might say, or do, if he kept acting like a 10-foot oblong table sitting 4-feet off the ground was an obstacle for a Chuck Norris scooter to scale. She could clear the table effortlessly, clipping sophisticated worshippers holding hand blown crystal goblets commfortably.

So he looked across the table and asked, "how's your ribs No-No? Are they so juicy and tender they're melting in your mouth," he teased.

"This stuff ain't meltin' in my mouth nothing. It's gittin' all over my fingers and sticking to my teeth," she shouted.

Oh boy. He walked into that one. He turned away, hoping the napkin she held up to her mouth wasn't to pull out her dentures and drop them in the water goblet. No-No had zero filter. Her shame meter had to be the lowest of mankind.

But while No-No fixed her palette... indeed pulling out her teeth and dropping them in the goblet, a real stomach curler caught his attention. From across the room he recognized the knock-kneed gait headed his way. Looked like an ostrich toting a bouncing vulture, both flapping its wings.

"Finally," she screeched, arms outstretched and red wreathed teeth exposed. "My baby brother is saved and a part of the family!"

'All be damn' he was, though he hopped up without being poked and fell into her embrace. Eyes closed it felt like bones and chit'lins wrapped around him.

"Aww...Wouldja' look at Stang...him and his sista' makin' up," No-No grinned, vigorously rubbing her teeth with a napkin. How his food stayed down he had no idea. But he didn't recoil. It was more disturbing seeing Merda than watching her teeth doing laps in a glass.

When the ostrich released him he turned his head to avoid noticing the dark rings around her eyes, and red lipstick smeared over her teeth, and loose skin beneath her neck wobbling in concert with her flapping tongue broadcasting the last time he'd been to church and how she wished her parents were alive. "Mama and Dada would be so proud of you," she beamed.

He couldn't tell what that beam really looked like because his eyes somersaulted over everyone but her. Two women sitting on either side of No-No appeared constipated. Another lady sitting next to one of the clogged up ladies had her head buried in her purse. It looked like she might be mining for gold, giving how deep and earnest she plowed the purse, but ended up pulling out an itty-bitty white pill she popped in her mouth.

Two women seated behind the pill-popper and clogged ladies also turned around. An arm each draped over the back of their seats, both admired the sibling re-union, alternating glances from No-No and Tebby, to him and her, utterly entertained. He even caught in his periph-eral view the First Lady and pastor peering over at their table, semi amused. Pastor Edmonds waved, but he didn't wave back.

"How ya' feel Stang, now that you done made up wif' yo' sista?"

His best answer. Mama taught him to play his hand close to his heart, while Pops reminded him to keep his relationship with God a private matter. This mix of values kept him from being deceived by the same ole' rigmaroles. "I feel like hearing *'How I Got Over'* one more time," he hooted, pumping his fist for the benefit of anyone who sung that morning.

Those tuned in laughed, Merda included. It was a welcoming compliment, even if he knew once he got home it was going to be the same ole' dialogue; same ole' Grejeckulas. She was going right back to scoffing 'the pastor needed to stick with scripture'…and did he see that woman jumping out of her bra? She hated women who had more going on, which was just about everyone. The First Lady she kept top on this hate list, disdaining her most. According to her, 'the pastor needed a First Lady, not a sometime Christian!'

Every single person sitting in the massive dining hall were going to be called out and judged. Whether it took an hour, a day, or the second he stepped foot outside the church, or turned his back, this level of duplicity was going to revisit like it had the day before, and the day prior to that day, and the one absolute that hadn't failed.

But back to the question, *'how did he feel?'*

For the first time in his life he felt nothing. He wasn't hot or cold. The food was tasty, but he wasn't full. He also was no longer anxious, but was neither without his usual observations. He felt absolutely nothing. No hurt or pain. No anger. No animosity. No plotting revenge. As God was his witness, he felt like he was walking on cloud nine. Whatever the probate court decided, Mama and Pops would rest well knowing he at least had Tebby!

Other Books *by the* Author

Memoirs

Black Table
God Be the Glory
****NEW Babies Raising Babies*

Novels (Series)

Leiatra's Rhapsody (I)
Something Xtra Wild (II)
This One I Got Right (III)
Rye n the Rump (IV)
My Love (V)

Other Fiction

Pretty Inside Out
Tehuelche
Pleasure
Double Dare
Lock Box
Big Bully
Copy Cats
Mindless
****NEW Painted Cats*

Short Stories

My Blackberry
Storytella

Poetry

Atlóta
GEM
A Blast From the Past
Civil Talk

About the Author

RYCJ is a book reviewer, blogger, publisher, and storyteller. Since 2009 she has written dozens of books in a mosiac of genres, and has read and reviewed hundreds of books. She is the ultimate book lover, passionate about reading and writing stories that educates, entertains and inspires.

CPSIA information can be obtained
at www.ICGtesting.com
Printed in the USA
LVHW100042160222
711257LV00025B/1092